THE TRIAL OF ALEX LORD

by

Ray Blackston

The Trial of Alex Lord

Copyright © 2011
Ray Blackston

Cover illustration by Mona Roman Advertising
Cover and Interior Design by BookMasters

Published by Bay Forest Books
An imprint of Kingstone Media
PO Box 491600
Leesburg, FL 34749-1600

www.BayForestBooks.com

Printed in the United States of America by
Bay Forest Books

Library of Congress Cataloguing-in-Publication information is on file.

ISBN: 978-1-936164-34-9

1

A HERON TOOK FLIGHT OVER THE POND AND BANKED ACROSS the fairway just seconds before we teed off on the first hole at Grand Cypress. As usual, it was just the two of us, Austin in his perfectly pressed pants and tan argyle shirt, serious as always, calculating how he might win back the eighty bucks he'd lost to me the previous Friday.

We'd been at it since our second year of law school, a regular Friday afternoon game, sometimes 18 holes, more often just nine. Today, 5 years after graduating number two and three in our class, we still wanted to beat each other's brains out—on the course, off the course, and most importantly, amid the plush offices of Powers, Morgan, and Greene.

Austin drew a tee from his pocket, flipped it end over end, and let it fall to the ground between us—our version of a coin toss. The sharp end pointed at my black Foot-Joy golf shoes.

"Hit it crooked, Alex," Austin smirked. "You're up."

I teed my ball and smashed it 260 yards down the middle of the fairway.

No comment from Austin. He simply teed his ball—he even borrowed my tee, the cheapskate—and promptly pulled his shot to the left, beyond a sand trap and into some adolescent palm trees.

"That's further left than Nancy Pelosi," I said and slid behind the wheel of our golf cart.

Austin stepped off the tee box, moseyed over to the rear of the cart, and slammed his Ping driver back into his golf bag.

I penciled in our names on the scorecard and said, "Hey bud, don't blame the equipment. It's the Indian, not the arrow."

"Shut up, Alex."

Fifteen minutes later, I had made par on the first and second holes, and Austin had carded a pair of bogeys. As we motored to the next hole, he steamed like Florida in July and was $40 poorer. Our standard bet was 20 bucks per hole—enough to make things interesting but not enough to cost anyone his house.

To say I got on a roll would be an understatement. The next five holes proved that sometimes, once in a purple moon perhaps, everything just falls into place.

My hooked drive rebounded off a tree and back into the fairway. My 30-foot putt on a sloping green rolled to the edge of the cup, hesitated, and toppled in, a stroke that almost saw Austin break his putter across his knee.

"No human being is this lucky," Austin said and wiped the sweat from his eyes.

The ninth hole proved to be my encore. There stood Austin, proudly leaning on his putter, his ball only 10 feet from the hole after he'd struck a tour-level shot over a pond from 200 yards out in the fairway.

In a rare moment of appreciation, I had applauded his shot. "Best shot I've ever seen you hit, Austin."

He said nothing—being a hundred bucks down after eight holes tends to silence a man.

The ninth was the longest par-4 on the course, and Austin stared down his birdie putt as if his entire worth depended on it.

I, however, had sent my Titleist into the greenside sand, a bunker so deep that I could only see the top half of the flagstick and the collar of Austin's argyle shirt. He stood so serious and tense, wishing me bad luck, determined to win back some of his money. For a moment there, I figured he would.

But then I swung and my ball rode upward on a cushion of sand, the explosion lofting the ball high over the lip of the bunker. I scrambled out of the sand and up a closely mown hill to see the end result on the green.

The result was my ball landing into a left-to-right slope then breaking with that slope as gravity exerted its influence, the ball rolling and rolling, slowing into the grain and, to my utter shock and glee, disappearing into the hole.

Caught up in exuberance and surprise, I laughed and pumped my hands in the air. Austin looked—honestly, this is how it seemed to me, and I'm not a violent man—as if someone had plunged an ice pick into his ear.

Of course, he still had a chance to tie me. And that's when Austin began to stalk. He stalked that 10-foot putt from the east, from the north, from behind the ball, and from the moneyed perspective of a young lawyer in debt.

He stood over his ball, gripping and regripping his putter, for what seemed like a day and a half. If this had been football, the refs would have called a delay of game penalty—perhaps two penalties.

Finally Austin stroked the ball, and it rolled so smoothly, so very smoothly did it roll; and then his ball peeked into the cup in much the same manner that Austin had peeked at my test paper during our real estate law class 6 years earlier. As if punishment had been delayed until today, his ball caught the lip of the hole and spun away.

Austin had missed—again. He'd finished behind me—again.

I won't repeat what he said, what he yelled, or even what he muttered as we walked off that ninth green and over a footbridge that spanned the pond and some random clumps of marsh grass. Just know that Austin Adam's words were not mild, and that the volume and repetition of those words rattled a foursome teeing off on the first hole.

My brief wave to that foursome sufficed for an apology. They looked like retirees, all of them in gaudy golf attire, everything from plaid knickers to awful green golf shoes. But that was the appeal of

Florida—the people with healthy retirement plans and ample savings could golf and fish and play shuffleboard year-round and do so in the most colorful of wardrobes. I could never see myself in knickers—put out to pasture on green fairways while the world yawned.

We crested the bridge single file, Austin striding off ahead of me, my head down in the obligatory pose of a humble winner faking his humbleness.

Just then Austin stopped, and I nearly ran into him. Without warning, Austin pulled a golf ball from his pocket, wheeled around, and heaved it back across the bridge, over my head, and sent it soaring out over the pond.

It was quite a throw; its length and arc more suggestive of Peyton Manning than a lean, once-a-week golfer. Belying the raw anger of its launch, the ball flew gracefully against the setting sun, then it splashed hard and sunk quickly, as golf balls are apt to do.

Austin stormed off toward the cart, but I remained on the footbridge, watching the ripples expand across the pond and wondering about the fate of that ball. A small gator lived in the pond, though on this day the little monster remained submerged, or at least inconspicuous.

I suppose we all have our secret gators. And some of us have the teeth marks to prove it.

2

T WAS A FRIDAY NIGHT IN MY UNIVERSITY APARTMENT—LATE
September of our sophomore year at the University of Florida, both
of us 19—when Austin and two other members of the baseball team
wandered in to play poker around my kitchen table. It was an open
party and in the adjoining living room three freshmen swimmers
played some sort of board game that involved language skills beyond
the reach of most athletes. We preferred having a few bucks on the
line—something to keep us interested.

Austin and I both played outfield on the baseball team, though
neither of us were starters. I had determined to change that by spring.
Tonight, however, was simply cards, brews, and guy time.

The beer was cold, the poker chips shiny, and the chatter frequent
as the four of us talked of tomorrow's football game between our
4–0 Gators—ranked second in the nation—and our rival, LSU. The
game would be played before ESPN cameras and a national television
audience, a level of fame and notoriety never experienced by us lowly
baseballers. We knew that the gridiron boys produced the revenue
that paid for the school's entire athletic budget, and we supported
them in kind.

Austin was dealing the cards for the first hand when two slightly
inebriated, rich kids from the third floor wandered in and asked if
they could play.

I pointed to a pair of folding chairs propped against the wall.
"Welcome, all ye gamblers."

Austin slid them some white chips. "Dollar ante, dollar raises."

The rich kids rolled their eyes as if dollar poker was so beneath them, but they wanted to play so they unfolded their chairs and sat to my left. Austin sat directly across from me, his poker face not yet pokered.

Austin and I had met at baseball practice during freshman year, although in those days we rarely hung out beyond the white lines. By sophomore year he'd moved into the same apartment complex, and the weekend poker games had become for us a regular event to mute the pressures of studies, grades, and our shared quest to get into law school.

"Ready to lose again, Alex?" Austin said as he dealt cards around the table.

"You don't look good in orange, Austin," I replied. "Washes you out, much like I'm about to wash you out."

The previous week, Austin had won my last 10 bucks on a bluff that was more stupidity than skillful poker. After his win, he'd counted out my dollar bills one at a time, slapping them down on the table as if they were spikes driven into my ego.

This weekend would be my revenge, and in more ways than just a card game.

Grades, poker, women—what we did in college was *compete*.

To my right and left sat the four other guys, two of them sober enough to know what they were doing. Austin and I couldn't afford to play golf very often, but this poker thing, yes, this we could do.

By the fourth hand I was seven dollars ahead and Austin was down five. The inebriated rich kids could afford to lose every hand, and they acted like it. Their attention kept wandering to the growing gaggle of freshmen in my living room—the three guys plus the two freshmen girls who'd just joined them from down the hall.

During the next hand, one of the freshmen guys started playing a harmonica, but he wasn't bad so I didn't ask them to leave.

Plus I vaguely remembered doing laundry next to the bru-nette girl, and I'd already met the other one—Karen, the willowy blond—the same night Austin had won my 10 bucks. She'd been his date that night but I was sure they were no longer an item.

"You in or out, Alex?" Austin asked as he noted my distraction. He had not so much as waved to her.

"I'm in."

Just then the five freshmen in my living room began singing Johnny Cash's *Ring of Fire* as the harmonica guy lit into the chorus. They sat in a circle on the carpet, sipping Yuengling in between bursts of lyrics. Karen was the worst singer of the bunch, though her volume and enthusiasm led me to believe she'd never once considered where she ranked on the scale of bad to good.

"I'll raise a buck," I said to the guys, and just then the rich kids folded and said they were going to make a beer run—they were out of some 5-dollar-a-bottle import that probably tasted like mulch.

"I'll call," Austin said and slowly dropped a chip into the pot as if to intimidate me. "And I'll raise you a buck."

I looked over the top of my cards and caught Karen's interested gaze. A brief smile and she went back to singing. I noted for a second time the blond swirls of hair curling over her shoulders and the soft curve of her lips before turning my attention back to the cards.

The other two baseball players folded, and after all the cards were face up and the numbers tallied, I'd secured a pot of 17 crumpled dollars. Austin slumped in his chair and shook his head. The other baseball players suggested we change the game to Texas Hold 'em.

I, however, sought a different kind of change. It was time for another beer, time to scoot on to my living room carpet beside Karen and her friends, and time to introduce myself and make a lame attempt to sing like Johnny Cash.

✳ ✳ ✳

The entire gang from the apartment party—all 11 of us—sat together high in the student section for the LSU game. Blue and orange filled every nook except for a couple sections of cheap seats occupied by the hated purple and gold Cajuns.

With my meager winnings from the poker game, I offered to buy Karen a Coke and a slice of pizza, which she readily accepted. We'd just finished eating when one of our wide receivers made an impossible catch. It was only 2 minutes till halftime and I high-fived Karen, our fingers interlocking for the briefest moment.

By the fourth quarter I felt the side of her leg pressing against the side of mine, which may well have occurred much earlier in the game. However, the score was tied 24–24 and I was largely ignorant of all but the happenings on the field.

With four minutes left, LSU kicked a field goal to go ahead 27–24. The crowd sighed. Karen and I sulked together. Then I leaned forward and looked down the row, past three others and up at Austin.

"We gonna pull this one out, buddy?" I asked.

He wouldn't look my way. "Probably," he muttered.

I detected envy, but Karen had sat next to me of her own accord; it wasn't like I had bought her a specific seat. Besides, this was the University of Florida. Available women were everywhere, and Austin was handsome enough to meet his share.

The Gators drove methodically down the field as time ticked away, and with 6 seconds remaining we called our last time-out.

Everyone in our crowd expected a pass. But before the fans knew what was happening, our quarterback handed off to the tight end, who looped behind the line and pitched the ball to our speedy running back, who evaded two lineman and a safety and bolted for the end zone.

I stood and played the role of play-by-play announcer. 'He's to the ten…the five!…touchdown!"

The student body rushed the field, pouring out on to grass and slapping the shoulder pads of the giants we so admired. Most of our row bolted down the concrete steps toward the excited throng, though Karen and I stayed behind and absorbed the triumph from on high. The crowd forced Austin ahead on the steps, and for a moment he turned and looked back up at the bleachers, where Karen and I still stood by ourselves in row 47 of section T.

We sat for the longest time and took in the celebration, answering the gator chomp with our arms extended, then just talking and people-watching as players and coaches completed their hugs, high-fives, and media interviews.

Soon delirious fans streamed into the exits, and exhausted players disappeared into the tunnel. Karen and I never budged.

There were only a few dozen fans left in the stadium and several workers toiling on the sidelines when Karen turned and whispered into my ear. "Alex, do you know how I like to celebrate huge wins?"

I took a breath and turned to her. "Um, not really, but I have a feeling I'm going to like—"

Her lips met mine and they tasted of Coca-Cola—a first kiss followed by giggles and a resumption of victorious lip-lock.

"What are you giggling about now?" Karen asked, and looked me in the eyes with the wry smile of a young lady who is exactly where she wants to be.

"Meet the girl, win the poker game, win the football game," I whispered. "It's been a great 24 hours…and I hope the clock never stops."

My last comment must have been what she wanted to hear, at least if measured by the intensity of her next kiss.

After a good 10 minutes of smooching, I peeked over Karen's shoulder and down to the empty football field below. An ESPN camera guy was packing up his gear and loading it on to a cart. He wrapped an extension cord around his arm and looked up into the stands. Then he made eye contact with me, saw Karen's head burrowing into my neck, and gave me the most enthusiastic thumbs up I'd ever received.

I returned his gesture and resumed kissing on Karen, until finally we both looked down and saw a completely empty stadium—no one but us—except for the burly security guard waving at us from one section over.

"Okay, you two, I've been patient enough." He pointed to the exit. "Scram!"

I stood, grabbed Karen's hand, and said, "Sir, we were only celebrating."

He waved us away. "I know," he said, hands on hips. "My wife and I have the same tradition. But at least we wait till we get *home*. Now scram!"

We scrammed—all the way across campus until we were slow-dancing in Karen's dorm room.

Already I knew she was the woman I wanted, and I intended to keep her.

3

As Austin and I left the golf course in my BMW, I wanted to leave the match at the course and talk about work, but Austin refused to talk—about anything. He only stared out his window and twirled a golf tee between his fingers. His serious attitude about our wagers seemed so unnecessary; it wasn't like we had bet our homes and cars.

Austin owned a two-story townhouse in east Orlando, an area that had suffered a mere 40 percent drop in average sales price, compared to over 50 percent in many communities. He never mentioned his bad timing in buying the townhouse, but at least he took pride in its appearance. I pulled into his driveway and noted the manicured lawn and tightly trimmed bushes. Austin was even more of a neat freak than I was; I even imagined his golf shirts arranged in his closet by color—a cotton rainbow of conformity.

I popped the trunk and we both climbed out and met at the back bumper. He lifted his Ping golf bag from atop mine, flung it over his shoulder, and turned for his sidewalk, a brief over-the-shoulder wave sufficing for goodbye.

"Hey! I need the hundred and twenty bucks you owe me, Austin," I said and shut my trunk.

It felt horrible to have to ask him to pay up; golfer protocol requires the losing party to initiate payment, and I was big on protocol.

Now halfway to his door, Austin turned slowly and peered over his clubs. "I'll get ya' tomorrow."

Palms up, I tried to gesture my frustration with him.

Upturned palms did not sway him.

"Yo,' Big Money," I said, employing what little ability I had to mimic street talk. "You sayin' you don't have the cash? Successful young lawyer turnin' deadbeat? Man!"

From his steps he stared back, blank-faced and defeated. He pulled another golf ball out of his pocket, and for a moment I feared he might throw it at me or at my car.

But no, he just kept squeezing that ball harder and harder, as if it were a Surlyn-covered lemon from which he'd extract one last drop of juice. Finally, he turned and unlocked his front door.

"Seeya' at work," he said into his foyer.

I didn't press him any further, only envisioned him throwing that golf ball against a mirror to alleviate his anger. I didn't lose to him very often. Perhaps I should have.

Truth be told, the timing of his payment mattered little to me. I had happier people with whom to interact. One in particular—who lived under my roof and to whom I'd been married for three-and-a-half years.

Her name was Karen Lord, and though she practiced often in the shower—and sometime we even attempted a duet—she still couldn't sing.

* * *

The marble hallways of Powers, Morgan, and Greene echoed my footsteps until I turned a corner and centered my route on an oriental runner. Our hallways boasted the kind of brooding artwork that hinted strongly at aristocracy, interspersed with framed portraits of partners long dead. After passing the last of their stoic mugs, I summoned a deep breath and mentally rehearsed my entrance into Conference room C. Ten seconds to show time.

There are many moments in an attorney's life, where he or she prepares to enter a conference room without knowing the mind-set or the demeanor of the party who initiated a lawsuit. If I knew beforehand when I entered the room that I'd be met with narrowed eyes and pursed lips, I too would enter with pursed lips. (I saved narrowed eyes for the courtroom, rude door-to-door salesmen, and golf games with Austin.)

Likewise, if I knew beforehand when I entered the room that I'd be met with a fake smile, well, I could summon fake smiles with the best of them.

I turned the brass handle and pushed open the door.

My first glance met the competitive gaze of Mort Anderson, a sixty-ish blue-collar worker who sat uncomfortably on the far side of PMG's massive mahogany conference table. Mort's same-aged lawyer, Teddy DePasquale, filled the seat next to Mort and nodded a greeting at me.

"Alex."

I approached the table. "Teddy."

Teddy worked for a smaller firm, and from the look of his suit he was only scraping by as an attorney. Still, he had experience on his side, and as my opponent he deserved and received respect.

I sat opposite them and opened my briefcase.

"Mr. Anderson," I said and pulled papers from a file, "my clients think your lawsuit is absolutely baseless. They believe you're trying to squeeze them for a few dollars in order to goose the quality of your retirement."

Mort Anderson's eyes widened in shock. "Horsefeathers."

I was expecting 'That's BS,' or perhaps, 'That's a load of crap.' But no, he'd actually said 'horsefeathers.' If money hadn't been at stake, I would have laughed.

Instead, I met his stare. "Your work deteriorated, sir."

He shook his head as Teddy D pursed his lips.

Mr. Anderson banged a fist on the table. "Thirty-seven years! For 37 years I slave for them, and then they throw me away like an old shoe. My work was still as good as—"

I raised a hand to halt him.

"Mr. Anderson, I'm not here to debate what occurred over the span of your career. I'm here to see if we can settle the case."

Teddy D knew it was time to intervene, and intervene he did.

"What are you proposing, Alex?"

I arranged three documents neatly on the table. "I have here a release, a notice of voluntary dismissal, and a check." I reached out and tapped the papers for effect. "Mr. Anderson signs the release, you sign the dismissal, and the check is his."

I slid the check across the table's glossy surface and stopped it a foot from Mr. Anderson's left hand, which nervously moved to pick it up.

Teddy D, however, beat him to it. Teddy snatched the check, and the two men huddled in their chairs and eyed its sum. I watched them for a reaction and was reminded of Austin as his birdie putt slid past the hole—a growing disappointment followed by tight-lipped frustration.

Disappointment was a major export of Powers, Morgan, and Greene. To our opponents we shipped out disappointment with all the regularity of teenagers sending out texts. Just this week, the junior associates had exported disappointment to a fast-food customer suing because her apple pie was too hot; to a pay-at-the-pump customer who'd given himself a skin rash by squirting gasoline on his leg; to a fishing boat captain who'd rammed his boat into a dock; and to an illegal immigrant who thought he'd been discriminated against when the City of Orlando refused to grant him a business license.

At this moment inside the stucco walls of PMG, various lawyers sat in a dozen other conference rooms having the same conversations with our adversaries—how to settle as cheaply as possible for our clients.

Even Austin was probably sitting in a nearby conference room, settling some labor versus management case, or perhaps a foreclosure. Good Lord, were we inundated with foreclosure cases—Floridians had collectively lost enough home equity to buy Australia. The backlog was so deep, the banks so overwhelmed with the sheer quantity of people ceasing to pay on their underwater loans, that people were staying in those homes for 6 months, 12 months, and even longer before their case reached the point where they were kicked out for not paying their mortgage.

Today, however, my goal was to kick out Mort Anderson and Teddy D, though I suspected the brunt of the kick would be softened by the $30,000 sum printed on the check, the same check they gazed at in unison, frowns stretched across their faces like Halloween masks of doom.

"This ain't right!" Mort Anderson protested. "It just ain't right."

He was right about that.

The disappointment we exported did not always hit at once; sometimes it crept upon a person over a span of years, as he realized that he'd had his shot, had met with legal resistance, and ultimately signed away his rights for a pittance. Most of our opponents were familiar with time-release capsules, so we at Powers, Morgan, and Greene sought also to familiarize them with time-release disappointment.

Teddy D leaned across the table and narrowed his eyes. "This is a poor excuse for settlement, Mr. Lord. In fact, it's less settlement than excrement."

I couldn't help but smile. I appreciated spontaneous wit. "Good one, Teddy."

"Don't 'good one' me, Alex."

"It just ain't right!" Mort repeated, as if the aging turntable of his mind had its needle stuck on one phrase.

I nodded, not to agree with him, but to convey that I understood that he felt that way. Then I looked at Teddy for a couple seconds, then at Mort for a few more. "Juries decide right and wrong, gentlemen. This is about money."

"This is about getting screwed!" Mort shot back, his needle unstuck.

He was right again. But each man in the room knew that Mort wasn't going anywhere. He did, however, attempt a bluff. He rose from his chair and turned for the door, though he never extended his hand to grip the knob. He just stood there, frozen in a chasm of choice—to take what was offered or risk going to trial and getting nothing at all.

Across the table, Teddy D said nothing. He just held the check in both hands and shook his head as he imported disappointment and calculated his cut.

"Let me explain something to you, Mr. Anderson," I said with resolve. "Logan Aerospace is a *Fortune 500* company, and they defend lawsuits with vigor and tenacity."

Mort huffed and folded his arms. "More like with thuggery and with two-by-fours rammed up their opponent's ass."

Teddy D raised a hand of wisdom to his client. "Mort, let's calm ourselves here."

It was time to apply the real pressure. "Powers, Morgan, and Greene is one of the largest firms in the country, and if necessary we'll put 50 lawyers on this case who will work insane hours for the next 10 years dreaming up defenses that your attorneys have never heard of. If you choose to go forward, just know that you'll get crushed."

Mort Anderson took a step toward me and clinched his right fist. "Don't you threaten me, you—"

Teddy D rushed around the end of the conference table and put an arm around Mort. "Shhh," he whispered to his client. "Fistfights won't solve a thing."

I remained seated and assumed a nonaggressive pose. Knowing I had them on the ropes, I slouched a bit in my chair and interlocked my fingers across my stomach. "Look, Mr. Anderson, I'm not threatening you. Even your attorney knows that this case has holes wide enough to drive his Volvo through. But let's assume for a minute that a miracle happens and you do win. You may not even be alive to see it or celebrate it. It would likely take years—and every dollar you have—for that to happen, and it would not be a pleasant trip."

He turned to face me. "Hell of a way to make a living, Mr. Lord…screwing people out of money all day long."

That was all I could take. "Fine. Try your luck in court." I stood and closed my briefcase. "David beat Goliath once, and it was so amazing that we're still talking about it."

For a moment I regretted using the David and Goliath line. Behind that analogy, way back in the mind of an attorney who rarely made it to church, was the fact that David used great violence, a high-velocity stone propelled from a sling and striking a bull's-eye in the center of Goliath's forehead. As if I could not stifle my thoughts, my mind raced ahead and I saw Mort Anderson suddenly thinking himself a vengeful David, perched atop an adjacent building not with a sling but with a sniper rifle. He was peering through its scope, about to launch a high-velocity bullet at one Alexander Lord.

No. Control your thoughts, Alex. At PMG, we don't do fear.

We faced each other at the doorway, and I decided then that Mr. Anderson was not only nonviolent, but also, from all observable evidence, pretty much nonintelligent.

As we sized up each other, there were no intimidating gestures from either side. Mort Anderson just slumped his shoulders, looked sadly at me and said, "How do you sleep, son?"

His words rattled me but I did not show it. I could not show it. Even though I was half his age and respected my seniors, even senior *opponents*, I could not show it. Still, for a brief moment I wondered how I did sleep. Perhaps the firm had brainwashed all compassion from its young lawyers. More likely, however, the young lawyers saw compassion as an obstacle to reaching our holy grail—partner. Austin and I were in a race to that pinnacle of prosperity, and I was determined to win again.

Today, however, I just needed to win this hand of attorney poker. "Mr. Anderson, there will not be another offer. Take a long look at the check I left on the table. It's the last check from Logan Aerospace you will ever see."

Two minutes later I left the room and retraced my route down PMG's plush, marbled hallway, the oriental runner cushioning my steps as I strode toward my office. I took one last look behind me and saw my opponents board the elevator at the far end of the hallway, their twin stares of defeat containing enough angst to turn me back around again.

I wasn't lying to Mr. Anderson. He would have been destroyed in court. Fighting solo against an army doesn't mean you're brave; it means you're an idiot.

I stopped at the sprawling desk of my assistant, Carol, and handed her the signed papers. Carol was just north of 50 and perhaps the most efficient person in the entire firm.

"Carol," I said, with a trace of a victorious smile, "please file this dismissal today, and copy Logan Aerospace as well."

Carol nodded like the team player she'd always been. "Mr. Anderson took the check, huh?" She checked the signatures and nodded again. "Congrats, Alex. I'm glad he didn't spoil your big day."

I tapped the corner of her desk. "That guy couldn't spoil my day no matter how hard he tried."

I strode into my office to find 10 blue and orange balloons bulging with helium tied to my flat screen monitor, the largest balloon inscribed with *The Big 3-0!* A card was attached, the congratulatory note professional and encouraging.

I went to my door and stuck my head into the hall. "Thank you, Carol! Nice touch. You're the best."

She waved me off as if it were nothing.

I hadn't noticed the small gift waiting for me in the desk chair, the thin little box impeccably wrapped in silver paper, a twirl of blue ribbon in the top left corner.

I shed the wrapping paper and opened the box to find a silver pen with an *L* inscribed on its clip.

A note rested in the bottom of the box:

This pen cannot be used for anything legal! Consider it an investment in our future. Someday, Lord willing, we will be parents, and this pen is for us to use as a couple to write down memories to share with our children.

Happy 30th! Looking forward to dinner tonight.
Much love,
Karen

It too was a nice touch, having a gift waiting—and the thought of writing memories for our future children was something that excited me—but I also saw the invisible wording between Karen's lines. She was as anxious as ever to conceive a child. We'd been trying for 8 months, although the last time we'd tried, well, she'd only been *physically* present. During our first year of marriage, perhaps that was okay with me, her being only physically available. But by year three that wasn't enough; I wanted all of her now—her mind, her body, her soul.

The enjoyment of past attempts were turning over in my head when Austin bolted into my office and tossed a box of cigars on to my desk.

Shocked that he'd remembered my birthday, I pointed at the box and then at myself. "For me?"

Austin folded his arms and smirked. "Before you even ask, just know that the hundred and twenty I owe ya is in the box."

"Ah," I said and reached for the box, "cash with a scent of Colombian…nice, Austin. Thank you." I opened the box, drew out the money, and noted a couple of cigars were missing from the neat rows of 10.

"I helped myself to a couple," Austin said, with hardly a trace of shame. "They're really good."

Neither of us had noticed Richard Sterling, one of the firm's silver-haired and super-intense partners, standing in the doorway.

"Alex!"

Austin turned to face the voice.

Sterling eyed Austin from head to toe. "You're not Alex. But then, all you young guys look the same."

Austin and I chuckled, but only because we felt it was our duty.

Sterling shifted his attention to me and leaned a bit to his left to see around the balloons. "I need to see you, Alex. Five minutes, my office."

"Yes, sir."

He left in a blur, and Austin made sure he was gone before whispering, "Must be very important, golden boy."

I closed the box of cigars. "You know it, man."

Private meetings with a partner could be anything, but between Austin and me, they meant the other had pulled a step ahead. I knew I wasn't in any trouble with Sterling; the man was so competent and informed that he probably knew already the minute details of the

Logan settlement. Perhaps now he wanted to trust me with a bigger case.

I pulled my jacket from the back of my chair and slipped into it just as Austin spotted the Ping putter leaning against my book-shelf. He grabbed the putter, assumed a golf stance, and took a practice stroke atop my rug. "What time are we drowning olives tonight?"

We'd celebrated his 30th birthday 3 months earlier with a couple of martinis, and he'd told me that he wanted to reciprocate. I'd forgotten his offer, which he'd served up two days earlier as we passed each other in the men's room.

"I'm supposed to go to dinner with Karen."

Austin made another practice stroke. "Go to dinner *after* drinks. You really need to go out, man. How long's it been since we did happy hour...4, 5 weeks?"

I frowned and straightened my tie.

"Don't be a wimp," Austin chastised. "You're going for drinks. I'll tell Tatiana to wear something sexy."

Where Austin met these women was a mystery to all the other associates, including me. If Tatiana was like the previous one, she'd giggle at whatever Austin said, order whatever he ordered, and not know the difference between lawsuits and linguini.

"You still seeing her?" I asked, watching the clock until I met with Sterling.

"Three weeks and counting," Austin said, and set my putter back against the bookshelf.

I hurried around him and out into the marble hallway. "Sounds serious."

He followed me out, turned the opposite direction, and spoke over his shoulder. "Yeah, right. See ya' at 7. Bring Karen with you."

Karen had told me—months before our marriage—that during college she'd had two dates with Austin, and that the most romantic they'd ever been was just a kiss goodnight on the steps of her dormi-tory. This just 2 weeks before I'd made out with her in the stands after the football game.

Although Austin would never admit it, my being with Karen had got to him, and deep down I suspected that he wished she had a twin sister.

With 2 minutes to go before I was due in Sterling's office, I pulled out my Blackberry and called Karen. I had stopped in the hallway and faced one of the partner's portraits hanging on the far wall. His look seemed so refined—the patented attorney mug. Before Karen answered I glared up at the framed partner and said, "Happy Birthday to you, too, Smiley."

"Karen. Hey."

"How's the birthday boy?"

I pictured her at her drafting table, designing some state-of-the-art building. She liked her work but loved even more the thought of being a stay-at-home mom.

"I'm good. Loved the pen. Thank you."

"You're quite welcome. Carol had the balloon people drop it off for me. Tell her thanks for me."

"Sure. Hey, let's meet a couple friends for a drink before we go to dinner tonight."

Her pause was not a great sign. "I thought tonight would just be you and me, then dessert in our birthday suits."

Oh man, how she could sway me. "Tonight *is* just you and me...I mean it *will* be. C'mon, Karen, Austin gave me a box of expensive cigars and I kinda' hinted that we'd have one drink with him. Just 45 minutes or so, then we'll go eat."

Another pause. "Is he bringing whatshername, the one who wears the skanky clothes and couldn't spell 'cat' even if we spotted her the c and the a?"

I chuckled and stared up at the stoic partner painting. "Austin will be with a different whatshername, but yeah, basically the same woman as before."

Her sigh of resignation induced in me only mild guilt. She'd be fine. After all, Karen liked Austin; she just wasn't crazy about the women he dated.

"Okay," she said. "But only one drink. Besides, it's *your* birthday."

"You're the best."

"Tell me that after dessert."

* * *

Richard Sterling's corner office seemed large, chilly, and well-appointed, just like its occupant. His back was turned to me as he sat in his bulbous chair and glared out the window at the city beyond. He looked like a Master of the Universe, one of the few characters in Orlando who thought himself more important to the city than the Mouse.

Personally, I liked the Mouse. I had proposed to Karen in a park at Epcot one night, after arranging a place of solitude with one of the park managers.

Today, however, was not about solitude but about obedience. I always felt like a third-grader in the principal's office when I entered the opulent realm of Mr. Sterling. I had no clue why he wanted to see me. My best guess was some wildly complicated and complex assignment for which he'd demand a due date of last Thursday.

I sat in his guest chair and he spun around in his own.

"Alex, an individual named Abner Plott is suing our firm and the Hammond National Bank."

No surprise that he'd summed up the entire reason for our meeting in one sentence. Sterling was a man of few words—unless he was presenting a case to a jury. There he became one part Jay Leno and five parts Johnny Cochran. It was all an act, of course, but that act had earned him millions of dollars.

Someday I expected the name of the firm to elongate to where it became Powers, Morgan, Greene, and Sterling. Twenty years later, of course, I hoped it to read Powers, Morgan, Greene, Sterling, and Lord.

Richard Sterling slid a file across his ample desk. I opened the file and read the document inside, which did not resemble anything legal. It was just one solid paragraph of capital letters, raw emotion, phony presumption, and underlined clauses:

> *Hammond National Bank and POWERS MORGAN AND GREENE KNOWINGLY committed <u>GREAT FRAUD</u> and costed one ABNER PLOTT his HOUSE at 1223 SHADOW PALM LANE and also costed ABNER PLOTT tens of thousands of dollars. The recklessness and aggressive actions of HAMMOND NATIONAL and POWERS MORGAN AND GREENE causes me to sue for the sum of <u>NINETY-FIVE THOUSAND DOLLARS</u>, whether it comes to ABNER PLOTT from EITHER ONE of the above or is SPLIT and <u>PAID EQUALLY</u> BETWEEN THEM.*

The document was the legal equivalent of turning in a Master's Thesis written in pencil and scrawled onto a notepad without indentions.

Incredulously, I peered over the paper to the glare of Sterling.

"Alex," and he let my name linger for a moment, "Mr. Plott decided that he simply did not want to make any more of his mortgage payments, and so Hammond National foreclosed. Now he sues us for representing Hammond."

I looked again at the title of Plott's document. "Complaint for Damages of Constructive Bank Fraud, whatever that means."

Sterling leaned back in his chair and put his hands behind his head. "I want this to disappear, understand me? I want this gone, and gone immediately. File a motion to dismiss, and do it before you leave tonight."

I set the odd document back into the file and closed it as if it were a trivial matter. "Are you going to argue the motion, sir?"

Sterling smirked. "Alex, when you become a partner, you'll have associates handle all the nuisance cases…just like I do."

"I understand."

His nod told me our meeting had just ended.

I stood and told him that I'd get right on it.

In a gesture I did not expect, Sterling stood also and reached across his desk and shook my hand. "This case won't be a big deal,

Alex," he said and let go of my hand. "You might even find it somewhat amusing. Mr. Plott is just a wee bit unusual. Some might call him 'eccentric.'"

A nutty old man, I figured. No problem.

"I'll handle it, sir." I turned for the door and nearly made it there, but just as my hand gripped the brass knob, he halted me with one word.

"Alex!"

Oh, man. What now? I turned to face him. "Sir?"

Richard Sterling pointed an index finger at me. "Happy 30th."

"Thank you, sir."

4

USTIN AND TATIANA WERE SIPPING MARTINIS AT A SOFTLY LIT table for four when Karen and I strolled into the bar. Their postures and the way they scanned the room without moving their necks made them look more like part of the décor than a couple out on a date. I took Karen by the hand and led her in their direction. En route I noted Karen's curious expression as she observed Tatiana's low-cut orange dress—so low that it might qualify her for skankdom.

"You're sure that isn't the same woman as last time?" Karen whispered.

"I'm sure."

We began with small waves and sat quickly—Austin to my left, Karen to my right, and Tatiana directly across from me in all her voluptuous glory. By the time the ladies had been introduced and a waiter had taken our order, Austin raised his glass and said loudly. "Here's to our good friend, a lucky golfer, and the second most important associate at PMG, the one and only J. Alexander Lord, the—." Austin had stumbled over his toast. "The…thirtieth."

He surely meant 30th birthday, because there weren't 29 other J. Alexander Lords in my family tree. Still, the rest of us met his glass with our own and clinked them above Tatiana's spring rolls, which she'd barely touched.

Austin sipped his drink before leaning toward me and addressing me in a low voice. "Maybe by your 40th birthday, you'll be a partner. And then you really will be lord."

"I'll be there long before then, my friend. And long before you."

Austin reached for my glass, held it below his nose as if he knew what he was doing, and sniffed the contents.

"Bargain Mart Winery," I said to him. "They make great vino."

"Stop, just stop," he said in mock disgust. "I wanted to work on that case. Do ya' have to bring that up again tonight?"

Austin wasn't jealous; he was just trying to put on a show. But at that moment I saw Karen running a hand through her hair—her signal that I was not to spend the evening discussing work with Austin.

Still, I couldn't resist one last whispered jab to Austin. "When I make partner, the first thing I'll do is to inform all the other partners what a sick individual you've become."

Austin's eyes widened and he feigned shock. "Oh yeah, sure, let's pull each other up the ladder, buddy."

Tatiana leaned forward until her ample bosom pressed against the table. "What's the big deal about making partner? Is that all you guys ever talk about?"

"It's a career goal for Alex," Karen offered. "He's worked hard for it."

My wife—the steady one, the calmer of storms, the reasoned thinker among ignorant fools.

"Tatiana, Tatiana," Austin said and shook his head in rebuttal. "You are so very naïve."

Tatiana sipped her martini and sat back in her chair with a look of offense.

"It's the gold at the end of the rainbow," I said. "And sometimes we associates feel like Leprechauns with lead in our shoes."

Austin banged his empty glass twice upon the table. "Four years of college, busting your ass to get into a decent law school. Then three more years re-busting your ass to land a job with a good firm. Then, after those seven years of torture, you get to take the bar exam, which is kinda' like rectal surgery."

"So that's why you two have been walking funny, " Karen said.

I chuckled, but my fellow associate gave Karen a look of disapproval, as if no one at the table really understood the obstacles that

Austin Adams had endured in his underprivileged, country club life, never mind his underdeveloped maturity or his overly starched shirts. "Then," he said, with great emphasis. "*then* comes seven years minimum of 70-to-80-hour weeks to become a nonequity partner."

The light kick to my ankle was from my wife, informing me with her size-six heel that this little meet-for-drinks event was not to her liking; she was fine with my ending it—at my discretion—and escorting her to dinner.

Austin was not finished. He clutched his empty glass as if it were his last friend in the world. "Then after three or four more years of butt-busting, maybe they let you in the club and call you a partner."

Tatiana turned to him with her latest revelation. "Your butt must really be sore by the time you get there, huh?"

"Sure," I said, "but Austin would tell you that it feels better with all the associates kissing it for the rest of his life."

"There's something to aspire to," Karen said.

I turned to her and could not stop myself. "I suppose you'd be happy if I worked at a gas station and walked through the door at 5:30 sharp every night?'

As she diverted her gaze to her lap and said nothing, I immediately regretted my comment. Birthday or not, I had embarrassed my wife. I reached under the table and patted her hand. Sorry, baby. After a slight delay, she squeezed my fingers.

Austin, being Austin, tried to capitalize on my mistake. "Oh yeah, Alex, she'd love crawling into bed every night with a guy who reeked of motor oil and axle grease."

Karen gave Austin a smirk and looked away.

His eyes remained on her, as if checking to see if he'd scored points, and right then I knew it was time for dinner. For two.

∗ ∗ ∗

It was nearly midnight when I undressed, crawled into bed, and sat up with my back against a pillow. I pulled from the foot of the bed my big gift—a new leather briefcase, which proved even more impressive as I admired its plush interior. Even after two bottles of champagne at dinner, I was still sober enough to appreciate quality.

Karen had given me the gift in her car as we'd parked at Gargi's. Italian food had long been a favorite of mine, and she'd reserved a corner table with a view of the water. As soon as we'd been seated, she'd admitted that she was glad that the awkward and shallow nature of our double date in the bar was a distant memory. I, in turn, had admitted that I was glad to be apart from Austin and Tatiana, who seemed like they had struck some kind of deal with each other. *I'll wear sexy dresses and be your escort if you'll take me to nice places and pay for everything.* Karen and I agreed that the two of them had little chemistry, but that they probably deserved each other.

The manicotti and lasagna had settled—as had the champagne. I ran a finger across the shiny leather top of my briefcase and began thinking of dessert.

"Karen," I called into the bathroom. "This is such a great gift. Really awesome. I can't imagine what you paid for it."

A faucet spewed and cut off. "What'd you say, honey?"

"I asked if you were going to sing for me on my birthday."

"Only if you wish to go deaf." She stuck her head out the bathroom door, a towel around her neck. "Besides, even if I *could* sing, I wouldn't be in the mood after your little gas station comment earlier."

"C'mon, Karen! I told you I was sorry while we were sitting there with Austin and whatshername."

She remained in the bathroom for another 5 minutes. Five minutes became 10.

Impatient, I called into the bathroom again. "Karen, come to bed with me. It's getting lonely out here."

She came out of the bathroom in a plain blue nightgown, walked past the bed, and closed the curtains that overlooked the pool. I should have closed them myself but I'd been too busy admiring my briefcase. I set it on the floor and watched my wife ease around the bed to her side.

I fluffed her pillow for her and spoke to her in a whisper. "You're so beautiful that it amazes me to think you're mine."

"Alex, please."

She crawled into bed and turned her back to me.

There was no denying the message. What I'd said to her at the bar had acted as an anchor on levity; the celebratory dinner seemed awkward as soon as we lifted our menus and held them perhaps an inch higher than usual. Austin's comment about my coming home smelling of gasoline had lingered around our date like an unwelcome whiff of unleaded. No matter what I'd said at dinner to soften things, no matter the length and breadth of my apology, Karen remained subdued, trying to steer any and all conversation to the fact that most of our similarly aged friends were already parents—and we were rapidly falling behind.

I reached under the covers and began stroking the side of her hip. "You know, honey, when we left the restaurant I was looking forward to some birthday love, and I still am."

"Can we just go to sleep?"

I stroked her hair, then her back. "You said we'd enjoy all the frills tonight. You even sounded pretty excited about it."

"I was—earlier today."

I turned onto my back and stared up at a dark ceiling. "We're never going to get pregnant if we don't do it."

Long seconds of silence passed. "I'm thinking of going back on the pill."

"Well, if you're sure that's what you want to do."

Her head turned slightly on her pillow. "You know it's not what I want to do."

"Hey, no need to go there. We've been trying. You wanted to try...so, we're trying. It's fun to try."

Now she turned to face me full on, and the length of her sigh served as a warning for me to listen close. "Alex, I think we should wait another month or two, perhaps seek some wise counsel because we're not interacting as one. Two become *one*, remember? But we're still *two*, and in that state we'll never model a unified marriage to a child."

Oh, man, she'd broken out the kind of language she summoned when she needed to make a point. She had this reservoir of relational instinct and marital language that she'd downloaded at some point in her past. Probably from church or family or some of both. Who knew? It wasn't like either of us jumped out of bed on Sunday mornings to get each other to church. I wasn't even sure where the church was located. Regardless, her comment about two not becoming one got to me, so I did my best to deflect the topic.

"Karen, please tell me what—"

She sat up and faced me. "Alex, what did I wear tonight?"

"Huh?"

"At dinner tonight, what was I wearing?"

"Look, if you don't want to do it tonight, just say so."

"You have no idea what I wore on your 30th birthday, do you?"

I rolled over and faced the curtains. "This little talk is going nowhere."

For long minutes, I toggled between a black dress and a green dress, but sleep overwhelmed me before I could embarrass myself with a guess.

5

ARK GREEN.

The courthouse steps glinted brightly in the morning sun, and I took them two at a time, my wingtips clicking as I passed a bell ringer with a plastic bucket—a volunteer perhaps—raising money on the sidewalk to benefit the homeless. It was only September; it wasn't the Christmas ringers, although they may have started early due to the recession. On the top step I glanced back down at the bell ringer but knew there was no time to stop and be charitable.

Judge Robert Hancock's waiting room was my destination, and when I arrived, his judicial assistant set her phone in its cradle and answered my nod of greeting. "Good morning," she said.

"Good morning. I'm Alexander Lord, here for the ten-thirty."

She perused a schedule and ran a finger down its page. "Very good, Mr. Lord. The judge is running just a few minutes behind."

"No problem," I said and retreated over to guest seating. Six chairs—three and three interrupted by a corner table. I sat nearest the table, set my briefcase in the adjacent chair, and drew out the file for one Abner Plott.

His name kept orbiting in my mind. *Abner Plott.* It sounded so backwoods, and it conjured for me a man in dungarees, tromping through the hills of Tennessee with a double-barrel shotgun, huntin' himself a squirrel or a possum for his dinner. A man named Abner Plott probably spent his weekends engaged in Civil War re-enactments and always insisted he get to play a Confederate soldier. *Kill the Union.* Spit, spit.

I knew him as soon as he walked into the waiting room. Without a glance my way, he shuffled to the judicial assistant's desk. His back was hunched in a way that made him teeter to the right with each step. He was probably in his early 70s, his wrinkled gray suit probably in its 30s. But he looked neat—his hair damp and combed into place, hands cleaned, and shoes polished. He stopped several paces short of the assistant, a bit further back than most people would have stopped, as if he were cautious of this entire building and its educated occupants.

"Can I help you, sir?" the JA asked.

"Hello," he said in a kind of monotone. "I would like to speak with the judge, please."

"Are you here for a hearing?"

"A what?"

"Sir, are you here for a hearing? On a motion?"

He looked at her as if she spoke a language from the jungles of New Guinea. "They took my house away."

The secretary looked at him with a lot more compassion than I would have mustered. "Did you receive something in the mail telling you to be here today, at this hour?"

Abner Plott reached into his coat with the deliberate nature of a man reaching for his pocket watch. He drew out a folded piece of paper and handed it to her.

She looked a bit miffed that he had not bothered to unfold it and read it himself, but she remained professional and read it herself.

"You are Mr. Plott?" she inquired.

"Yes. I'm Abner Plott."

"Have a seat, sir." She motioned my way.

"Thank you," he said.

Mr. Plott loped across the waiting room and sat two seats away, only my briefcase and some stale air separating us. I could feel his stare, and it was neither hate nor affection. What I felt from him as I checked messages on my Blackberry was a kind of yearning for justice.

Attorneys often detect such vibes from opponents: They think we're supposed to understand, that deep down we know they are right, and we have no business representing the defense.

His head tilted down a tad, and I knew he was staring now at my new briefcase and calculating how much it cost. The man probably didn't even know the difference between a partner and an associate. From the detail and quality of that briefcase he was figuring me for a Mercedes, a five-bedroom stucco in Windemere, and vacations in Belize.

"Hello," he said, in a measured tone. "I'm Abner Plott."

I glanced his way and saw him begin to extend a hand, as if he weren't sure if we should shake or not. My hands remained resting on the arms of my chair. After an awkward moment, Mr. Plott withdrew his hand and settled back into his seat.

"Hello." My reply was intentionally flat, though I thought it a bit colder than I'd intended.

His gaze left my briefcase and shifted to my face. "Have I done something to offend you, sir?" He said this with a faux innocence that I'd heard before—always from blue-collar plaintiffs looking for any way possible to back a young attorney into a corner.

I turned to him and met his stare. "Powers, Morgan, and Greene does not like to be sued."

He nodded in the manner of an innocent child. "Oh, I see." Then he looked me over from toe to head. "And which one are you?"

I wasn't sure if he was trying to get under my skin or if he truly thought I was one of the founders. I went with the latter answer. "None of the above. They're all long gone."

"Oh, I see." He seemed to rock back and forth in his chair now, as if methodical movement brought clarity to his thoughts. "Then why do they care about getting sued?"

Answers to his ridiculous question eluded me, and I felt relief when the door to the judge's chambers pushed open and a stocky bailiff emerged.

He quickly scanned the waiting room, saw the two of us, and called out in an authoritative voice, "Plott versus Powers, Morgan, and Greene."

I grabbed my briefcase and snapped to my feet. Without so much as a sideways glance at Abner Plott, I walked blank-faced past the stiff-lipped bailiff and into the judge's chambers.

Judge Hancock looked tall even as he sat behind his desk and read the file. I imagined him up on the bench—already towering over the courtroom—and how intimidating he might appear to both sides. A long table, set perpendicular to his desk, gave the room the appearance of a giant T. I moved along the left side of the table, took a seat nearest the judge, and hoped he wasn't teed off about anything.

"Good morning," I said, in as professional a voice as I could muster. "Alex Lord, Powers, Morgan, and Greene. Judge, I believe we met at the Lake Nona member-guest tournament last April. You have one heck of a golf swing."

"Thanks." He looked out the window to his right and appeared to be reflecting. "Ah, I remember now. You played with Commissioner Monroe, and you tossed part of your sandwich to that gator in the pond."

I smiled at his recollection. "That was me, sir."

His attention shifted back to the file. "You shouldn't feed those things."

Plott had wandered in behind me and sat down at the far end of the table, where he was the maximum distance from me, but more importantly, from the judge. We now had Plott at the bottom of the T, me in the middle, and Judge Hancock at the top, which made for a lot of head swiveling on my part.

At least for a few seconds—until the judge thought better of it.

"Sir," he called to Plott in a loud voice, "Why don't you come up here and have a seat across from Mr. Lord? This way none of us has to shout."

The bailiff gripped the back of Plott's chair, waited for him to rise, and pulled the chair back to assist in the transition. Plott shuffled up the right side of the long table and sat dutifully across from me, his gaze remaining on the table. He appeared to be deep in thought.

"Mr. Lord," the judge announced, "This is your motion."

I nodded to him and, just to appear professional, to Plott. "Thank you, your honor. We have before the court Powers, Morgan, and Greene and Hammond National Bank's motion to dismiss Abner Plott's pro se complaint."

Mr. Plott glanced at the judge, then at me, then back to the judge. "Pro who?"

I knew the question would come. The words "pro se" were to Abner Plott the equivalent of Mandarin Chinese—foreign syllables of raw jibberish.

Judge Hancock cleared his throat. "'Pro se means you do not have an attorney."

"Oh." Recognition flashed in Plott's face, and he sat up straight as if competence was now fully restored. "No, I don't have an attorney anymore."

Time to interrupt. "Judge, if I may. This case is nothing but pure retaliation." I reached for the complaint, held it high for all to see, and then lowered it and began reading. "In the first paragraph, Mr. Plott alleges that Hammond acted, and I quote, with intent to defraud Abner Plott from his private property without no cause of action promulgate by the head of the agency to foreclose—" I stopped not only to take a breath but also to let the ridiculous nature of the words settle upon Judge Hancock, whose eyebrows had twitched at the grammatical screech, 'without no cause.'

He'd likely heard worse in his years on the bench, but right then, he looked as if this were a first.

I continued quoting. "'And for failure to justify the promulgate rules regarding the implementation of foreclosure statutes.' I mean, to allow this to go forward, Judge, would..."

He cut me off with a wave of his hand. "I've read your motion. Now I would like to hear what Mr. Plott has to say to us this morning."

Abner Plott stood, adjusted his tie, and tried to press the wrinkles from his worn gray suit. "Thank you. Sir, to begin, this man seated across from me is not authorized to practice law in the state of Florida, or anywheres else."

Anywheres. Not only was he spewing lies, he was butchering his own spew. I looked at the judge, whose face relayed a measured confusion, caught as he was between trying to hear both sides while at the same time deciphering the muddled ramblings of Mr. Plott.

Plott continued. "The certificate to practice law issued by the state Supreme Court is not a license issued by the office of the secretary of state promulgate rules to practice law as a common right."

Judge Hancock looked at Plott, sighed briefly, and shook his head. "Mr. Plott, let's just assume for a minute that Mr. Lord is able to practice law in the state of Florida. Tell me *why* you are suing his firm and the bank."

Plott nodded, paused, and nodded again. I assumed he was attempting to remember something he'd memorized. Or perhaps he was making it all up as he went.

"Certainly, Judge," Plott said, and pointed at me. "His firm is operating under false advertising malpractice, and operating as actual shysters as defined by *Black's Law Dictionary*. They also did not take corrective action regarding personnel whose vicious propensities were notorious."

Who's vicious propensities were notorious? I had to jot this one in my notes, just to show Karen the kind of people with whom I sometimes deal. The wording was so absurd that I figured it might even draw a laugh from Austin.

Judge Hancock slowly closed his file, pursed his lips, and narrowed his eyes into a decision. "Mr. Plott, I understand that you lost your home. That is an unfortunate circumstance for anyone, and I do sympathize with you. However, the bank and the law firm acted within the law." His attention shifted to me. "Mr. Lord, submit an order."

Our little meeting ended seconds later, and Abner Plott looked deflated. He stood and walked with his head down toward the door. Then he opened the door and looked back at the judge, at me, and then he just stared at the floor for what seemed like a full minute. Finally he turned and walked away without a word spoken to anyone.

By this time I had collected my papers into my file. I shut my briefcase quickly but then reconsidered a hasty departure; I wanted to linger a moment there in the judge's chambers to give Plott enough time to move through the waiting room and reach the elevators and disappear. He'd be out of my sight for good, gone back to his raccoon huntin' and his Civil War re-enactments.

File in hand, I thanked Judge Hancock and made my way down the length of his long table and reached to push open the door.

"Mr. Lord." The judge's voice hammered me from behind like a gavel. I could already guess what was coming.

"Yes, Judge?"

He placed his elbows on his desk and leaned forward. "Just as you shouldn't toss part of your ham-on-wheat to reptiles with large teeth, you likewise should not make condescending facial gestures to an opponent who has lost his home."

He was right, and I admitted as much. The foreclosure crisis was so much worse than I'd figured. Every day the Florida newspapers printed horror stories of families finding their locks changed, their stuff on the curb, their homes worth half of their mortgage balance. I had kept the Sunday front page photo of a house whose owner had spray-painted a message onto its white siding the day he was evicted. *My house was underwater before the waters began to rise.*

But despite my sympathy for victims of the real estate debacle— Karen and I had seen the appraised value of our home fall from $340K to $260K—I left the judge's chambers knowing I'd won my little battle with Abner Plott.

The waiting room was empty and the secretary nowhere to be seen as I entered an empty hallway, its light gray tiles glossy and polished. The elevator beeped, and while I waited for it to open I returned a call to Austin. "Hey," I said, "no can do on golf this week. Too much on my plate, plus I need to make more time for Karen."

Austin muttered something about his workload and a lawsuit brought by some ne'er-do-well.

"That's nothing, Austin. You should have witnessed the crap I just flushed from Judge Hancock's chamber. 'Statute obtain promulgate shyster blah blah blah.' You would have laughed out loud. A little bit of knowledge is a very dangerous thing."

The elevator door opened, and I stepped inside, phone to ear. If there were footsteps behind me on the tiles, I never heard them.

"But still it's a victory, Austin," I went on. "Hardly the greatest victory of my career, beating some whacked-out old man, but a victory nonetheless. As for the gym, sure, I could use a workout."

The elevator closed, and when I turned to press the lobby button I saw him. Abner Plott stood beside me, staring straight ahead at our reflections in the elevator door.

He'd heard everything I'd just said. In the reflection I saw him tug at his zipper, and I knew I had been presumptuous in figuring he'd already left the building. In reality, he'd stopped to visit the men's room.

A surge of blush-inducing embarrassment ran up my spine and into my neck. Then the elevator bell signaled that we were underway, our slow descent in sharp contrast to a second surge of embarrassment jolting upward from my gut.

Plott stared into his reflection. I stared into mine.

"Are you happy?" he asked in a monotone that hid well any anger he might have felt.

I turned to face him but he did not look back at me. "We have nothing to say to each other, sir."

Plott tapped his left foot a couple times, then three more times, a gesture lacking rhythm but perfectly in character for him. "We will."

What did he mean by that? I could not believe this old man had just threatened me, so I stared at him for a sign of clarification. After a couple of seconds he turned and stared back at me, no expression at all in his face. His was a countenance devoid of anger and reason. Perhaps this was an early sign of a man who had lost it all and had reached a state of numbness. But my day was full and I just wanted the elevator to reach the lobby and allow me to step off—off and out of the life of one Abner Plott.

The bell rang, the doors opened, and in a brief moment of grace I decided to allow Plott to exit first. I looked at him but he did not move. So I started forward, and when I did, Plott paralleled my first step and tried to cross in front of me.

We hit hard.

My left shoulder rammed into his right and he caught his shoe against mine. He sprawled out of the elevator and on to the floor. My briefcase landed under him and burst open—papers scattering on tiles.

"Mr. Plott, you—" My mental cursor clicked 'delete,' and I did not say what I wanted to say.

But I felt sure he had orchestrated our collision, lying as he was on his side, the soles of his shoes grasping for traction as he made a weak effort to right himself. I wanted to shout at him, but the stocky bailiff rounded a corner and was striding for us.

I kneeled to pick up files and papers. Then I whispered to Plott. "You did that on purpose, didn't you?"

He reached for his back, as if in pain. Then he looked up at me in some kind of false ploy for sympathy, but I could not, would not, offer him assistance. The bailiff arrived and leaned over and asked Plott if he wanted help. Plott nodded and tried to stand. The bailiff assisted him from behind, grasping him under the arms and pulling him up. Plott stood without difficulty. Then he glared at me for a moment and reached a hand around his waist and felt his lower back. He winced, glanced at the bailiff, and winced again.

I gathered the last of my files and papers—some had landed under Mr. Plott and were now visible after he'd rolled off of them and stood. The papers were crumpled and creased, and as I tucked them back into my briefcase, I frowned in disbelief at what had just transpired.

"You okay, sir?" the bailiff asked me.

"I'm fine."

One quick glance at my watch, and I left Plott and the bailiff there in front of the elevator. The old man was not just whacked out but also had a vindictive streak in him. He'd had his little vindication, and now that our competition was over I strode confidently out of the courthouse, down the steps, and into the rays of a noontime sun.

* * *

Richard Sterling—he of plush corner office and impressive wardrobe—appeared out of place in a windowless room with concrete floors. We had all gathered inside the basement of Powers, Morgan, and Greene, six lawyers and four paralegals seated evenly on each side of two folding tables, boxes of files against the walls, a huge dry erase board behind Sterling who commandeered our meeting from the end of the second table. There was nothing here to distract anyone, no opulent furniture or original artwork to remind us of our economic status. This was our war room, and we were about to go to war for Bargain Mart and defend the 80 million dollars they held in cash reserves. Everyone knew that words and facts were the weapons of this war. *If they say X, we say Z.*

Sterling pounded a fist on the table: "The Bargain Mart trial is exactly 4 months from today, and we are not ready." He motioned behind him to the dry erase board, where names and dates were written in red and black marker, and in fonts large and small. "Did you hear me, people? We are not yet *ready*. We have got to get our act together. Defending a 200 million-dollar class action is not an easy task. Therefore we're going to try it with a test jury in 3 weeks, and I want everyone present to focus on the date and prepare for that date as if it were the real thing. Am I clear?"

Heads nodded in unison.

I was seated two chairs to Sterling's left, a paralegal between us. He turned to her—a perky, curly-haired blond whom Austin had likely already hit upon—and she gripped her pen and held it above a yellow legal pad.

"Are we set up?" Sterling asked.

She nodded firmly. "We have six rooms right across the street from the courthouse, all of the rooms are on the same floor. We also have a suite with extra phone jacks for computers and faxes. Plus I've got catered food deliveries set up for all meals—breakfast, dinner, midnight, whatever we need."

Sterling looked satisfied. "Good. We'll be in that location during our mock trial as well. Tell your families and neighbors to remember what you look like, because none of them will be seeing you for a while."

Nervous chuckles echoed against concrete walls, but only briefly.

In the collective pause that followed, I noted nine wedding bands in the room; only the paralegal was single. I wondered about the long-term costs to those nine marriages from the mega hours imposed on us by the firm. Then my thoughts tightened from macro to micro and I considered Karen's increasingly hostile comments about my time allotment to the firm versus my time allotment to her. I even chastised myself for thinking in terms of *time allotment* when it came to my wife.

Sterling pointed to the board and was about to say something else when the door to our war room opened. Carol stuck her head in and peered about with quiet sensitivity.

Sterling frowned at the interruption and met her gaze. "Yes, Carol?"

She pointed at me. "I need to talk to Alex—just for a moment."

Sterling was not about to let her—or me for that matter—off so easily. "What's this about? Can't it wait till later?"

The normally unflappable Carol paused as if she just could not conjure a believable lie. "Um, there's someone here to see him."

I caught various glances, subtle frowns, and the slow shake of Sterling's head, like he figured my wife or mother had shown up with oatmeal cookies and tall glasses of milk.

Carol extended her right hand into the room, palm upturned. "Mr. Sterling, it's a policeman."

Sterling rocked back on his heels, as surprised as everyone else. "I suppose a policeman trumps a partner." His glance directed me to the door. "Hurry back, Alex."

I stood and moved toward the door, a double dose of embarrassment weighing on my spirit, the first from being called out of a meeting with a partner, the second from the knowledge that a policeman had paid me a visit. It was probably my car. It had already been broken into once in the past year, and with Florida's economy teetering on the brink of depression, the thieves and burglars remained busier than ever.

Sterling continued commandeering his meeting, asking a pair of associates where we stood with the preparation of Bargain Mart's expert witnesses.

I closed the door behind me, hurried up a flight of stairs to the lobby, and saw waiting an officer, smartly dressed in navy blue, a large sidearm affixed to his side. He stood in marked contrast to the soft pastels of our lobby sofas, though his expression perfectly matched the hardness of Mr. Morgan and Mr. Powers, our long deceased partners whose portraits graced the far wall.

"I'm Alex Lord. What can I do for you today, officer?"

The officer squared his shoulders to mine. "Mr. Lord, I'm placing you under arrest for battery."

Austin! This was his belated birthday joke. A day late, but nonetheless effective. I smiled at the officer. "Austin Adams put you up to this, right?"

"I don't know any Austin Adams." He recited my Miranda rights, reached to his belt, and rested a hand on a pair of handcuffs. "Mr. Lord, I'm not joking at all. You're being placed under arrest for battery, and you need to come with me to the police station."

I bristled and took a step back. "Nope. No way. You have the wrong guy."

The cop took a step toward me but stopped and folded his arms in front of him. "Mr. Lord, were you downtown at the courthouse earlier today?"

I nodded in the affirmative. "Yes. But what does that have to do with—"

"A man named Abner Plott told us that you threw him to the ground. We followed up with the courthouse, and a bailiff said he saw Mr. Plott fall out of an elevator, and that you were right behind him. No one else was on that elevator, Mr. Lord."

Abner, the obsessed scoundrel.

My hands rose in protest, and again I stepped backward, my instincts urging me to distance myself from false accusation. "No again, officer. You're nowhere close to the truth here." I glanced at my watch and thought of the impatient Richard Sterling scrawling on his dry erase board and doling out assignments to my peers. "Can I call the station or come down there in about an hour and straighten all this out?"

The officer moved toward me until I could retreat no further; the wall pressed against my back, and it was then that his hands produced the handcuffs.

"Give me your wrists," he said, and he meant it.

As he snapped the handcuffs shut, I looked over his shoulder into our plush lobby and saw sitting there a bevy of clients, all of them executives from various Orlando corporations, all of them movers and shakers, all staring at me with puzzled expressions, as surprised by the scene as a congregation watching their pastor being shackled and escorted out of a sanctuary.

My march out of our lobby would have been bad enough, except for the elevator bell ringing a short distance behind. I looked over my shoulder to see not one but three partners stepping out, all three stopping and staring at their associate being escorted from the premises by law enforcement, the cop's hand pressed into the small of my back.

Outside on the sidewalk, a pair of pedestrians also stopped and stared. My instinct was to explain myself to anyone who cast a doubtful glance. But I fought that urge and moved peacefully and silently beside my captor.

"Duck your head," the officer said. The back door to his squad car pulled open, and I was nudged inside. Oh, that smell.

The drive to the jail took me past working-class folks hurrying to lunch, homeless guys rattling tin cans, bus drivers and shoppers and the unemployed, people running their resumes door to door in order to fight the poverty brought forth by the real estate crash. At that moment I would have traded places with any of them—the backseat of the cop car was filthy. I sat amid ashes and dirt and the stench of dried beer. Who knew the range of drunks and hookers, pimps and thieves, lowlifes and lawyers who'd ridden in this very seat, all of us staring out longingly at common freedoms we'd moments earlier taken for granted.

We pulled into the police station lot and the officer got out and began talking with another officer. He just left me sitting in that hot vinyl backseat. As seconds turned into minutes, I pondered the consequences of returning to the office. Assignments for which I should be favored—now doled out to others in my absence. Meetings for which I was expected, now proceeding with an empty chair in the room. I kept thinking of what this misunderstanding might cost me, and the cost rose substantially when I reflected upon the looks on the partner's faces as they stepped off that elevator and saw me in handcuffs.

Powers, Morgan, and Greene had just imported a large crate of disappointment, and my name fronted the return address.

6

AFTER THREE-AND-A-HALF YEARS OF MARRIAGE, I HAD QUASHED all notions of being able to predict my wife's mood. Sometimes I played a little game with myself: As I would pull into the driveway, I would pick a number between 1 and 10—with 1 being her toughest, don't-even-look-at-me mood, and 10 being her greeting me in a slinky red dress, a glass of wine in one hand, her other hand pointing upstairs to the bedroom and urging me to hurry.

This evening, I turned off the ignition to my car and saw the lights on in the living room; I guessed '4.' After all, I had missed dinner, though the tardiness was not entirely my fault.

At the front door, just before I turned the knob, I upped my guess to a very neutral '5.' Then I turned to admire the twin gardens flanking our front steps. She'd planted a multitude of yellow things, some taller blue things, and it all made for a more attractive entrance.

Slowly and with a smile, I pushed open the door; Karen was to the left, reading a book on the sofa. She had a pair of fluffy beige pillows under her right side with the lamp turned to provide maximum light on the novel in which she'd lost herself. I assumed she was lost in the fiction because she never looked up. Not even when I shut the door did she look up. My numerical labeling of her mood descended to no more than a '3,' perhaps to even a rare and dreaded '2.'

"Hi, honey. The garden looks great."

She smiled my way, waved once, and continued reading. "Thanks."

"Sweetie," I said, still in the foyer, my briefcase settling on ceramic tiles. "I was, um, I got arrested today."

She must have thought I was trying to make her laugh and had failed miserably—she only rolled her eyes and kept reading her book.

I walked behind her to the kitchen and plucked a bottled beer from the fridge—some amber imported thing I'd picked up at the grocery store a week earlier. Then I took a long swig and went back into the living room and stopped at the far end of the sofa. "Karen, I wasn't kidding. I got arrested today."

At this second mention she placed her book in her lap and raised her lovely eyebrows a smidgen, just enough to acknowledge that she'd heard me.

"Yes," I continued, and sat in a chair at our dining table. "This crazy old man who had tried to sue our firm followed me into an elevator, then when the door opened he fell in front of me. Then I got arrested for assault and spent an hour in the city jail, discussing street economics with Rosco-the-pimp. He's a Florida State fan and enjoys walks on the beach and drive-by shootings. How was *your* day?"

She set her book on the coffee table. "Was he hurt?"

"Rosco-the-pimp? No, he's perfectly healthy."

"I meant the old man in the elevator. You said he fell."

"Karen, please!" I stood and stared at her in disbelief.

She looked incredulous. "What is wrong with my asking a simple question?"

I walked around the dining table and stopped in front of the sofa, only the coffee table separating me from my wife. "It's like this—half of the firm saw me get escorted out of our building in handcuffs, I missed the Bargain Mart meeting, and now you're asking me if *he* was hurt! Where's the compassion?"

She hugged a beige pillow and rested her chin on it. "I'm sorry you spent an hour in jail. That's...horrible. But you did say he was old and he fell down."

"People fall down all the time! Especially old people! The man tripped...it wasn't a big deal, okay?"

"Then why," she said, and her voice softened with each syllable, "are you shouting at me?"

I pinched the bridge of my nose in an effort to squeeze the pressure out of my life. There was no reason at all for me to be shouting at my wife, especially over a situation to which she wasn't privy. "I don't know," I said and sat on the sofa a couple feet from her, which felt like 10 miles. "I suppose today just meant one more thing I have to deal with. It's all cumulative, ya' know."

She turned toward me, her arms still clutching the beige pillow, her girlish chin still in repose on the pillow's border. She looked as if she wanted to say something profound, but she only stared at me, her eyes a moist blend of sorrow and bewilderment.

"What?" I asked.

Her brand of bewilderment—I knew this from experience—derived from her disbelief over what had happened to us. The couple who had lived with such affection and spontaneity had become a couple weighed down by the increasing demands on their time. At least that's how I saw things.

"What?" I repeated. "Come on, what?"

She lifted her chin from the pillow but still did not speak. This was bad. Even for a guy who'd had a terrible day at work and spent an hour in the slammer, I knew this kind of silence required something of me that would ultimately sting—my being vulnerable. She was drawing it out of me with those soft brown eyes that begged for masculine authenticity.

I scooted a foot closer to her, my right arm on the back of the sofa. "Karen, what, last night? Is that what this is about...last night?"

"Don't pretend you don't know or that you can't zero in your compartmentalized mind on the real issue. I wanted some time for *us,* Alex." She let her gaze fall to the floor for a moment, then let it meander back to my chest though not to my eyes. "For *us.*"

"I tried last night to make time for us. You didn't seem very interested."

The beige pillow came at me on an arc, not hard and vindictive but with just enough force to let me know I was off on a tangent from the real issue. "Alex, our drinking with Austin and his tramp-of-the-week doesn't make me feel very close to you."

I pressed the pillow into my lap and looked into my wife's face and decided to be as honest and authentic as Alex Lord could be after a day at the county jail. "Okay, then tell me when have you felt close to me lately?"

She sighed, and for a moment her lips quivered. "I don't know. Maybe on our picnic last month, when it was just you and me."

The pillow fell to the floor as I moved closer to my wife and took her hand in mine. Even a logical, left-brained lawyer knew there were times when words were insufficient. Our fingers interlocked, and her thumb began moving against my palm.

We sat there for long minutes, feminine thumb and masculine thumb taking turns, searching for connection in a slow caress of digits.

This was not an on-ramp to the marriage bed; as much as the primal instinct could dominate my senses, I knew we were not about to go into our bedroom and love each other with great passion. These flexing fingers and circulating thumbs were for us an attempt to regain companionship, to stop looking at each other in disbelief but instead stand side-by-side and look out together at the world before us. That was what I remembered most about our wedding day—right after we'd kissed in front of all those friends and family members, right after the preacher pronounced us man and wife, we had turned together, hand-in-hand, and faced for the first time as a couple the world at large. *Team Lord against the world*—it was what we laughed about as we walked the beaches of Sint Maarten during our honeymoon.

I squeezed her hand and waited for her to squeeze back. It took her a couple seconds, but finally she did reciprocate.

"We'll spend some time together, Karen."

For the first time since I'd arrived home, I saw genuine hope in her face.

"Saturday?" she asked, and her voice affirmed that hope. "Are we going away somewhere next Saturday?"

Like a tsunami halting a stroll on white sands, so did the word 'Saturday' stifle thoughts of togetherness. The Bargain Mart trial, the 12 other cases to which I'd been assigned, and the Abner Plott fiasco all came crashing into my quiet living room and stood like a brick divide between us.

While she waited for my answer I reflected on the growing brevity of our vacations. The week skiing in Utah had withered the next year into four days in Boston, which had withered this past year to two days in Destin, and now I couldn't even make time for a Saturday night trip to—anywhere.

She must have sensed what was coming, because before I even spoke the first word she looked into my face and, seeing something familiar, slowly pulled her hand from mine. She hugged again the fluffy pillow and sunk into her corner of the sofa.

"Alex, I do appreciate how hard you work. Really I do. But it's causing me to feel distant from you. If you cared about our relationship, you'd make time for it." She pulled a fleece blanket from the back of the sofa and covered herself with it. "I think I'll just sleep here tonight."

7

ARRIVED AT WORK EARLY IN THE HOPE OF AVOIDING ANY PARTNERS asking questions about the handcuffed associate they'd seen being escorted from the building a day earlier. My plan worked. By 10:30 A.M. I'd been at my desk for four-and-a-half hours without anyone so much as stopping by to say hello. The attorney life had bred in me the focus and alertness of a morning person, and today I was focused on devouring as much detail as possible to prepare for the Bargain Mart trial.

The trial would be my opportunity to redeem myself in front of the firm. Over the past 3 months I had read thousands of pages of pleadings and deposition transcripts, and still another thousand pages awaited me. I'd become a human sponge, absorbing detail after detail, pushing myself toward some unquantifiable level of excellence.

Before I could give myself a grade of excellent, however, a knock on my door shook me from my studies.

"Come in," I said, not bothering to stand up, guessing that the knocker was not a partner.

Right again. Carol stuck her head in, a mask of sympathy frozen onto her face. "Alex, I really hate to be the one to tell you this, but there's a sheriff down in the lobby and he's here to see you."

I stared over the top of my file and then up at the ceiling. Perhaps I was hoping to see some Divine presence up there, offering heavenly assurance that all would be well, but all I saw was a tiny sprinkler head, shiny and steel and waiting to save me should a fire break out.

I was sure there would be fire; the sheriff was the smoke rising over the treetops. "Another sheriff," I mumbled, "to see me."

Carol nodded slowly and with concern. "He wouldn't say what it was about."

I stood and dropped my file onto my desk and sighed the sigh of an interrupted lawyer.

Carol took a step toward me, her head cocked to the side. "Alex, are you okay?"

"I'm fine, and I'll handle whatever the good sheriff wants to ask me." I thanked her for her concern and made for the door, but stopped and turned to her. "By the way, have you seen my address book?"

She shook her head and followed me out. "Have not. But I'll look for it while you're talking to the sheriff."

The sheriff stood between the firm's receptionist and a potted plant. His arms were folded in front of him and he did not look particularly concerned that I might be the violent type or one who might flee. Instead he appeared as if he visited law firms on a regular basis and, from his learned experience, had little to fear other than the possibility of some young attorney trying to deflect his agenda with five-syllable words of legalese.

I had no such words. I walked up beside the potted plant and said, "Hey."

He sized me up for a moment. "Are you John Alexander Lord?"

Anxious and wary of what might be coming, I nevertheless determined not to show fear. "Yes, I'm Alex Lord."

His arms unfolded from his chest, and I saw that his left hand held papers. "I have five civil summonses to serve on you, sir."

He handed me the papers, and I gripped their end as if they were used Kleenex. "Oh, only five. Great…just great."

The sheriff nodded, his work done. "Good day, Mr. Lord."

"That's it?" I asked. "Not even, 'Sorry I have to give you these summonses?'"

The sheriff shrugged and stepped toward the exit. "I'm just doing my job, sir."

Yes. And that is exactly what I'd been doing—my job. I was doing my job when Abner Plott wedged his way into my life; I was doing my job when he threatened me; and I was doing my job when good Sheriff Stoic walked in and served me my five summonses.

Plott. He was probably sitting on a porch somewhere, a smirk on his face as he ate ravioli from a can and downed it with a cola he'd purchased with his food stamps. Ten percent of Orlando was on food stamps—and we were doing well compared to the rest of the state. We still had the happy mouse and the happy duck, who together employed a sizable chunk of the citizenry. And yet a huge portion of the citizenry, just like Plott, had purchased homes that were now worth far less than their mortgages. I had once told Austin that if we installed bumper stickers on our cars which read *Honk if You are Upside-Down*, the horns would never stop blaring. Most people, however, were still paying on their mortgages, not walking away like some petulant child and seeking to fling blame at someone who had nothing to do with their decision to abandon fiscal responsibility.

The door closed behind the sheriff, and my cell phone buzzed. I checked the sender and saw that it was Austin, wanting me to meet him for lunch—probably to ask me for a golf rematch.

✳ ✳ ✳

When I entered Momma B's Giant Subs at lunch hour and took my place in line, I did not expect to be met with charity, especially from the likes of Austin. But there he sat in a corner booth, waving me over.

He had already ordered for me. A full plate awaited my arrival.

"You ordered for me?" I asked. "This is a first."

"Turkey wrap with Swiss, light mayo. It's your usual, right?"

I stood there in semi-shock. Austin Adams never sprang for lunch.

He motioned for me to sit. "It's on the firm, Alex. They asked me to take you to lunch today."

I sat and tucked a napkin into my lap. "This beats the partners asking you to push me in front of a bus."

He snickered as if he thought the scenario ridiculous. And yet on another level—continued losses on the golf course—he'd likely already considered it.

Austin bit into his steak sandwich and studied me as he chewed. Finally, after he swashed down the bite with a swig of sweet tea, he leaned forward and spoke in a hushed tone. "Alex, the partners asked me to talk to you. They want to know if you can ask all your law enforcement friends to stop hanging around our reception area. We're running out of free donuts."

Hoohah, really funny, Austin. Lure me in and then unload the ol' sarcasm.

Not only was I not amused, I didn't even want to eat with him. But I was hungry, so I lit into my wrap and ate without comment.

"C'mon, Alex!" Austin chided. He met my stare with a cheesy grin. "Lighten up, buddy. You got served with *five* summonses? *Five*?"

It did seem unbelievable on the surface. Not so unbelievable, considering the mental deficiencies of Abner Plott. "The five suits were filed in five different counties. Work-wise and marriage-wise, this couldn't have come at a worse time. I'll be running all over the state of Florida dealing with this crap."

Austin sat back and nodded as if he could relate. But he could never relate—single, skirt-chasing attorneys do not relate to married, non-skirt-chasing attorneys. "So, what is Mr. Plott suing you for this time? And how many times did he use the word 'promulgate?'"

"Who the heck knows," I said and crunched a potato chip in my fingers. "It's the same kind of nonsense he was spewing last week."

I thought Austin would have more to add, but as he gripped his tea glass and brought it near his mouth he stopped and turned in his seat.

A shapely blond waitress passed beside him, and his eyes followed her like a pair of guided missiles locked in on their target. "Good gracious, Alex, they're everywhere!" Then his face locked into a kind of mock seriousness. "I must meet her," he deadpanned, his tone robotic. "I must. I must make her mine."

I might have laughed had I been in a better mood. Still, he was a sad case. "Austin, aren't you still seeing Tatiana?"

He nodded. "And that's important, how?"

The waitress returned with a pitcher of tea and refilled my glass and then Austin's. He winked at her as she poured. I suppose her brief smile was a kind of victory for him, a white light of affirmation logged into his flirtometer.

The waitress left to serve other customers, and it was then that Austin turned serious. "Okay," he said, and clutched his tea glass with both hands. He stared into the depth of melting ice and appeared—if I read him correctly, which was not often—to be considering the consequences heaped upon me. "Just where does a guy like Plott get the bucks to file all those cases? I mean, filing fees are at least one-fifty a pop, aren't they?"

I lost my appetite. "Not if you're indigent. Plott just signs an affidavit and then proceeds to sue the hell out of me…for free."

Austin admired the second half of his sandwich and spoke around it. "Ya' know, the system should not be open to poor people."

I had no will to discuss the economic prerequisites of the legal system. Somewhere in the back of my mind I knew the system should treat everyone with equality, although PMG certainly had no poor clientele. At PMG, money did not just talk, it cross-examined, rebutted, shouted, and swung the gavel. After a moment of reflection on just how severely money directed my life, I flicked a crumb from my Oxford and redirected our chat. "Austin, I believe that Mr. Plott has my appointment book."

Austin's eyes widened with surprise, as if I'd missed out on the technology boom. "You don't keep all your appointments on your Blackberry?"

"It's just backup, Austin. Plus, I like to jot notes in it."

"But how in the hell would he get a hold of it?"

"It was in my briefcase at the hearing. He might have taken it there, or maybe he grabbed it when we collided leaving the elevator."

Austin studied me again. I knew he was really trying because the blond waitress passed by again and he never flinched—not even a glance her way. "Paranoia will kill you, my friend. It'll kill you right after it saps all the happiness from your life. And life, Alex, is so very short."

Just shoot me. Mr. Lust just morphed into Mr. Philosophical.

I pushed my half-eaten turkey wrap to the center of the table and motioned at it to see if Austin wanted to finish it. He shook his head, and I dropped my crumpled napkin onto the plate. "I haven't seen that appointment book since that morning, and there's no way it just wandered off."

"I'll give you five bucks. Buy another one."

"You don't understand. That little book had my information in it—license number, insurance info, even a credit card number."

Austin set his fork on his plate. "Wait, just hold right there. You mean that you actually fill out the little page in the front? The page with all those categories in the teeny tiny font?"

I frowned and looked out the window.

"Oh. My. Goodness."

"Austin, don't."

"Alex Lord actually fills out the little categories in the front! I've heard of being anal, man. Maybe for Christmas I'll buy you an App for your Blackberry. But wow…no wonder the firm loves you. I'd bet you even fill out your time sheets every night too."

"I need to talk with Sterling about how to handle this."

Austin guzzled more tea and said, "Old man Plott is really starting to get to you, isn't he?"

I chewed my lip and embraced denial.

Austin pointed a finger at me. "What you should do, buddy, is go on the offense." Now two fingers pointed at me. "Maybe you can even sue that crazy old bastard. Yes, you can counterclaim for intentional infliction of emotional distress! Then counterclaim for abuse of process and anything else you can think of."

His enthusiasm neither swayed nor encouraged me. "And just what could I get for my efforts? The guy has no money. Did you hear me, Austin? No money. Even if I got a judgment, it wouldn't fatten my wallet by a single Benjamin."

Austin looked incredulous. "So what? Teach the old man a lesson."

"Yeah, that would look so good, wouldn't it? A lawyer from PMG going out to the sticks to clean out some poor old man's house. Now wouldn't the press just love that story? I can guarantee you the firm would not."

He picked up our check and reached for his wallet. "Well, I'd sue him in a heartbeat. Mr. Plott has to learn that there are consequences to his actions."

Austin could sound so practical at times. It made me wonder why he chose to date the kind of women he did.

* * *

I left the deli feeling much like my lunch—half eaten—and began the two-block walk back to the firm. Horns honked in crowded streets, and the smell of bus exhaust lingered in the heat. At the intersection of Orange and Central, I waited for the light to grant permission to walk, but before it did, my peripheral vision caught sight of a partner—Richard Sterling, striding toward the deli I'd just vacated.

Stay or go? Go or interrupt? One-on-one time with a partner outside the office was a rare opportunity, so I hurried over and caught up to him.

"Richard."

He looked mildly surprised to see me. "Hey there, Alex. Nice tie."

"Thanks."

"Did you finish that memo this morning?"

Memo? Oh, that memo. "Ah, yes sir. I'll have that memo waiting for you when you return from lunch."

He glanced down the block toward the deli's front door as if searching for someone. "Good," he said, and turned his attention back to me. "We need to make a decision on that one, and we need to do it soon."

I strode along with him, his pace quickening even as I put more and more distance between myself and the office. "Richard, do you remember that case from last week, the one with Hammond and that oddball named Abner Plott?"

He smiled and weaved around slower pedestrians, the sun glinting off his silvered hair and starched white shirt. "That one is all gone, I assume? Fully flushed?"

I nodded in the affirmative and fudged my answer. "The case itself is gone, sir. But Mr. Plott has now filed five separate suits against me personally—plus a criminal complaint."

Richard Sterling never broke stride, and soon I noted that he was not going to the deli for lunch; we had just passed its entrance. He also seemed unaffected by my confession, and I supposed this too was to be expected. He had mastered the mannerisms of the well-heeled partner, an important man allowing himself the leisure of measured thought. "The unfortunate part of being a PMG lawyer, Alex, is that when you are the best, everyone wants to take a shot at you. You should expect such obstacles."

I nodded and matched his pace. "Well then, what I should I do about Mr. Plott?"

"Defend the suits," he said with confidence. "Sure, it'll be a pain, but you're smart and you'll work through it quickly. It's really no big deal."

I pressed him further. "What about Hammond? Do ya' think they would help with the cost to defend?"

Richard Sterling stopped on the busy sidewalk. Fellow pedestrians weaved around us. His easy manner turned serious, and he appeared skeptical of my question. "Hammond didn't get you into this, and they are not the one suing you."

"I know," I said, trying to agree while at the same time calculating how to state my case. "But what I meant was...."

Sterling's raised index finger cut me off. In the awkward moments that followed, that experienced finger remained aloft, an obstacle for me to overcome, hovering between us as people brushed by and frowned at the blockage we'd created. "Alex, Hammond is a valuable client. Very valuable. Every major firm in Orlando would love to have them."

His finger folded in with its mates and he walked onward, his pace quickening again. He spoke over his shoulder. "Understand that we are not going to approach Hammond about this matter."

From a step behind I blurted, "I understand."

"Open some non-billable files, and we'll deal with that criminal charge if need be."

"Oh, man, more non-billable matters on my record."

Sterling nodded as if he could relate to my plight. "Part of the job, Alex. Every partner in the firm has been there. All sewers run downhill, haven't you heard?"

He smiled at me and stopped in front of the University Club, upscale dining for the city's elite. I should have known that Richard Sterling would not eat lunch at Momma B's Giant Subs.

The doorman, replete in blue jacket and gold buttons, opened the door and motioned Sterling inside, as if expecting him. Who knew? Richard could have owned a chunk of the club—a silent partner, perhaps. He could certainly afford such investments. His was a level of success that not only spurred Austin and I to compete with each other but also served to raise the bar for every associate in the firm.

Sterling ran a hand through his silvered hair and motioned for me to lean in close. "I meant to tell you one other thing, Alex. The corporate guys from Bargain Mart are flying in here Saturday for our report on the trial preparations. Be in the office by 11:00, and also plan on going to dinner with us. We'll take them somewhere fancy." He patted my shoulder. "See ya' then."

Sterling greeted the doorman like he would a longtime friend and disappeared into the club. I reversed course and made my way back toward the office, realizing as I walked that I should have finished my lunch. Sometimes the lawyer life burns more calories than golf and gym-workouts combined, although lately it was only law and the gym.

In a desperate attempt to get energy into my system for the afternoon, I stopped at a street vendor and bought a hot dog with chili.

I liked my chili hot, and as a second bite followed the first, I remained in the shadow of the street vendor's roofed cart, afraid to try and walk and eat. An associate showing up at PMG with a huge chili stain on his oxford was almost as bad as getting arrested.

I was about to gobble the second half of my hot dog when someone tapped me on the shoulder.

"'Scuse' me, sir, but could I talk with you?"

Before I turned around I knew this was a street beggar. Downtown Orlando played host to hundreds of them, each unique in his scruffiness and foul scent, yet all of them bonded by poverty.

My initial instinct was to shoo him away like some fly that had tried to light upon my meal. But as pedestrians whisked by us and the hot dog vendor filled orders for his growing line of customers, I met the hollow gaze of the beggar and figured he was looking at me like I had just looked at Richard Sterling—someone ahead on the economic ladder, who with a simple gesture could wildly affect the trajectory of the day.

"You need a couple bucks?" I said, and finished off my hot dog with one last, very large bite.

"I fought in Viet Nam," he mumbled. "Benefits all ran out now."

Viet Nam, Korea, Baghdad. These guys knew the military angle and they played it for keeps. I half expected one to someday tell me he'd fought alongside Robert E. Lee, and had simply preserved himself well.

I wadded my hot dog wrapper into a ball and tossed it into the street vendor's trash can.

"Did two tours in Viet Nam," the guy said. "I'm just a hungry man needin' a break." He tapped my shoulder and pressed his case. "Half my platoon got burnt up with napalm. Can't you give some love to a veteran?"

I doubted the guy knew napalm from a nectarine. Regardless, I paid for his lunch, and as he admired the steaming dog and gripped his drink he thanked me for doing my patriotic duty.

8

A T FIRST I ONLY REMOVED MY SHOES AND SOCKS.
Still in my work clothes I stood next to the pool stairs, between the water and our picture window, staring into those waters and watching the moon's reflection shimmer in the ripples. Karen and I had both worked a long Monday, and now I waited for her to finish her shower so that we could complete our plans for a weekend getaway. The pool had sold us on the house—the tall wooden fence for privacy and for swimming sans suits; the French doors leading out to the pool from the bedroom; the view of blue water and brushed concrete through the oval window in our den. Alone or together, in the water or out, the pool was where we unwound.

I rolled up my black slacks until they gathered at my knees. Then I sat on the edge of the pool and plunged my legs into the water up to my calves. Behind me, I heard the shower cut off from our bathroom, and I knew that when she joined me poolside I could use the setting and the moonlight to try to soften the news that I could only go away with her for Friday night; I would have to be back in Orlando by 10:30 A.M. on Saturday. Karen was figuring that by late Saturday morning we'd be snuggling in the coziness of some B&B. In reality I'd be seated in a conference room with seven other associates, Richard Sterling, and four executives from Bargain Mart.

I tossed a small pebble into the center of the pool and watched the ripples expand until they became for me the waves from a storm named Abner—vindictive misfits surging forward to cause as much damage as possible for Powers, Morgan, and Greene.

"I've been thinking about our trip, Alex," came Karen's voice from behind me.

Before I turned to her I tried to guess what she was wearing: the standard silky blue pajamas, or maybe the sexier low-cut red nightie, or perhaps her lime green bikini or even nothing at all. I went with door number two—the red nightie—and turned to see that I had guessed correctly. My wife was beautiful. There in the ten o'clock hour, her hair damp and falling across the thin straps of her gown, she looked as fresh-faced and vibrant as she had that first night I'd met her after the poker game back in Gainesville.

"Hi there."

She came over and pulled a chair up behind me. Soon I felt her feet brushing against my back. "If we leave early Saturday morning, we can make it to St. Augustine by mid-morning and have a late break-fast at that cute restaurant by the river. I just love that place; they have the best French toast. They serve it with blueberries, remember?"

I remembered the blueberries and the view of the river—both were fantastic—and stared into the pool and nodded to show her that I was listening to her every word.

She ran a toe slowly from my neck down to my lower back. "We can check in around noon, then take a nap or lounge on the porch, whatever we want. Then maybe we'll go for a hike in the af-ternoon…or perhaps we can rent a boat and go exploring. What do you think?"

Her toe spelled out the word 'LOVE' upon my back. She'd done this before, but this time I figured she meant it because she used capital letters.

I could not bring myself to tell her. Not yet, not tonight. In my head I knew that Saturday would not bring me a late-morning nap with my wife but an all-day meeting with Bargain Mart. And instead of a boat rental and a relaxing exploration, I'd be arguing trial strate-gies and listening to exposition—from Sterling, who would not toler-ate my taking Saturday off to work on my marriage.

So I reached a hand behind my back and stroked Karen's foot. "Sounds good," I said. "We'll do whatever you want to do."

An explanation could wait until tomorrow, or perhaps the next day, but not tonight. I needed tonight.

I motioned to the pool and unbuttoned the top two buttons of my shirt. "Wanna go for a swim, pretty lady?"

Karen stood beside me and let her hair fall over one shoulder and curl atop the thin strap of her nightgown.

"If we're going to exercise," she whispered, and pointed back into the bedroom which fronted the pool, "why don't we do it in there?"

She took my hand and pulled me up and we practically ran to the bedroom. So welcoming was I to physical touch that I didn't even bother to close the curtains. Karen pushed me onto the bed and I lay back in semi-darkness, her fingers attacking the last three buttons on my shirt.

Yes, my wife was beautiful, and as she unfastened my last button I lost myself in her beauty and admired her feminine silhouette against the shimmers of our pool.

✻ ✻ ✻

Tuesdays were always Karen's day to go in early, and today she left the house 10 minutes before I walked out to my car. Skies brightened over Orlando, and I felt rejuvenated—great sleep and exercise always had that effect on me.

I backed from the driveway and drove down the block and craned my neck as a rusty El Camino passed me, not the sort of vehicle we were used to seeing in our neighborhood. But then a glance into my mirror revealed shovels, rakes, and a fertilizer spreader sticking out the back of the car, just another yard guy hired by a neighbor.

With the unemployment rate in Florida stuck upward of 11 percent, anyone with a decent back had taken up landscaping and lawn maintenance to try and earn a few bucks.

I motored along Edgewater Drive in the fast lane and weaved deftly around and between slower cars. I felt, for the first time in days, a renewed confidence in the important facets of life—with Karen, my workload, and my ability to handle irritants. Confidence, however, was on this day as fleeting as last night's dream.

Waiting for me at my desk at Powers, Morgan, and Greene were not partners or Austin or even a voice mail from Karen, but instead a letter from the state Supreme Court. I slumped into my chair and opened the letter, aware that such missives were usually not good news.

Re: Inquiry of Ethical Complaint
John Alexander Lord, III
Fla. Bar No. 991007

Dear Mr. Lord:
An ethical complaint has been filed against you. The Florida Bar is currently conducting an investigation into this matter. You, or your attorney, are instructed to respond to this office in writing within thirty (30) days. Please provide a detailed response to the allegations set forth in the enclosed letter.

The second page almost made me regurgitate my coffee. There in a block paragraph of emotion were the bolded words, countless exclamation points, and red underlines from the pen of one Abner Plott.

I supposed that a bolded word with an exclamation point meant Plott was mad; a bolded word with two exclamation points meant boiling anger; and a bolded word with four exclamation points *plus* a red underline meant his head had exploded in rage against a system that had specifically sought him out and done him wrong, with no responsibility at all assumed by him personally; he'd only stopped paying his mortgage. Such a trivial matter—non-payment.

I dropped the letter onto my desk calendar and wondered how many Floridians were of a similar mind-set—that the system had screwed them. Yes, all ye frustrated Floridians, the system had rigged the real estate market and inflated the prices to artificially high levels, lured you in with cheap teaser rates on your mortgages, and then collapsed the market on purpose in order to steal everyone's home out from under them.

The victim mentality had become a spreading disease across the fruited plain, but here in Florida it was epidemic.

Across my desk calendar I drew a short flowchart of the epidemic:

Greed => excessive debt => foreclosure => fling blame => sue somebody.

I worked through lunch on trial preparations, a rare day without interruptions—until mid-afternoon when my Blackberry buzzed and I saw a voice mail from Karen waiting for me—probably more details about how she wanted to spend our time in St. Augustine. My plan was to explain things to her tonight after work using my workload and Abner Plott as twin excuses to back out of the weekend getaway. I decided to wait a while to return her call.

The universe, however, had other plans. Carol called me out into the lobby, and there was my new friend, the sheriff.

"You, again," I said.

"Me, again." He showed me a stack of summonses, and I totaled their sum as he handed them to me in a kind of exaggerated countdown, as if he were already tiring of playing delivery boy. "Two. Three. Four. Five. Six...*and* Seven."

"Seven new summonses," I said. "Nice. Maybe I can collect them like baseball cards. Store them in shoeboxes and pass them on to my kids."

He tipped his cap. "Again, just doing my job, Mr. Lord."

We bid each other good day, and then he bid Carol good day and added a small wink.

The elevator door closed in front of him and I turned to Carol. "That sheriff winked at you."

"Yes."

"And you winked *back.*"

"Yes, Alex. The sheriff has been giving shooting lessons to me and three of my girlfriends."

I tucked the seven summonses under my arm. "Shooting lessons. My assistant shoots pistols in her spare time? Why did I not know this?"

Already back to work, Carol nodded and began typing into her keyboard. She seemed a whir of efficiency. "It's fun to shoot. Makes for great stress relief."

I had never thought of stress relief via handgun; my method usually involved whacking golf balls at a range. In seconds, however, I filed the thought away in my not-feasible file, as I had no time for such pursuits. Heck, I didn't even have time for nine holes with Austin. He'd already e-mailed me twice about scheduling a rematch.

Back at my desk I spread the seven summonses like a poker hand and wondered if Plott were bluffing. The man had become Nuisance No. 1, and yet there were no hours available for nuisances—Bargain Mart and improving my marriage would consume my hours. Or so I thought.

Carol buzzed in on the intercom and I leaned into it to speak. "Yes, Carol?"

"Alex, Karen is on line one and she sounds upset."

Uh oh. Perhaps a hurricane was headed for St. Augustine and she feared having to cancel our plans. We were going to have to cancel anyway, due to Bargain Mart, but a little help from the weather would be welcome news, a saving grace even.

I pressed the line one button. "Hey there. What's up?"

"Alex, I think…." Her voice broke, and she struggled to finish. "You need to come home."

A quick glance at my watch revealed 3:07 P.M. "Are you kidding? It's the middle of the afternoon. I leave now and the partners would tackle me on the front steps!"

She sniffled twice. "I really think you need to come home. Someone attacked our house."

"Attacked? With weapons?"

"Well, I mean more like attacked our yard. Just come home, Alex. It's awful."

I ran out of the building without telling anyone where I was going or when I'd be back. Into the parking deck I sprinted, and into my car

I jumped. Seconds later the tires of my BMW screeched around tight corners and into the street.

Three red lights and countless yellows passed in a blur of acceleration—a left on Ivanhoe, a right on Edgewater—I sped through the suburbs and onward toward 27 Osprey Lane.

I didn't even make it up the driveway. Our yard was devastated, most of the grass covered with an inch of fertilizer—the south end burned and yellowing, Karen's new flowers yanked from their beds. Even worse, our bushes and Japanese maples had been hacked off at the ground, their raw, exposed nubs sticking up like severed thumbs. On the driveway ran streaks of dirt and trails of leaves where someone had dragged our beautiful shrubs around the house and toward the backyard.

I climbed from my car and stared over the hood at the chaos. It looked as if a small tornado with a singular purpose had dropped down onto our yard, inflicted maximum damage, and disappeared without marring a single leaf in the rest of the neighborhood. Being a lone victim felt awful, for I knew that other homeowners on the block—regardless of any sympathetic gestures to come—would likely stifle their own outrage in deference to fear that their homes would plummet further in value.

The front door pushed open and Karen emerged in a pair of old jeans and yellow T-shirt, her eyes reddened. She was barefoot and she moved slowly down the four steps from our porch, her head shaking, her numbed gaze on the sidewalk in front of her.

She stopped midway down the sidewalk. "Who would do this to us?!"

Her words barely got out before she burst into tears.

I ran across the fertilizer and wrapped my wife in a bear hug. "Don't panic. You're not hurt, and that's the most important thing."

I said this as I imagined pressing a foot unto Abner Plott's neck and pouring fertilizer down his spiteful throat. Intuitively, I knew that the bitter old man had committed this crime.

Karen squeezed me and whispered into my ear. "I loved my plants. I spent so many hours getting this yard right." Her tears wet my neck and I could not think of anything to say. So I just held her.

It only took seconds, however, for my internal rage to trump spousal affection. "You haven't called the cops yet?"

Karen pulled away and shook her head. "I'd only been home for 2 minutes when I called *you*." Through eyes wincing with pain she looked again at the carnage that was our front yard. "I'll go call them now."

Karen went inside, and I kneeled to dip a finger into the fertilizer. It smelled like industrial strength Drano with a dash of urine, or perhaps the odor was the stench from the far end of the yard, which appeared chemically scorched.

From behind me, in the distance, a weak voice called out. I stood and turned to see Mrs. Fox, our 90-year-old neighbor from two houses down, slowly moving up the street in a flower-print dress, white cloth sneakers adorning her feet.

I met her at the curb as I didn't want her to have to inhale the awful smell emanating from my yard.

"Hello, Alex," she said, and paused as if to catch her breath.

I met her hand and held it gently. "Mrs. Fox. Have you been around all day? And did you see anyone come into our yard?"

"Oh yes," she said and let go of my hand. "I've been here all day. I don't drive anymore, you know. My niece takes me for groceries. And sometimes we stop for ice cream. I like the kahlua flavor...with sprinkles on top."

Determined to stop her tangential ramblings, I moved closer, palms extended. "Mrs. Fox, did you see *anyone* in my yard?"

She squinted at our scorched earth. "Oh...oh yes. The poor fellow worked and worked all morning and all the way through lunch. He hardly ever took a break! I almost brought him lemonade, but he didn't seem to want to stop."

"What poor fellow are you talking about?"

She looked past me at three stubs all raw and protruding from the corner of the yard. "I didn't think he should cut them all down, Mr. Lord. You did tell him to leave a few, didn't you? It looks so sparse now, like a...a botanical holocaust."

I'd forgotten she was Jewish. "I didn't hire *anyone*, Mrs. Fox."

She pulled from her purse a pair of wide-framed sunglasses, very dark and thick, and slid them unto her face. "You mean you weren't planning to put in a new lawn? But then I have no idea why you would want to do that, since the old one looked so nice and all. I helped your wife plant two of those bushes, you know. We went to Home Depot together that day. I bought roses and she bought her bushes. Is she home, dear?"

"She's inside calling the police," I replied, and fought the urge to shake information from her. "Mrs. Fox, did you see what the yard man looked like?"

Neither the rub of her chin nor her two glances skyward brought clarity. But after several seconds of heavy thought, she said, "Yes. I believe he wore a big hat, floppy over his face, which is good for keeping the sun off. I'm going in next week to have a spot taken off my forehead. Too many summers at Daytona Beach, I reckon."

"What was he driving, Mrs. Fox? Do you remember?"

With a bony index finger pressed against her lip, she thought hard for a moment. "It was an old thing…rusty…not quite a car but not a pickup either."

The rusty El Camino. In the rush of my morning commute I hadn't noticed the driver. Plott had likely disguised himself.

Gently and persuasively, I put a hand on Mrs. Fox's shoulder. "Is there anything else you can remember? Anything at all?"

She shook her head and pressed her dark glasses higher upon her nose. "No, wait, yes yes, he had sunglasses like mine, with the sides that go all the way around."

"Anything else you can share?"

"No…no, not really. Not with my cataracts and all."

I looked up the street and down the street for anyone else who might be stirring about, but the street was empty except for the two of us. My 90-year-old witness would have to do. She had not felt the effects of the Plott tornado, but she at least had seen it light upon my yard.

I thanked Mrs. Fox with a light hug and a pat on her back, and she smiled and nodded her sympathy and shuffled off toward home.

Two minutes later I entered our living room. The phone rang before I could even find Karen.

"Alex?" She said from the kitchen. "Can you get that?"

In no mood to talk on the phone, I snatched it up from the receiver. "Hello?"

"You worthless, dirtbag, ambulance chaser. Where do you get off harassing decent Americans with your legalistic crap?"

Too stunned to reply, I turned to look through our bay window at the backyard and saw a sight nearly as ugly as our front yard—our pool filled with uprooted plants and severed bushes, all of it floating in a tangled mess, the water browned and grotesque.

I squeezed the receiver and forced it back to my lips. "You—"

"I've read all about you, Mr. Lord. I saw your pictures. You're just another egg-sucking lawyer, draining the life out of what was once a great country."

My mind ran from one negative to another and back again: The yard, the pool, the crazy man on the phone. If they'd come at me one at a time, I might have dealt with them with some semblance of reason. But now they had me cornered; the circumstances and the instigator of circumstances confronted me all at once.

I felt my body shake and convulse.

Karen entered the kitchen and saw the terror in my face.

Out of instinct I said into the receiver, "You ignorant thug. Why don't you show your face?"

Dial tone. He'd hung up on me.

Karen, still red-eyed and trembling, demanded an answer. "Alex?! Who was that?!"

I picked up the phone and dialed *69, but an automated voice told me the last number that called me was unidentified.

A quick jerk of the cord unplugged the phone, and I dropped it to the floor.

Karen reached for my hand. "Alex! Who was it?"

"His name is Plott and he's a certified nutcase."

Karen followed me out the back door and we stood side by side at the edge of our pool, trying to process disaster. What was planted and thriving hours earlier now lay chopped and withering in chlorinated waters. If I hadn't been so mad I would have cried.

Hands on hips and ticked off to the point of considering violence, I kicked a limb into the pool and joined it to the other debris. "This just takes the cake."

Instantly, I regretted saying those words, for I supposed that if there had actually been a cake, Abner Plott would have thrown it into the pool as well.

Karen clutched her arms to her chest. "I'm scared, Alex," she said and pointed at the floating wreckage. "This is serious psycho territory we've entered."

"I should have set an alarm back here. Are the cops coming out?"

She nodded. "Be here in a few minutes, or so they said." After wiping her sleeve across her face, she sat in one of the poolside chairs, her elbows on her knees, her head resting in her hands. "What if this Plott guy does something else to our house this weekend while we're gone?"

The time was now, and I faced her with as much sympathy as I could muster, given the situation. "We're not going, Karen."

Her face registered both shock and disillusionment. "What do you mean 'we're not going?' You agreed we needed to get away together! We need it for our marriage, Alex!"

"We're not going. Sterling is making me work. We have some important clients coming in on Saturday."

Karen stood and strode up to the pool and kicked another small limb into the floating brown mess, which now resembled a huge, unflushed toilet. "Well that's just great. Just great. Work comes first, always first."

To argue would have meant losing. The easy retort would have been the standard male default—that I was trying to be a good provider, and that my role sometimes entailed working hours I would otherwise not choose to work.

But Karen was too smart for that old-school logic, and if truth be known, I respected her intelligence too much to use that line. Life's rpm's had red-lined, and it was my own foot pressing the gas.

I went and sat in the pool chair she'd just vacated. "You need to know that it wasn't my idea to work on Saturday."

Her back remained turned to me as she stared into the pool. "Not only are you too busy to go with me on our trip, but you spend so much time at the office that I have to be first one home after Psycho Man does a Jack-the-Ripper on my Japanese maples!"

Karen labeling Plott as Pyscho Man caused me to consider again the idea of buying a gun, perhaps two—one for me and one for her. Besides, if whacking golf balls was good stress relief, then shooting targets with live ammo might be *great* stress relief.

Out of energy and consumed with frustration, I collapsed into the deck chair. "It's not like I have a lot of choice here, Karen. Not if I want to get ahead in the firm."

She spun around and faced me. "Well, *I'm* going. I'm packing tonight for St. Augustine, and I'll just go by myself." She strode past me and back into the house. "In fact, I might even take vacation time and leave tonight."

"Go," I said to the concrete. "Go ahead."

Alone with my brown pool, I reached behind me for our oldest chair—a green plastic thing faded by years in the sun—and lifted it over my head. Then I stood with that chair held high, walked forward to the pool, and heaved the chair halfway across the water until it crashed atop a half-sunken bush.

The heave felt good. For about two seconds.

But then I walked slowly around my brown pool, my eyes fixated upon the bushy heap all tangled in the deep end.

It was such an ugly scene, all that life cut off prematurely and left to die in chlorinated waters. Those waters had been so pristine—Karen and I both took great care of our pool. It was for us a place of refuge, our secluded time-out, and the location of our Saturday night skinny-dips. We had not skinny-dipped in months. We also had not cooked favorite meals for each other in months, or stayed up late talking into the wee hours, or snuggled on the sofa and watched a movie together. It felt to me as if so many facets of our marriage—the conversational, the physical, the sense of partnership—had been sabotaged.

After another numb walk around our chlorinated swamp, I stopped beside the stairs again and watched one of the exiled plants, weighed down and no longer buoyant, sink slowly toward the bottom, its slender leaves reaching for the surface as if gasping for one last breath. What I saw, however, wasn't a plant yielding to gravity but my most valuable relationship yielding to heavy circumstance.

Everything in my orbit yearned for oxygen, and as I took a deep breath and prepared to go inside and re-engage with Karen, a second plant succumbed and began its slow, eerie descent to the bottom of the pool.

9

ILENT AND POKER-FACED, JUDGE RAMOS REMAINED A PICTURE of concentration as he read the Abner Plott file. For 10 minutes we'd both been waiting on Plott to arrive, the two of us seated in the familiar T formation, the judge at the top, my seat below his bench, on the left side of a long table. Perhaps Abner's tardiness was yet another attempt to get back at the system, to inject chaos into legal proceedings in much the same manner as he'd brought chaos to my front yard.

It was good that he was late; the delay gave me more time to calm myself, to stifle my desire to slug him upside his head the moment he walked into the judge's chambers.

Two more minutes passed, and Judge Ramos looked up from his perusal of the file and said, "We've waited over 10 minutes now. Do you have any idea if Mr. Plott is going to join us, Mr. Lord?"

I shook my head. "No, Judge, I do not." The question felt to me like a small opening, an opportunity to briefly prepare the judge for what he might encounter over the next half hour of the proceedings. Boldness seemed in order, so I sat upright in my chair and became bold. "Judge, I must inform you that Mr. Plott is a bit of a lunatic. He has sued me—with suits just like this one—in 14 different Florida counties. If you're going to dismiss the case...."

"Mr. Lord," Judge Ramos said, and his voice boomed at me. "I do not appreciate you taking advantage of another party's absence to bend my ear in a manner that benefits you. It is unethical, and you, being a member of the Bar, know that."

Boldness withered into humility. I nodded to the judge to let him know that I agreed, and then, in a kind of silent apology, clasped my hands in my lap.

The knock on the door was almost inaudible, so soft it almost did not register in the chambers. I turned to see Abner Plott in a dated brown suit, shuffling into the room and over to the right side of the long table. He sat opposite me but close to the judge. At least he had learned where to sit.

I still wanted to slug him.

Judge Ramos eyed Plott for several seconds, letting him know that he was not pleased with being delayed. "Mr. Plott, I presume?"

"Yes. Good morning."

The judge turned his attention back to me. "Mr. Lord, you may now address the court."

I did not want to address the court. While I stifled inner rage against Plott and sought some kind of mental at-ease whereby I could function as a lawyer, I did not picture myself addressing this court. No, I pictured myself grabbing Plott by the collar of his jacket, marching him all the way to my front yard, and stuffing his head face down in fertilizer. *Breathe it in, Abner. Take a strong whiff. Gulp a hearty mouthful, and swallow what you've force-fed on to the House of Lord.*

"Mr. Lord?" came the judge's impatient prod.

"Yes, of course." I dismissed revenge and turned in my chair. "Judge, this complaint is a rambling collection of charges and accusations with no basis in the law. There is no way to respond to this."

Judge Ramos twitched his lip and re-read a portion of the complaint. Then he met my stare with his patented poker face. "For the most part, I agree with you." With a similar blank expression, he turned to Abner Plott and leaned slightly forward over the bench. "Mr. Plott, no cause of action exists for 'shysterism.' In addition, your hate crime count does not state any cause of action. But tell me, sir, what is the basis for the count you call 'attack?'"

Plott glanced at me, then raised his chin to the judge. "He threw me to the ground."

I gripped my armrests. "Judge, that's not true!"

Annoyed and not afraid to show it, Judge Ramos raised a finger to me. "Counselor, you are aware that your motion tests the sufficiency of the pleading. Facts have nothing to do with it; there are no facts for me to consider. I find the count called 'attack' states a cause of action for civil battery. The rest of the complaint is dismissed. Mr. Lord, please prepare an order."

I almost came out of my seat. Only twin death grips on the armrests prevented me from exploding. There had been no *civil* battery. But there had been yard battery, plant abuse, and tree dismemberment, all committed by the dysfunctional dolt seated across from me.

Plott stood and slid his chair gently beneath the table, as if he were leaving an establishment of fine dining rather than a judge's chambers. But perhaps he had dined after all—I was the main course, and the civil battery charge was just an appetizer.

Plott left the chambers in his familiar shuffle.

I gave him a 10-second head start. Then, without bothering to offer so much as a 'thank you' to Judge Ramos, I walked out and followed Plott to the elevators.

He didn't see me as he ducked into the second elevator. I checked the hallway and saw no one, waited for the door to begin closing, and thrust my hand in to halt its slide. Once inside, I pressed the lobby button and turned to see Abner Plott backed into a corner. A surge of adrenalin jolted my body, and it was all I could do not to pummel my adversary. Instead, I lessened the space between us until it narrowed to a couple feet—then 18 inches, then 12.

The elevator began its descent. I moved so close to Plott I could smell him, one fist clinched at my side. "I don't know what your game is, old man, but it better stop, and stop right now. Got it? *Right. Now.* No more suits, no more calls, nothing."

The musty odor from his old suit annoyed me—but not enough to make me back off or reconsider.

He just stared back, expressionless, as if my threats did not register.

I thrust my left hand against the elevator wall, inches from Plott's head. "Did you hear me, Mr. Plott? Did you? Either you cease your demented games, or I swear I'll—"

The elevator bell rang and we stopped. But we were not yet to the lobby. The door slid open and a stocky deputy, thirtyish and un-suspecting, stepped into the elevator. By this time I had removed my hand from near Plott's head and assumed a nonaggressive pose, the result being that the three of us now stood in a kind of forward-facing triangle, the deputy at the apex.

As the door closed, Plott said, "Excuse me," to the officer.

My whole body tensed and I prepared to defend myself to law enforcement.

The officer turned. "Yes?"

Plott looked at me, I looked at him, and the officer looked warily at both of us.

Plott tapped his wrist. "Do you have the time, sir?"

The officer raised a forearm and cast a glance downward. "10:52."

After my sigh of relief, I considered the size and caliber of the deputy's pistol. A part of me wanted to pull the pistol from his holster, press the black barrel to Plott's chin, and force the coward to admit all he'd done to try and wreck my life.

But I did none of that. The elevator bell rang, and the three of us stepped out into the lobby like total strangers. The officer turned right into a hallway, Plott turned left toward the twin exit doors, and I paused 2 seconds before following him again.

Or so I thought. New obstacles arrived in the form of two more police officers, who merged in from the hallway and pushed open the exit doors for Plott. He thanked them and departed, and I watched him shuffle off and climb into his old El Camino, parked in a handi-cap spot, right next to a squad car.

Today was not the day for retribution. That would have to wait.

I stood on the top steps of the building, awash in the hot Orlando sun, and heard my Blackberry buzz from my pants pocket. It was Austin, and his message lent a small dose of levity to the morning.

If you don't have time for me to beat you at golf, at least let me out-lift you at the gym.

I texted back my okay and made for my car. The gym around the corner from PMG contained a pair of punching bags, and once there I would take my Plott frustrations out with a few jabs and uppercuts.

* * *

Austin squatted under several hundred pounds of weights, working his legs and grunting through his final repetition. From the sweat that covered his face and dampened the moist triangle on the back of his sweatshirt, he'd been pumping iron for at least a half hour already. "That old man Plott whipped your butt, didn't he?"

I tossed my gym bag into a chair against the wall. "He most certainly did not whip my butt."

Austin stood, grabbed a towel, and wiped the sweat from his face. "Surviving your motion to dismiss most certainly qualifies as whipping your butt."

I pulled one leg behind my back and stretched. Then I backed up into the squat machine and did three reps. "Yeah, Austin, and you've never lost a hearing because some judge screwed up and pulled a ruling out of the sky?"

Austin smirked the way only Austin could—with equal part disdain and superiority. He grabbed a 40-pound dumbbell from the floor and began curling it in slow repetitions. "Sure, I've lost hearings, but there was always a *lawyer* on the other side of the table."

I managed four more reps, each one faster than the last, and mostly in reaction to the insult I'd just swallowed.

"Hey," Austin continued, "it could have been a lot worse. He could have made you do the order."

His comment annoyed me but I didn't show it. No way would I admit to Austin that the judge made me do the order.

For the next few minutes, neither of us spoke. We just took turns squatting and curling, then curling and squatting, until the volume of my sweat had nearly matched his own. We were so competitive that we even compared sweat levels.

I decided that weights offered less stress relief than pounding golf balls; at least with golf balls you could imagine the ball as someone's head launching into orbit, and if you didn't like the way their head flew or you wanted their head to fly higher, you could always tee up another and relaunch their head in a new direction.

I walked toward the rowing machines and, seeing that Austin was coming with me, spoke over my shoulder. "This Plott stuff is getting way out of hand—way, way out of hand. I've had freaks calling my home and scaring Karen, insulting us both. They even have my cell number now."

From behind me, Austin tried to offer advice. "Don't worry about it," he said. He paused to catch his breath from the workout. "Have you counterclaimed against him yet?"

I kneeled beside a rowing machine and retied my sneaker. "I'm trying to spend as little time on this as I can. The road to becoming partner should make as few passes as possible down Abner Avenue."

Austin chuckled and watched me slide into the rowing machine. "How's Karen?"

"She's fine," I shot back, the speed of reply masking the truth.

Austin examined the second rowing machine as if it were too feminine a task for him. He poked it with his foot and frowned as I began to row beside him. "You need to get this guy's attention. Throw a brick through his window, rough him up, intimidate him a bit. You know where he lives?"

I rowed twice more and stopped. "Yeah, I know about where he lives. His address is on the complaints he filed against me. An apartment out near the Citrus Bowl."

Austin pulled a plastic chair over beside the rowing stations and sat. "Figures he'd live somewhere like that. Slime area. The hood for old geezers." He removed a shoe and rubbed his foot. "Look, Alex, just get him alone somewhere and tell him you'll rip his ratty head off and feed it to stray dogs. Punch him in the gut if you have to, just do whatever is necessary to get him to believe you."

"You mean fear me?"

He slid his shoe back on his foot. "Fear you *and* believe you."

I began to row again, but my heart wasn't into it. Neither was my mind or my muscles. "You're full of great ideas, Austin. What you don't know is that some guy called and said that he read about me, that he saw pictures, though I have no idea what kind of pictures he's talking about."

Austin smirked again. "Maybe Mr. Plott has an 'I Hate Alex Lord' newsletter. No telling what a subscription might cost."

We made our way over to the squat machine again, and it was at Austin's suggestion that I agreed to wager on who could squat the most weight.

"Loser buys a Gatorade for the winner?" he asked. He assumed a stance under the bar and faced me with lips pursed, confident in himself and assured of victory.

I became worried when he squatted 340 pounds, with only a mild grimace to show for his effort.

"Not bad," I said, and knew that I was about to lose.

I traded places with him and changed out the weights to start with something lighter. Then I grunted under the weight across my shoulders, and managed, barely, to handle 280 pounds. No way would I even attempt more.

"You lose, Brotha' Lord," Austin said and reached for a towel. "I'll take my payment in orange flavor."

"The Gator alumni favorite," I said. "But then you never did look good in orange."

He tried to pop me with his towel. "And you're never gonna look good with those chicken legs too weak to clear even 300 pounds."

He was right. I had spent far too much time in my lawyer chair, stagnant at my lawyer desk, doing my lawyer duties and thinking of how to take lawyer revenge on Abner Plott.

Plott the plotter. He'd plotted against me like he had a Ph.D. in Terrorism, which seemed strange when I considered that Abner likely couldn't read past a third-grade level.

* * *

My shower was quick; my trek back to the office even quicker. If there really was some sort of 'I Hate Alex Lord' newsletter, it would not be in print but in the form of a blog, the author hoping it would go viral and build sympathy for his demented cause.

Austin wandered into my office with his wet hair slicked back, his right hand clutching the nearly empty bottle of orange Gatorade. "Find anything?"

"It's searching now."

The search completed its scan and turned up what I hoped it would not. But there it was, for all to see. *J. Alexander Lord – Shyster Supreme*. It sounded like a new kind of pizza, made especially for criminals: A Shyster Supreme. I clicked the site to find my company photo centered on the home page, my phone numbers, and address listed in bold red letters below the picture.

Austin guzzled the last ounces of his drink. "Oh, man…you're going to be famous very soon. If you're not already."

Already my hands shook as I moved the cursor to the right and scrolled further down the page—one large block of text, full of capital letters and underline—the signature markings of Abner Plott. With the Internet, this Abner was in fact quite large, very determined, and relentlessly focused on my destruction.

Teetering between shock and outrage, I began to read: "J Alexander Lord is a first class shyster, the Captain Commander of all Shyster Forces, and he works for the most vile, shysterish, and evil law firm on earth, the dreaded Powers, Morgan, and Greene."

Austin snickered behind me. "Well, Alex, at least you can't sue him for libel."

I ignored the insult and read the next paragraph: "This extraordinary collection of shysters—notice the all caps—has launched a vicious campaign in which they seek to extort, rob, and defraud hard-working American citizens from their hard earned monies, said monies having been earned with sweat and blood."

Austin moved around from behind me and stood beside my desk. "I've read all about this stuff on the web. Plenty of militia types and extremist wackos target judges, lawyers, and federal agents with this drivel. They usually aren't smart enough to come up with the phrases and vocabulary on their own, so they just copy and paste it off the Internet. There's probably a fortune to be made for an accomplished writer willing to contract himself out as a hatemonger-for-hire."

I could not take any more. I leapt from behind my desk and grabbed my Ping putter from against the wall. I stepped into the open space in the middle of my office and imagined Abner Plott in the room. I swung at his imaginary head—and would have decapitated him with the force of my swing.

Then I reared back and swung again. This time, Austin—who leaned against my desk and watched me with great amusement— clapped for my second effort.

"Nice, Alex. Did you picture his head bouncing down a par-4 or a par-5?"

"Down a cart path and into the pond toward that gator who ate your golf ball."

Austin chuckled. "You should use a 4-iron."

I gripped that putter with all the force I could muster. "Austin, I swear, I will not let this crazy, demented old man ruin my life." I glanced over at the picture of Karen and me on the beach. "I meant *our* life."

Austin turned for the door but stopped and admired my office. "Well, you'd better do something about this while you still have a little life left, *el shyster supremo*."

He departed in a blur but his chuckle lingered, leaving me to wonder if he actually felt compassion for me or if his shallowness and competitive nature had combined to produce a man incapable of sympathy. But Austin Adams was the best friend I had, and he was certainly right about one thing—if necessary—I would use the 4-iron.

10

I DIDN'T EVEN KNOW THE NAME OF THE BAR, ONLY THAT THE bartender's name was Otis, and I knew his name because he wore a name tag fastened semi-straight above the Bass Pro Shops logo on his ocean blue fishing shirt. Otis didn't engage me in conversation; he just went about his business, serving a strawberry concoction to two elderly ladies at the end of the bar and drying pairs of wine glasses with the care and thoroughness of one who takes pride in his job.

I'd come here for downtime. I'd come here for reflection and planning, and I'd come here because Karen did not want to talk to me. She said she was going by the house and was considering heading out of town early, perhaps right after work. She said she wanted to stand on a balcony overlooking a marsh and find peace in nature because she could not find peace at home. What was clear to me was that we sought comfort in opposite corners—me in a no-name bar in a nondescript section of Orlando; she in a coastal retreat. We were both flailing, and I felt certain that any happiness either of us found in hiding would prove as temporary as my last beer.

"Want another?" Otis asked from 10 feet away. He polished the bar's dark wood and motioned at the last ounces of golden liquid stagnating in my glass.

"Can I ask you something?"

He flung his rag behind him and into the sink, a no-look toss that he'd obviously perfected over the years. "Sure. What's up?"

I turned my beer glass slowly on the bar, as if its contents held 99 percent clarity instead of 6 percent alcohol. "What's the most difficult aspect of being a bartender?"

He rolled his large dark eyes, and a smile crept upon his face. "Whew. Good question, that one."

I took a sip and fondled my beer mug. "Take your time."

He leaned into the bar and stared past me at the empty tables. It was only 8:30 P.M., and the diners had departed. The remaining patrons consisted of the two old ladies and myself; collectively, we were doing a poor job of keeping Otis busy.

Otis ran a finger back and forth across the gray whiskers on his chin. He seemed deep in thought. Finally he raised that finger and used it to amplify what he was going to say. "The hardest part...hmmm...the hardest part for me, being a 61-year-old black male in Orlando, Florida...is finding time to date all the hot sorority babes who road trip down from Gainesville to visit me every Saturday night."

I almost spewed my beer across the bar.

Even the old ladies laughed.

"Cheerleaders, sorority girls," he said, aware that he had an audience, "independents, young associate professors, I can't keep up with 'em all anymore."

The old ladies slapped their knees, and Otis upped not only his narrative but his volume as well. "They texting me all hours of the night, wanting me to teach 'em how to dance, wantin' me to escort 'em to homecoming, help 'im shop for cute little outfits, share recipes with their mommas, play golf with their rich daddies, yeah, all that stuff combines to make up the hardest part of my job."

I shook my head at the detail he'd weaved into his story. "I wanna switch jobs, man."

"No, no," he continued, "seriously, the hardest part now is the hours. After I passed 60, my need for sleep went up. But I can't afford to hire more help, so most nights I close it myself. Gotta' keep the inflow above the outflow, ya' know?'"

I nudged my glass toward him. "So you're actually the owner? Part owner?"

"Half owner. But my brother let me name the place."

I turned to look back at the door and saw the blue neon flashing the name of the bar in distinct cursive. Otisology.

"Otisology." I said the word slowly, as if to decipher it between syllables.

Otis nodded and poured me another draft. "I offer each patron the opportunity to gain a degree in bartender wisdom. One drink is freshman course. Two is sophomore, three is junior, and eight is senior level."

"*Eight?*" I asked, shocked at the jump in volume. "That's an expensive degree."

"Yes, and at that level, most people will believe anything I tell 'em!" He slid me my third beer. "Now, what's the hardest part of being an attorney?"

My mug stopped an inch short of my lips. "I never told you I was an attorney."

"But you are, aren't you?" He turned and checked on the two elderly women, acknowledging their thumbs up with his own. Then he rapped his knuckles on the bar in front of me. "Knew it as soon as you sat down…the shirt, tie, briefcase. Yep, you a lawyer."

I drank and it was very cold, the way first sips are supposed to taste. "Does Otisology offer a course on vengeance?"

Otis turned serious, his eyebrows becoming one, then separating, then becoming one again. "You mean like payback?" He lowered his voice. "Somebody after you?"

I loosened my tie and decided to trust this stranger with a few details. "No, somebody already *came* after me. He ruined my yard, scared my wife. Now I'm getting threatening phone calls every day."

He studied me for all of three seconds. "Drug dealer, right? You put the dealer away, now his homies coming after you 'cause you cut off their flow."

I sipped again. "Nope. Older white man who lost his house. Hates lawyers, so he picked me to take out his vengeance at the system."

Otis took my mug away and poured the contents into the sink behind him. He returned empty-handed. "You ain't gonna solve that kinda' issue with more beer."

"No?"

"Your hair's too neat and your shirt's too nice for you to be some outcast from the legal system."

I held an imaginary mug in my right hand and offered him an imaginary toast. "Thank you for the compliment. Now can ya' give my wife a lesson in how to give those?"

Otis laughed. "Look, I'm gonna close early tonight 'cause it's so slow, but lemme' tell you what I think."

"Like I have a choice."

Here came that pointing finger again. It stopped just 12 inches from my nose. "If you're using my beers to soften yourself up so that you can return violence for violence, I want you to go to somebody else's bar. Got it?"

I hated being so transparent. "Yes, sir," I said to that brown finger. "I got it."

He lowered his head to where we were eye to eye. "But if you just want to apply Otisology, well now, that's a different thing altogether."

I played along and shrugged as if I could not resist what he was about to serve. "Give it to me, Otis. Gimme' the senior level course on how to deal with a vindictive old man."

His questions came quickly. "What he do to your yard?"

"Chopped down my plants, shrubs, and Japanese maples."

"Ewww. What else?"

"Threw it all into my pool."

"You got a pool?"

"Yep."

"A nice one? Like with both a shallow end and a deep end? And a privacy fence and stuff?"

"Just like that."

"Man, I always wanted a pool. After you clean out all them bushes and make it blue again, ya' think I can come over and we'll hang out and drink a beer?"

I couldn't help but chuckle at his initiative. "Might as well. I sure ain't using it with my wife."

Otis grabbed a towel and began wiping the bar in slow, rhythmic motions. "You own a gun?"

"No, but you're the second person this week to suggest it."

He folded his moist towel into a fine square and rested one elbow on it. "I ain't really suggesting you get a gun, but if some wack job ruined my yard and my pool, and he was still at large…yeah, I probably buy me a gun. I'd go with a 9 millimeter, concealed carry."

The two and a half beers had created in me just the slightest buzz, just enough to let me bring both hands together and form a pistol, both index fingers combining to make a barrel. I shot two rum bottles and a fifth of Jack Daniels.

"Anything else you'd advise, Otis?"

He picked up his squared towel and wiped his hands. "Yes. I would also carry a canister of pepper spray, and I'd stay away from places that…."

Crash! The sound of wood hitting wood. We both spun to see the second elderly lady backward on the floor. She had fallen from her stool. But her head had hit carpet and she lay on her back laughing. She looked up at her drinking buddy. "Oh, oh my, Glenda."

I hurried over to help, as did Otis, who ran in long strides around the bar.

We got the lady to her feet, and she only wobbled once before regaining her composure, dignity notwithstanding. In the aftermath, we decided she was less drunk than uncoordinated.

Her friend took her by the elbow, and they thanked us and made for the door, the sober one saying to the fallen, "We should stick to non-alcoholic margaritas, Bea."

Otis held the door for them and bid them good night.

I checked my watch, saw 8:52 P.M. and remembered I needed to stop for gas, look over some notes, and be in the office very early. "I'll stop by later in the week, Otis. Thanks for the crash course."

He used his foot as a doorstop and reached out and clasped my hand in both of his. "You take care, brother." He squeezed my hand

and let go. Then he closed the door behind me and I walked toward my car knowing that even though I hadn't solved my Plott problem, I'd at least made a friend.

Seconds later it didn't surprise me much when he called to me down the block. "'Hey, I like my pool water at 85 degrees!"

I waved over my head, but in reality the only thought I had about temperatures concerned Abner Plott. If somehow his body would assume room temperature, that would be as comfortable for me as an 85-degree pool.

* * *

Karen had left a note on the kitchen counter, informing me that my inability to travel with her meant that there was no longer any need for her to wait for the weekend. She'd taken two personal days off from work and would be back on Thursday afternoon. At least that was her estimate, depending on how she felt after some time alone in St. Augustine.

I saw the irony in her going away to the oldest city in America in order to deal with the oldest problem in America—marital disagreement. But I also knew that marital disagreements were best solved with both parties in the room, not separated by over a hundred miles of Florida and the pressures of work.

Karen rarely if ever added a P.S. to a note, but this one had a P.S: *I will pray for us, Alex.*

That one shook me. Not because the person closest to me mentioned that she'd pray, but that the two of us so rarely entered into the activity of requesting from a higher power such trivial additives as wisdom and guidance.

A second dose of irony washed over me as I considered that my wife had sought wisdom and guidance from God on the very day that I had asked for wisdom and guidance from—Otis.

I walked out through the French doors onto our patio and stared once again into our murky brown pool. I had forgotten to call the pool service, and Karen had not taken care of it either before she left town. The mess was even worse than before. Not only had most of the plants drowned and drifted to the bottom, but the bushes that still floated had now added offensive scents to their ugliness.

Perhaps Abner Plott had sprayed the bushes before he severed them. Or perhaps the smell was of botanical decay mixing with chlorinated water mixing with Florida humidity.

All I knew was that the sum of it stunk and stunk bad.

Plott. Pool. Work. Marriage. Life. Everything stunk.

I doubted the pool man would want to clear shrubs from the water, so I decided to do it myself. I shed my oxford, untucked my T-shirt, and fetched a rake from our supply closet. Then I walked around to the deep end of the pool next to the stairs and raked at the first water-logged bush and a Japanese maple. The maple was some 6 feet in length and proved a much easier rescue than the heavy shrubs. These I dragged out the gate one at a time and around the left side of our home, down the driveway and to the street, where a branch nicked my trousers and pulled a thread out above the knee. This ticked me off, so I kicked the shrub. Twice.

I recoiled from the second kick and was considering a third when two kids on bicycles zoomed past me in the street. I'd seen them around before but had no idea which house they claimed as home, or why they were out after 9:00 P.M. on a school night. They both looked 11 or 12, their mountain bikes outfitted in wild shades of green and purple.

The pudgy kid looped around and stopped in the street behind me. "What happened to your yard?"

I pulled the Japanese maple around by its base until it was parallel to the street. "My yard was sabotaged."

Pudgy perused the damage from end to end. "More like it got blown up."

The smaller kid on the purple bike pulled up beside his buddy and took his time studying my scorched earth. "Maybe we could make a video game called Yard Terrorist."

Pudgy laughed, and they both looked at me as if expecting a reply.

What I gave them was an offer. "You two wanna make a few bucks?"

"Sure."

I pointed at the pile I'd just begun. "Pay you guys 20 bucks each to get every plant and bush out of my pool tomorrow. You drag it all down to this pile, but make sure that neither of you drown in the process. Want the job? It'll be messy, but I gotta' work all weekend and I want this cleaned up as soon as possible."

The smaller kid said, "We swim in ponds all the time. Can't be worse than that."

Pudgy scanned my barren yard as if trying to guess just how many plants and shrubs lay foundering in my pool. "Twenty bucks each, eh? But how long you think it'll take us?"

A pint-sized negotiator, this was all I needed. "Okay, 20 bucks each, plus I'll leave a cooler full of Cokes beside the pool. Just have it all done by dark tomorrow, 'cause I'm calling the pool guy to come change out the water on Thursday."

I introduced myself and discovered that the pudgy kid's name was Marty, and the smaller kid was Jackson. Marty leaned over his handlebars and whispered something to Jackson. Then he turned his attention back to me. "For an extra fifty bucks we'll drain your pool and fill it back up with a garden hose."

Jackson snorted. Marty-the-negotiator looked dead serious.

"Ha, ha." I said with all the sarcasm of one who was out of patience and had just torn his best trousers. "You and Trump Junior can start with the plants and bushes. And be sure and wear goggles. That water has yard chemicals in it now, and I don't want your parents suing me."

Jackson addressed me in a whisper. "We don't tell our parents anything, mister. We just need some cash."

Marty nodded. "What time you want us to start?"

I spoke to the tear in my pants. "Right after you get home from school. By 4:00 at the latest. Shouldn't take you more than 2 hours. But you're going to have to feel around the bottom of the pool. You won't be able to see all the debris, because the water turned brown."

"Oh, great," Jackson complained. "Probably an 80-pound gator livin' in there by now."

Good grief. Next they would ask me for hazard pay. "I'll leave your cash in a jar on one of the deck chairs. Don't take it until you're done. Got it?"

They assured me they'd do a fine job and peddled off into the night.

I went to bed fearing Plott, dreading my next conversation with Karen, and envious of entrepreneurial youth.

11

THE SCENT OF MEN'S COLOGNE CIRCULATED INSIDE THE ROOM, and from a fourth floor window I stared out at the pink residue of sunset splashed over downtown Orlando. It was 7:00 P.M. on Wednesday, and my lofty perch was not in a bar or a nightclub; the view I enjoyed came from Richard Sterling's corner office, where we'd been discussing for the past half hour my next project with Powers, Morgan, and Greene.

"Alex," Richard said, and he closed his file drawer and returned to his seat. "You know about the Cypress Manufacturing trial, don't you? That it starts tomorrow—or at least it's *scheduled* to start tomorrow."

From his guest chair I nodded in the affirmative. "I've heard mention of it from the other associates."

With a fist clenched in confidence, he pounded lightly on the file, as if it were just another problem he could quash under his mighty hand. "Let me give you a quick rundown. Cypress is a long-standing client of ours, and we go back nearly two decades. Recently they've fallen on hard times and cannot afford this trial, nor can they at the present time afford to pay us to defend them. Tomorrow morning they'll be filing for bankruptcy, which will stay the trial."

"*Are* they bankrupt?"

Richard peered into the file for all of three seconds and shut it again—another soft fist-pound, a pursing of lips. "More or less."

He opened the file again and drew out a legal-sized envelope bulging with papers. This envelope he slid across the desk and I caught it as it tumbled toward the floor. "That envelope, Alex, contains the petition and the schedules. File it when the clerk's office opens. Be the first one there. Elbow your way to the front of the line if you have to, but I want you to arrive first. As soon as it's filed, you call me on my cell and we'll let the court know that the trial can't go forward."

I tucked the envelope under my arm. "You got it. I'll be there before they open for business."

He looked as if he'd gained back a smidgen of confidence in me, and when he said nothing more I figured it was time to go.

Not so fast.

"Alex, I've reviewed your numbers from last month."

Oh, man, here it came. PMG was all about the numbers. For that matter, everything in my life seemed about numbers: Karen and the number of hours we spent together; Austin and the number of pounds we could lift and the numbers we penciled on to our golf scorecards; Plott and the number of summonses he could file against me to make up for the lack of numbers in his checking account—due to the number of times he'd failed to pay his mortgage; and now the number of billable hours that Richard Sterling and his fellow partners had decided were my quota.

I stood behind the chair I'd just vacated and waited for him to complete his thoughts.

"I'm a little concerned, Alex. Your billables are off by quite a lot."

"I know my hours are down a little, sir."

He crossed his arms across his chest and sighed. "A little more than a little, wouldn't you say?"

"It's the Plott complications, sir." I gripped and re-gripped the file, my weak attempt at a stall. "Dealing with the attacks and the phone calls takes a lot of time."

To my utter surprise, he actually seemed sympathetic. "I know it's been a time stealer. But look, we all have hurdles to overcome. Someone close to us dies, you get sick, perhaps your kid gets sick. You don't have kids yet, but you know what I mean."

I absolutely knew what he meant. "I know. And sometimes there just aren't enough hours in the day."

Richard Sterling smiled knowingly and motioned out his window at the twinkling lights. "That's what nights are for."

I did not want to agree but I agreed anyway. "Yep."

"Call me when it's filed, Alex." He gave me that trusting look again and folded his arms in his lap. "And get those billables up for me."

* * *

Karen came home a day early from St. Augustine—at least that's what she'd said on my voice mail. Not that I was home *with* her. Hardly. The take-out box in my office trash can gave testament to my extended hours. I had volunteered for everything and anything in order to increase billables and get back on the good side of Richard Sterling and his numbers-obsessed partners.

By 10 P.M., the only billable I wanted was my bill for a stiff drink. I left Powers, Morgan, and Greene and drove around in a daze, my mind toggling between losing a chance at partner and losing my wife. One drink, one good drink, and I could make a plan and save it all. That is what Alex Lord had always been able to pull off—the incredible comeback from adversity. And I *was* Alex Lord. I reminded myself of this as I turned up the satellite radio and Elton John sang, 'Goodbye Yellow Brick Road.'

"I am Alex Lord!" I shouted above the chorus.

"I *am* Alex Lord!"

The liquor store I passed held more appeal than another visit with Otis—he was too lighthearted for my heightened level of anxiety—so I U-turned in the street and pulled in beneath the bright yellow lights. Posters greeted me from the windows: Jim Beam. Kahlua. Smirnoff. Corona.

I exited my car still wondering what to buy, and as I closed my door my Blackberry rang from the console. I retrieved the phone and closed the door with a push of my derriere. It was Karen.

"Hello," I said, a dash of hope in my greeting.

"Are you planning on coming home tonight, Alex?" Her voice sounded fragile.

"Maybe. What's up?"

"I'm just wondering if I'll see you before morning, that's all."

"Actually I'm on my way home now. Just had to make a brief stop at the store."

"How amazing—he's coming home."

Her lack of understanding felt like a kick to the groin. "Do ya' think I'm at a party, Karen? I really don't need sarcasm and condescension."

"And I don't need you using work as an excuse not to see me."

In front of the Corona poster, I seethed into the night air and failed to think of a single thing to say to my wife.

"Alex," she said, her voice softening, "I guess I'll see you when you get home."

I opened my passenger door and said, "Guess so."

Frustrated beyond sanity, I flung my phone backhanded into the passenger seat, watched it settle atop my briefcase, and slammed the door.

The chasm between us was growing wider with each conversation. The bridge back seemed crumbing at best, non-existent at worst.

Comfort called to me from the yellow lights, and between the Smirnoff and Kahlua posters I stared into the liquor store and wondered which beverage, if any, would spur wisdom.

Rum. Yes, rum would spur wisdom.

I strode into the store a confident man. But as choice overwhelmed me, that confidence faded until finally I reached high into a windowed cooler and selected a six-pack of an obscure microbrew called Golden Show Me. Brewed in Missouri, it promised an otherworldy sensation of liquid sunshine with a slightly hoppy aftertaste. All for just $11.29 per six-pack.

I needed other-worldly, in fact I hoped my consumption of all six of these pricey bottles would transport me to another world, a world of peace and justice where I could thrive as partner, succeed as husband, and delegate all cases involving Abner Plott to junior associates who could not afford my liquid sunshine with hoppy aftertaste.

I hoisted my Golden Show Me upon the counter and reached for my wallet.

"Hey," the clerk said in the monotone of a bored 20-something. He wore an oval earring in his left ear, his wavy hair dyed black like a rock star wannabe.

"Hey, what's up?" I replied.

He scanned the six-pack and frowned at the total. "Eleven seventy-six? Can that be right?"

I pulled a ten and a five from my wallet. "Sounds about right."

He pulled a paper bag from beneath the counter but stopped short of inserting my brews. Instead he read the label and glanced again at the cost displayed on his register. "Must be good stuff, man. I may try it myself some day when I hit the lottery."

I was in no mood to offer a smile of affirmation, but somehow I forced a small one and accepted my change.

"Is it strong stuff?" he asked, and handed me the bag. "I mean, it must kick butt for that coin. You could get six malt liquor talls for half that total and just get totally messed up."

I considered my lot in life—that of listening to a liquor store cashier with dyed black hair offering economic advice to assist me in achieving a state of drunkenness for the smallest possible out-of-pocket expense. Now *this* made me smile.

I clutched my six-pack as if it were my all-time fave. "It must be strong stuff," I said, and turned for the door. "It *has* to be strong stuff."

I pushed open the door and he called after me. "Hey, you like Green Day?"

"Love Green Day," I said to the night.

I set the six-pack on my passenger seat, next to my Blackberry, and opened the glove box to find what was, at least tonight, the most important hand tool in America—the bottle opener. I found it behind my car manual and registration. Then I opened the first bottle and drank the first delicious ounces. The hoppy aftertaste tickled my tongue and throat, and before I left the parking lot I'd reloaded with bottle number two.

Bottles two and three were finished off in my driveway, the BMW's headlights shining into the back bumper of Karen's Nissan Xterra. I half expected her to come out and curse me for drinking in the driveway, but no, that would require her to move *toward* me. Her default mode was to run away: St. Augustine. Ponte Vedra. Fort Lauderdale. Anything but to stay alongside me and try to understand the pressures that consumed her husband. I knew I was at least half to blame, and I knew that downing microbrews in my car was poor excuse for maturity. But it wasn't maturity I sought, it was comfort. And in the absence of a woman's gentle touch, a man can seek substitution in most anything. I had turned to Golden Show Me.

My warm buzz accompanied me inside the front door. Across the living room, Karen remained on the couch, her legs tucked under a pillow, a sky blue blanket spread loosely over her shoulders. She looked chilled, even in Orlando in September. In fact, the entire house felt chilled.

A hug would have been nice, but a glance and a smile sufficed as her greeting.

Already battling spousal nonchalance, I went over to the adjacent dining room and set the remaining three beers on the table. "How was your trip?"

"Pretty relaxing," she said, and snuggled into her blanket. "Short but relaxing. And your day?"

"Not so great." I pulled brew number four from the pack, removed my shoes, and walked in my socks to the recliner, directly across from her, the coffee table separating us. "I'm glad you enjoyed your getaway."

She smiled at me again, and this time she held my gaze a bit longer. "You'd like it there. They have a pretty golf course too. We should go back sometime. Maybe I can drive the golf cart while you play."

"Maybe I'd just want to ride in the cart with you and skip the golf."

I was hoping for a third smile, but something still bothered her and she only took seconds to share the source.

"Seven more harassment calls today, Alex," she said to the table. Then she pointed at our cordless phone. "*Seven.* The phone company says we can't get a new phone number until next week."

Without taking a first sip, I set my bottle on the hardwood floor and rubbed my eyes. Sleep had eluded me for three nights straight, and already I fought the urge to yawn. "We need to deal with it the best we can. Just screen all calls. If the number isn't familiar, don't answer."

She ran a hand through her hair and frowned. "You should listen to the messages on our voice mail. I've never heard such filth."

"Plott."

"They sounded younger."

"Plott is behind this. All of this."

"He's not the problem, Alex."

"No? Really?"

"He's just bringing it all to a head. He didn't just bare our yard, he bared what's wrong with our relationship."

There she went, using her patented twist on language to heap guilt on my head. "So I'm supposed to thank him for filling our pool with shrubs?"

Karen shook her head and pulled the blanket tighter around her shoulders. "The plant mess isn't in the pool anymore. Thank you for moving it all to the street."

"I paid two kids to do it."

She nodded and turned her face into the softness of the blanket. "They did a good job."

Silence crept upon our chilly abode, awkward seconds combining with my diminishing buzz to produce in me a late-night candor. "Karen, I firmly believe that our issues are largely a result of timing. The trial is coming up, and that's distracted me, and now Plott and his insanity distracts me further. But we'll work through it, sweety. We've worked through difficulties before."

Her countenance registered disagreement. "I'm afraid that by the time the trial is over I won't even know you."

"I'm doing my best to provide for us, and I know I need to do a better job of protecting you from Plott and his thugs."

She peeked out from the folds of her blanket. "You got the first two p-words right. Every woman craves provision and protection. But there's another 'p' I want too."

"Black-eyed or sweet?"

She dismissed my attempt at humor. *"Pursue.* I want you to pursue me, Alex. Even though the culture would say you already 'caught' me, I still want to be pursued, to go on dates and weekend getaways. I want to share a feeling of adventure with you."

Provide. Protect. Pursue. That was way too many "p's" for a lawyer with three Golden Show Me's in his belly, a faltering career, and a yard that looks like Hell's half acre.

I reached for my untouched brew on the floor but reconsidered and left it there. "I wish Plott would simply drop dead, or at least get hit by a bus or something."

She abhorred violence, and her frown reminded me of her sensitivity. "Don't say that."

"I want him gone. That much is true."

More frowns. "Real nice, Alex. A man causes you problems, and you in turn want him dead."

I got up out of the recliner and paced to the dining room and back. "A guy like Plott doesn't contribute to society. He's really just waiting to die."

She yanked the blanket from her shoulder and wadded it into a large ball. "He's a *person,* Alex."

"And you think his life is worth more than ours?"

She put her hands over her ears as if she could not listen anymore. Several seconds passed until her hands found their way back to her lap. "Did you ever think about asking him what he wants? Did that thought ever cross your mind?"

She had entered the realm of reverse female logic, a form of logic with which I was largely unfamiliar, even after nearly four years of marriage. "Please tell me you're kidding. You are kidding, aren't you? What Plott wants to do is drive me insane. Drive *us* insane."

She sat up straight and brought her knees together. "He's doing these things for a reason."

I paced again, slower, my steps heavy with doubt. "Sure he is. And perhaps I should ask him his reason. Maybe I'll just invite him over for quesadillas one night, okay?"

She rocked for a moment, as if comprehension eluded her. "Are you so far gone into your little lawyer world, attacking and fighting with people so often that you've lost the ability to show compassion and understanding?"

"If I go to Plott, then I'm admitting he wins."

Her gaze began hollow and drifted into incredulity. "So what if he wins?"

"So, I'm just not gonna do it."

She spoke over the top of her balled-up blanket. "Rather than try to understand him, you're just going to let him keep destroying everything you have? Sure, just keep hoping the man dies. You fear he might *win*? Earth to Alex—he's already won."

"That is a complete and total crock."

She motioned to the front door, to the yard beyond, and then to us. "Look around you. Our yard resembles moon craters, I'm afraid to leave the house, and I feel like I need a police escort just to go to work!" Her voice echoed off the walls. "You need to find out what Plott wants, and go give it to him!"

She'd never shouted at me like that. I decided to counter her volume with a more reserved tone and a two-second delay. "And what if I *do* talk to him, and the attacks and phone calls don't stop?"

"In that case, all you will have wasted is your breath."

"Plus my dignity."

"More news for you, Alex. When you sit around your house with a six-pack of beer and spend your time wishing that some sad old man will croak, your dignity is already long gone."

She left the living room and disappeared into the guest bedroom. I slumped into my recliner and grabbed my beer from the floor. I didn't finish it, however. Just one gulp and I took the bottle into the kitchen and poured it out into the sink, golden liquid swirling into the drain along with the last fragments of my dignity.

The porthole window over the sink offered a fresh view of our pool, and it appeared free of debris but not its taint. The kids had done their job. The pool man, however, had disappointed me by failing to show, thus the waters of the Lord estate remained brown and murky—visibility almost zero.

12

D ARK ROAST COFFEE SCENTED THE KITCHEN, AND ON 4 HOURS of sleep I tried to clear my head with a second cup. A gathering of small birds chirped from the patio, louder and louder, as if to summon not only the sunrise but also Karen, still asleep in our guest bedroom. I pulled her favorite mug from a cabinet and set it out with the vanilla-flavored creamer, her must-have additive for hot java.

The quiet sounds of morning, however, vanished in an instant.

A sound like wood smashing metal echoed from the front yard. I set my mug on the counter and ran through the house to the front door. I jerked the door open but saw no one. Down at the street, however, my mailbox leaned at an odd angle, a huge dent in its side.

In the distance, a car engine, but the car was already around the corner. Barefoot in my trousers, my shirt untucked, I made my way down the sidewalk to the street and inspected the damage. Plott, or one of his goons, had caved in the mailbox's side and door, the gnarled lid jutting out like a metallic tongue frozen in place.

"Hey!"

I turned and saw the pudgy kid, Marty, approaching me on his bike, his hair sticking up on one side in a glorious case of bed-head.

"Hey, mister!" he called and pedaled up beside me in the street. "I think some guy bashed your mailbox with a baseball bat. I ran around my house to see but he pealed out."

I stooped to inspect the underside of the mailbox, the screws partially pulled from the wood post. "Was he driving an old rusty car?" I asked the kid.

He pointed up the street. "El Camino. I know those cars anywhere 'cause my Uncle Mikey has one. He's got a 454 under the hood."

I needed a .357 under Plott's head.

Marty started to peddle away but he circled back and stopped beside me in the street. "You seem like a busy guy, mister. So for another 20 bucks each, my buddy and I could bike over to Lowe's and get you a new mailbox. We're out of school today, so we'll even install it."

The kid's penchant for prosperity was downright inspiring. "How 'bout 15 bucks each?"

"Deal, mister." He held out his hand, fingers flexing.

"No way," I said. "I wanna see the thing installed before I pay up."

The kid frowned like only a kid can frown. "I meant the money to buy the new mailbox. You can pay our labor when we're done."

I drew my wallet from my back pocket and pulled out a pair of twenties.

He shook his head at the two bills and took them as if they were only a pittance. "Forty bucks only buys a trailer-park mailbox, not a lawyer mailbox."

I gave him 20 more. "Find me a bargain, kid."

He seemed satisfied with the amount and tucked the bills into his pocket. Then he pulled out his cell phone and hit speed dial. "Jackson, meet me in front of my house. Lawyer-dude just gave us a new job. We gotta' go to Lowe's."

He peddled away into a morning sun, and I hurried inside to explain to Karen what had happened.

When I arrived in the kitchen she had just taken a strawberry yogurt from the fridge but had yet to open it. She set the container on the counter and reached for the comfort of flavored coffee. "I saw the damage, Alex. I looked out the window after I heard the smash."

"I'm thinking of buying us a gun. One of us may need it soon."

She appeared displeased at the idea, even as she lifted the coffee pot and refilled my mug for me. "If you do buy one, don't tell me."

"If I do, I'll get something small, something you could handle if you had to."

Contemplative, she opened her yogurt and savored a bite. "You know, I don't think I'd feel safe staying here tonight. Who knows what they'll try to smash next. Our cars? Our furniture? Our heads?"

I could tell she was frightened, though she hid it well.

In an effort at compassion, I kissed her on the cheek and urged her to get to work and not return home until she heard from me.

"I'll leave for work at my usual time. Plus, I have pepper spray in my purse, remember?"

The woman could put up a tough stance although I could not figure out if it was a shield against fear or if it was also a wall to protect her from our relational inconsistency. Over the past 8 hours I'd showed up buzzed, she'd shouted at me, we'd slept in separate rooms, and I'd kissed her on the cheek instead of the lips—not the stuff of marital harmony.

I brushed my teeth over the first of the twin sinks in our master bedroom, a simple act that reinforced the air of division in our home. On so many mornings we'd brushed beside each other in our shared rush to get to work, and now I didn't even see her toothbrush. I supposed she'd taken it to the guest bathroom.

The faucet ran in the guest bathroom as I left for the office. Yet when I reached my car and the lock chirped and I climbed inside, a sense of dread met me before I even buckled my seat belt—my briefcase was not on the seat. Not in my hand, not on the ground beside the car, and not laying flat on the roof. Neither was the briefcase on my floorboard or laying horizontal in the backseat.

Its absence was not a mere annoyance. That beautiful new briefcase, the birthday gift from my wife, contained the bankruptcy papers which I'd assured Richard Sterling would be filed first thing this morning. My wrist shook as I checked my watch. The clerk's office opened in 31 minutes.

Panic jettisoned my hangover, and my mind spun into manic reflection. *I entered the house last night with just my three remaining beers. I'd last seen the briefcase at the liquor store. No, I had a buzz when I got home, so maybe I did take the briefcase inside. Karen will know.*

I bolted back into the house. Wingtips slid on hardwoods and I nearly splattered myself into a bookshelf.

The kitchen table. No.

Beside the recliner! No again.

The counter! Nope.

Karen came out of the bathroom in her orange robe and saw me searching, my motions frantic and hurried. "What?" she asked.

"Have you seen my briefcase?"

She shook her head. "No."

I blew past her and looked in the bedroom. Nothing.

I ran back past her in the hall and went to the kitchen window and looked out into the pool area. Empty.

I turned and met her stare. "It's not in the car, Karen. It's not anywhere. And I have to file something hugely important in 30 minutes."

She stood with her back against the dining room door, hands on hips, her hair still damp. "Are you sure it's not in the car? That's where you usually leave it when you come home late."

"Yes, I'm absolutely sure. Did I bring it in with me last night?"

Karen sighed. "All I saw was the beer."

I could have done without the insulting comment, but my rush to find what was missing overran my desire for confrontation.

Instead I ran out of the house and jumped into my car and burned rubber in the street. En route to the office I called Carol.

"Mister Lord's office," she said.

"Carol! It's me! See if my briefcase is sitting in my office."

"Are you okay, Alex? You sound flustered."

"I'm beyond flustered. Please check for me—right now. I can't find it."

She put me on hold. I drove like a madman, despite being forced to listen to B.J. Thomas sing '*Raindrops Keep Falling on My Head.*'

Ten seconds grew to twenty, and twenty became forty. Hurry up, Carol!

'But that doesn't mean my eyes will soon be'. ... B.J. stopped singing. "Alex," Carol said, nearly out of breath. "It's not there. I looked everywhere."

I braked hard and U-turned in the street.

"Alex?! Are you sure you're okay?"

"No." I shouldn't have hung up on her, but further talk was useless. The briefcase was somewhere in my house, and I had to be in court in 22 minutes.

Karen emerged from the kitchen in a navy pantsuit, her left hand gripping a container of yogurt, her right spooning breakfast to her lips. "Did you leave it at work?"

"No, I did not leave it at work and right now I need you to stop eating and help me and not ask redundant questions."

Her narrowed eyes cast a gaze worthy of light sabers. One swoosh of those eyes might have cut a lesser man in half.

Palms extended in a plea for mercy, I blurted. "Please go look in the bedroom while I search back here."

She didn't move.

"Go, Karen! Look for it! Now!"

She stayed put and clutched her yogurt container in both hands. I couldn't tell if she was stunned by my tone or amused at my zeal.

I rushed past her toward the bedroom. "This is unbelievable."

My search expanded in a rush of panicked thought. Under the bed—No. In the closet—Negative. Beside the vanity—No again.

It wasn't here. The bankruptcy petition I needed to file was in that briefcase, and already I could picture Richard Sterling sitting in a courtroom and glancing at his watch, confident of receiving my call within a few minutes. I was ready to break something and curse Mickey.

No room, closet, or shelf held my briefcase. I bolted past Karen toward the front door until something—perhaps the knowledge that I was fast becoming an out-of-control monster—forced me to stop and look back at her.

She still stood in the kitchen entrance, clutching her spoon to her chest, her yogurt container now sideways on the floor, its contents melting.

A single tear, and then a second, ran down my wife's cheek.

I knew I should stop and go to her but now I only had 16 minutes to get to the clerk's office.

I ran out of the house to the car, and seconds later my tires barked my departure.

I made a right out of the neighborhood and immediately passed Marty and Jackson on their bikes. They were peddling toward Lowe's at a leisurely pace, both of them tilting a Dr. Pepper for breakfast, the morning sun bright on young faces. I wanted to switch places with them, to be carefree and 12 again.

Instead, I sped past them without honk or wave, my mind fixated upon Richard Sterling, and how I was going to tell him that the papers with which he entrusted me did not get filed. I imagined him listening on the phone to my excuse, his fist clutched in frustration, his silvered hair damp on the sides from the anger boiling up out of his ears.

A left turn past a black El Camino reminded me that one individual had sent my life reeling, and I wanted more than ever to remove that individual from society. My growing rage enabled such thoughts. I wanted to believe that Abner Plott had painted his car to hide himself, but no, as I braked to look it became evident that the black one was occupied by a young Hispanic guy, jamming to music and munching a donut.

I was losing it, ready to cast blame at anyone, for any reason. I sped through a yellow light and muttered, "Abner Plott, you will not get away with this."

I stared at my Blackberry, dreading the call I was about to make. There was no explanation acceptable to Sterling. I had failed—plain and simple.

Before I could fully confront failure, however, God sent an interruption. My speeding through a residential neighborhood had attracted the attention of a cop. Blue lights flashed in my rearview mirror.

I pulled to the shoulder and pounded my steering wheel.

My briefcase was gone, my career about to unravel, though I still had my wallet and registration.

13

RICHARD STERLING DIDN'T JUST HAVE A COW; HE HAD AN ENTIRE herd of heifers. Just before noon he summoned me to his office and gestured to his guest chair. No greeting came forth, just a pointed finger instructing me to sit.

I sat.

"This is inexcusable, Alex," he said, his face a centered mass of frustration. "Whenever we tell a client that a certain thing will get done, then that thing *gets done*. Period. No stories, no excuses, no tall tales of how the dog ate your homework. I'm so ticked at you right now I can't even see straight."

From my seated position I summoned courage and paired it with a respectful tone of voice. "My briefcase was stolen."

"Then you *allowed* it to be stolen!" He'd never sounded so harsh. "And just where was it stolen, Alex? From your house? Your car? Right out of your hand?"

"I stopped last night on the way home for about two minutes, three at the most. It must have been stolen then."

He crossed his arms and exhaled his disgust. "This whole thing I find just incredible. Incredibly immature and stupid. You didn't even notice it was missing until today?"

Wild thoughts invaded my head. I wanted to nuke the entire firm. Just be done with all of it. But somehow I clung to a hope for mercy. "It might not have been stolen last night, but that's my theory."

Sterling sighed to the ceiling. "Had you taken the time to notice last night, we could have had another set of papers signed and still had them filed on time."

My effort at hands-in-lap humility may or may not have made a difference. "Richard, I'm certain that Abner Plott or one of his hired goons stole my briefcase. I've been followed and harassed for days now."

"It was your job to see that your briefcase was not stolen." He unfolded his arms and leaned forward until his elbows rested on his desk and his eyes were level with my own. "Things like this just cannot happen at PMG, not if you desire a future here. You cannot get arrested in our own lobby in front of clients. And then you cannot use some deranged man like Plott as your excuse. It sounds weak, and that in turn makes the whole firm appear weak. We don't tolerate weak associates. Never have, never will."

My posture morphed into one of pleading. "Do you know what Plott has actually done? Did you know about the Bar complaints, the harassing phone calls, plus the Internet site focused solely on my destruction? Did you know he also destroyed my yard? I have two neighborhood kids pulling Japanese maples out of my pool!"

I could not tell if he grasped the magnitude of my sufferings, but at least he wasn't frowning. "Alex, come on now."

Further efforts to defend myself seemed futile. I matched his next sigh with my own and added a well-paced shake of the head. Words escaped me, and logic felt as foreign as marital bliss.

Long and awkward seconds passed, until Richard raised an index finger of caution. "Please tell me that one of our senior associates doesn't expect a leave of absence just so he can deal with some little old man?"

"No, that's not what I'm asking. I simply want you and the other partners to understand that I'm not using Plott as an excuse—my life is being destroyed."

Perhaps I should have toned down my narrative.

"Don't get melodramatic, Alex. I mean, you're good, and you're also sharp, but this is an extremely competitive firm."

"I know that, Richard."

That finger kept scolding me, warning me like some wise digit from afar. "You can't afford to make mistakes, and today was a big one. Huge. You either straighten this all out and get back to being a producer, or the other associates will step over you and on top of you, and then one day you'll just fade into oblivion and be gone."

I so wanted to explain further my circumstances and the fallout from the Plott debacle. But I figured he had heard enough. Time to suck it up and say what needed to be said. "I understand. What happened today should not have happened at all, and I promise that it will never happen again."

Richard Sterling pursed his lips and nodded, and I knew that was my cue to leave.

My day neither brightened nor improved when I saw Austin loitering next to the administration desks and reading the monthly report given out to all associates. His brief smile changed into a knowing smirk. "Alex, you old man, I absolutely dominated you in billables this past month. And now I've nearly caught you for the year as well."

I didn't need this, although our competitive history demanded some kind of rebuttal. In addition, our rivalry at least felt grounded in reality, whereas everything else around me spun out of control like some ill-conceived fantasy.

I stopped between Austin and a potted plant and decided to give him a backhanded compliment. "Wowwee, Austin, what a complete and dominant stud you are. I have the worst month of my career after enduring attacks on me, my wife, and my house, and you're *still* behind for the year."

His eyes widened as if he'd never seen me in such straits. "Whoa, man, take it easy. I was just chiding you a bit. Like we always do."

I strode past him and down the hall toward my office.

"Hey, Alex," he called after me, "lighten up, man. Let's grab some lunch."

I kept walking.

"Maybe tomorrow then, buddy."

* * *

I didn't remember the elevator ride down to the lobby. I only wanted to spend my lunch hour as far as possible from PMG, and to eat somewhere beyond the orbit of fellow associates and hardnosed partners.

I pushed open the door to our front steps, and a blue Florida sky greeted me like a blank canvas of limitless possibilities. For a moment I wished I owned a skywriting plane and could scrawl 'Right now, life sucks' for all to see.

A block south of our building I merged into a mass of humanity moving toward the eating establishments. It felt safe among this striding horde, no one talking to each other, many texting or lost in their thoughts.

I rejected four restaurants on my left and crossed the street. Then I hurried through an alley and onto a nearly barren and less-affluent street. A corner bar and eatery called Tanqueray's beckoned to me, and when I saw that its entrance required a descent down a flight of concrete stairs, and that those stairs led down below street level, I knew I'd found my place of seclusion.

This was not the place for expensive microbrews; this was bar food and Budweiser, an establishment where a ham-on-wheat and a Heineken would be considered upscale and snooty. The hardwood floor, which fronted a small stage, felt welcoming to feet shod with wingtips. But I paid it no further attention and made my way to the bar and sat at the far left end, five empty stools to my right.

A mustached bartender came over, sleeves rolled up over hairy wrists, and slid a menu toward me. "What'll ya' have?"

"I'll start with a diet Coke. Thanks."

He brought me a paper placemat and some silverware wrapped in a napkin. During the two seconds that my attention focused on spreading the napkin in my lap, I paid no attention to who had entered and sat three stools to my right. I only heard him speak to his buddy.

"Ya' know, that is so, so typical," he said in a voice heavy with ridicule. "The bartender serves the yuppie wimp in the business suit but ignores working stiffs like us."

His buddy said, "Yup," and he too spoke much too loudly.

I glanced at them and saw two white guys, mid-twenties, T-shirts and cheap tattoos, their heads turned my way, their gazes on the menu in front of me.

"I wonder what's good here," said the guy nearest me. "Guess I'll never know since the rich guy got the only menu."

I glanced at him again and wondered if he were mentally ill.

He raised a finger and pointed it at my head. "Don't you ever, ever look at me again, you understand?"

The bartender interrupted the warning and slid menus to the pair.

The second guy pushed the menu back toward the bartender. "How 'bout some drink service, man?"

The bartender sighed as if he'd rather not serve troublemakers. "Okay, what'll you have?"

The first punk looked at the second and said. "Two shots of bourbon." Then the first punk pointed at me and said to the bartender, "Put it on his tab."

I didn't flinch or smile. I just shook my head and said, "Nope. I don't think so."

While the bartender poured, the first punk reached deep into his faded Levi's and removed some crumpled money. He pressed the bills smooth on the edge of the bar and handed them to the bartender as if they were sacred treasures. Out of the side of his mouth he said to me, "Thanks for the drink, you white-collar wuss."

I tried to ignore him, choosing to read the menu over quarreling with a low-class thug. I thought of how I'd chosen this place to escape the heat inside of Powers, Morgan, and Greene, only to find equally hot temperatures—and perhaps tempers—here at Tanqueray's.

Ignoring punks rarely deters them, and my effort today was no exception.

The first punk turned to his fellow punk and spoke in the voice of a bad actor. "Ya' know what really ticks me off about these lawyer types? They make all this money and yet they never buy you a drink. Man, they won't even look at you."

Uh oh. His mention of the word 'lawyer' gave him away, and just then I felt adrenalin surge through me. These two were not just lunchtime lowlifes looking to pick a fight; these were hired hands.

Punk #2 leaned back on his stool and peered at me around his buddy. "Whatsa' matter, man? Don't you like us?"

"I'm just trying to order some lunch, all right?"

He rolled his eyes like he'd never heard something so ridiculous. "Don't let us disturb your little feast. And don't get ketchup on your prissy little tie, either."

I could eat elsewhere. I dropped three ones on the counter for the Coke and wondered if Plott was waiting in the stairwell.

It was time to find out.

I made for the exit door without even a glance over my shoulder. Still, the first punk could not help himself. "Oh, lookie here. Yuppie boy has to leave because we were being mean to him."

I pushed the door in front of me and found an empty stairwell. Then I hurried up the stairs to street level and searched in all directions for Abner Plott. He wasn't here.

Then I thought of Karen and wondered if she too had been harassed by thugs. My plan was to return to the office—if I could get there—and call her en route. I was still three blocks away when I reached Karen's voice mail. "Karen, call me as soon as you get this."

If she were in trouble, she'd let me know. Even if she were mad at me, she'd call. But the hired punks weren't after my wife, I was fairly confident of that. Plott aimed for me, and me alone. To Plott, Karen was just an amusing sidebar. Collateral damage.

A crosswalk halted my progress, and once again a crowd gathered. I looked behind me for any sign of the barstool punks. But no, they had not followed.

The WALK sign turned white and I stepped into the intersection with a throng of pedestrians. One more look behind me, and here they came. Both punks heading my way, perhaps 30 yards behind and closing fast.

I remained centered in the crowd and moved forward, glancing back every few steps. They closed half the gap in mere seconds, and now another intersection halted progress.

I pushed my way to the front of the curb. A bus roared past.

Another glance backward. Both punks pushed through the crowd, now thick behind me. Others in the crowd seemed to be staring at me, holding my gaze far too long for strangers on lunch hour. The punks advanced further, maneuvering just 10 feet behind me. I heard people complain as they were passed and shoved aside.

A motorcycle blew past. A second bus. The stubborn light would not budge.

I ran for it anyway.

I charged across the intersection and saw the light change. What I didn't see was the cop car trying to beat the light. I never heard his siren.

Tires screeched. My right hand cushioned the impact. His front bumper took my legs out from under me and I rolled across the hood.

For a moment I felt aloft, spinning into an awkward descent.

My head hit just below his windshield. I tumbled over the passenger side and landed shoulder first on the street. Blue sky faded to black, then sky swirled into a jumbled sea of concerned faces. Then the sky sparkled randomly and faded to black again.

"Sir, are you alright?"

I felt a hand on my arm.

I worked open my eyelids and saw a black police officer looking down at me, a worried expression plastered upon his young face. "Sir?"

"Wha?" I mumbled. "Me?"

In what would turn out to be the low point of my day, I rolled my head sideways on the sticky concrete to check again for my pursuers.

No sign of the punks.

"Sir, you okay?" a teenager said as he moved in close for a look. All I saw was a Subway badge, the name 'Blair' fading in and out as horns honked and the cop kneeled beside me.

"Sir," the cop said loudly. "What is your *name?* Can you hear me?"

I managed to shift my weight to my elbows, the gravel piercing into my joints. I raised my head and said, "Alex Lord. I was being chased by some punks."

The cop waved the crowd on and helped me to sit. Still dazed, I at least had enough sense to know that blood streamed from the left side of my forehead, and also from my lip. I tasted the blood and tried to scrunch the pain from my face.

The cop dabbed at the blood with a handkerchief.

I winced and shut my eyes. Then I opened them again, just in time to see the Subway kid stuff a coupon into my shirt pocket and run off as if he were late to work.

I had no clue how long I remained in the street. I heard some sirens, and then two paramedics scooped me like a sausage patty from hot concrete and set me flat on a stretcher. In mere minutes I was wheeled into Florida Hospital.

Before I could call Karen, however, a nurse strapped me to a blood pressure contraption.

She checked the gauge. "Hmmm. Let's try this one more time."

She squeezed the air from the cuff and repumped it, while at the same time someone else placed a bandage above my left eye.

"I really should call my wife," I said, and noted for the first time that my shirt was torn at the elbows, my pants ripped at the knee. *Two pair in two days.* Life had not only grown chaotic but also expensive.

"Wow," the nurse muttered to the gauge. She met my concerned glance. "Mr. Lord, do you have any history of high blood pressure?"

"No, not at all. Why?"

"Because you sure do now."

They released me at 2:45, and on the way up the stairs to Powers, Morgan, and Greene, I paused and left a voice mail for Karen. She was probably in a meeting, with no clue as to the happenings of my day.

My nature was to protect her from the harsher details, so I embraced my role and did my best to leave a message that diluted reality: "Hello, dear. Today I was accosted in a lunch deli by two punks who followed me into the street and into an intersection, where during my escape from said accosting I was upended by a police car, rolled onto the pavement, and busted my head. The punks were likely hired by Abner Plott, so please prepare yourself for my recommendation that you and I both purchase handguns. I'm returning to the office now in torn clothes and will have to work late, so if you get home before me and see two kids working beside our driveway, know that I hired them this morning to install a non-trailer-park mailbox, and we owe them 30 bucks. Total, not each. And please don't worry about my dinner because I have a coupon for a free Subway sandwich and can survive on that until I get home to sit beside our brown pool and numb my pain with a strong beverage. Peace be with you. Alex."

Embarrassed by my appearance, I pushed open the front door to PMG and ducked into an empty elevator.

✳ ✳ ✳

I had endured stares before—from homeless guys, Florida State fans, and of course the punks in the deli. But the stares from fellow associates and fashion-conscious secretaries jolted me like no others. I stepped off the elevator, nodded to everyone in the hallway, and made for my office. Not until I passed Carol did anyone speak.

"Great day in the morning, Alex!" she said, and looked me over from head to toe. "What happened to you?"

My posture forced her to view my good side, never mind the tear in my shirtsleeve. "I'm fine. Just have to get to an associate evaluation committee meeting." I checked my watch. "Which started 5 minutes ago."

I ducked into my office and grabbed my coat from its hanger. At least I could partially hide my appearance now.

"Alex, I really need…."

"Not now."

Rudeness was not my nature, especially when it came to Carol. But I was late and would apologize later.

The three partners seated on the far side of the conference table were dressed as conservatively as Presbyterian deacons. Who knew, perhaps on weekends they *were* Presbyterian deacons. Today, however, they were my judges, the approvers of progress and the determiners of my fate.

I approached the conference table with all the confidence of a bandaged man who'd spent his lunch hour being rolled over the hood of a police car. One by one the three partners noticed my unkemptness. Their eyes registered shock at my appearance, all three pairs focused on the left side of my head, where I knew from my brief glance into the hall mirror that a smudge of blood had seeped through the gauze.

I sat opposite them and clasped my hands in front of me. "Gentlemen, I'm very sorry about being late today. I was involved in a small accident."

The partner on the right, Jack Lesley, said, "Are you sure you're okay? Do we need to reschedule this meeting?"

His suggestion surprised me. Compassionate comments from a PMG partner were about as common as an August snow in the Keys. But perhaps this partner was sympathetic to my plight. Perhaps he too, during his associate years, had sought refuge in an out-of-the way pub and been accosted by hired thugs and spent an hour in the hospital having gravel picked out of his skin. At least I tried to convince myself of such history.

"No sir," I said to him before returning the nods of the other two partners. "I'm fine. Really."

Jack Lesley at first appeared not to believe me. But then his compassionate face faded to neutrality. "Alex, you've been around here long enough to know how this process works. This is your annual review. We've examined your numbers and we've solicited comments from other attorneys about your work, and now we would like to discuss our observations with you."

Sidney Thame, the partner seated in the middle, slid a sheet of paper to me and I picked it up and saw before me a numerical history of my past year. "Your numbers for the year have been very good, with the exception of the last two months."

I perused the decline from July to August, and from August into September. "I know. Believe me, I know. And these numbers will come back up."

A sigh from the left. Wayne Haubert, perhaps the most efficient number-cruncher of the bunch, was about to speak. All I knew about Wayne was that he didn't speak unless he had something important to say, and that he had the biggest marlin in the firm mounted on the wall of his office. The man practiced law to support his fishing habit. Powers, Morgan, and Greene was full of offshore fishermen and fisherwomen, but no one could hang with Wayne Haubert.

"The firm looks for consistently high production, Alex," he said over interlocked fingers. He emphasized "consistently high" in a manner that told me I was already considered inconsistent. "Drops like yours raise flags to us, especially when you're considered partnership material, which for you could be only a few years away."

He'd managed to wrap a compliment inside a loaf of criticism, a skill praised often around the PMG water coolers.

I cleared my throat and addressed his concerns with all the courage I could muster. "Look, ever since I arrived here I've consistently billed as many or more hours than any associate at my level."

"True," Jack Lesley said, "which is why this trend is so troublesome to us."

I was determined to retain an aura of control. "It is not a *trend,* Jack. I've been working more hours than ever the past 2 months, just not as many billable hours. If you doubt me, ask Richard Sterling. I have...."

Sidney Thame raised a finger of interruption. "There are also some comments about you appearing distracted."

Before I could even answer Sid, Wayne Haubert tapped on the table. "And what is this I hear about you missing a filing deadline this morning?"

News at PMG traveled at light speed and recirculated through the air vents. All I could do was smile at the flow of information. "Wow, does associate news travel fast around here or what? Yes, I did miss filing something. It was stolen from my car last night."

The three partners stared back without sympathy, as if I'd just told them that my Labrador ate my briefcase. I didn't even own a Labrador—or any dog for that matter. And I was glad I didn't, because the unfortunate pooch would likely have been found at the bottom of my pool along with my severed plants and lost billable hours.

No more excuses. I would tell these pinstriped amigos what they wanted to hear. "I am confident, gentlemen, that my non-billable matters will soon be wrapped up, and that my production will return to previous levels."

A trace of a smile from Jack Lesley. "Good. That's what we like to hear."

Wayne Haubert stood and said, "Let's schedule a follow-up evaluation so we can stay on top of this."

My hand met his across the conference table. Simple nods to Jack and Sid, and my review was over.

I made it back to my office without encountering anyone, not even Austin, who would surely poke fun at the trials and tribulations of his golf buddy. I closed the door and moved to my desk and sunk slowly into my chair. A new ache had surfaced in my lower back, and all I wanted to do was take a long nap.

My office door pushed open, however, and Carol rapped lightly on the wall. "Can I come in, Alex?"

"Can this wait a while? I just got back here."

She brandished a beige envelope and waved it like it held something I needed to see.

"Have you seen a doctor?" she asked, and walked to my guest chair and stood behind it. She appeared truly concerned for me.

"Yeah, I have. And I'm fine. Roughed up a bit, but fine."

Carol pulled my chair around and sat, an act she'd never performed before without my first offering her a seat. "I need to talk to you, Alex."

The lowered tone of voice alarmed me. I knew I needed to get to work and bill someone for something. "I'm really not in the mood to talk right now."

Carol scooted her chair closer to my desk. "I wish I wasn't the one to tell you this, but I guess it's better coming from me than anyone else."

"What are you talking about?

She brought the envelope up to eye level. 'I got this envelope in the mail today. It was addressed to PMG with my name on it, but lots of others in the firm got similar envelopes. Just about everyone in the office, I believe."

Her grimace told me this was bad, possibly very bad. She handed me the envelope, and I saw the familiar bad handwriting.

"I put the photos back as soon as I saw what they were. I'm really sorry that I saw them, Alex."

I opened the envelope and removed five photos, each of them of Karen and me—in our bedroom, Karen in her red nightie, then removing her red nightie. The photos were taken from our pool area, from an elevated perch over the fence, and shot through our sliding glass door on the night we'd been in too much of a hurry to close the curtains. I felt ashamed and embarrassed, even more so for Karen.

I glanced up at Carol. "How many of these envelopes arrived here?"

"Dozens, I'm afraid. Many of them went to partners."

"How long ago?"

"Less than an hour."

Speechless and enraged, I jammed the photos back into the envelope, words eluding me while Carol watched me for a reaction. I rolled the envelope up like newspaper and thought of the many ways I could eliminate Abner Plott from the gene pool.

Carol noticed my growing hostility. "I tried to get the mailroom to stop delivery, but the firm has a policy, plus it was too late. We all feel so terrible about this."

I grabbed a 4-inch pocketknife from my top drawer and bolted past Carol and out of my office.

"Alex, wait!" she called.

No more waiting. No more questions. No more theories, and no more legalese.

I would end Abner Plott's little reign of terror. One way or another, I would end it.

14

SURPRISED MYSELF BY DRIVING SLOWLY. THE PACE ALLOWED ME more time to consider my strategy.

Buying a gun sounded good. But a baseball bat might be threatening enough. I'd already tossed the pocketknife under the seat, as it was way too small, plus I had no idea how to win a knife fight. I figured that Plott, being as mean as he was, likely had a bigger knife anyway. *Or the lunatic might have a compound bow with poison-tip arrows.*

I turned my BMW off the freeway and exited on Orange Blossom Trail, my GPS blurting orders. A right and a left led me into view of the shabby apartment building that housed Mr. Plott. But before I reached the apartment, I slowed the car in an effort to not draw attention to a lawyer in a BMW cruising a lower-class section of town. The next block of emptiness was followed by a block containing a small Baptist church, its lawn filling with an elderly crowd, most of them toting food and setting it upon picnic tables. One of the ladies actually turned and waved as if she knew me.

In reply, I lowered my sun visor.

What day is this, anyway? I had no idea, but even in the midst of my wrath I noted the surreal nature of passing a Baptist potluck dinner en route to threatening my tormentor into a cease fire.

I also had no idea what I was about to do. All I knew was that confrontation would precede explanation, and that if things went awry, explanation might well follow aggravation.

I parked on the curb, rolled up my sleeves, and exited my car—a man of purpose and resolve. Seconds later I yanked open the entrance door to the shabby complex and bounded up a gray stairwell to the second floor.

Apartment #262 appeared, from the outside at least, just like all the others, except for the doormat. Plott's doormat beamed to all who stood over it—a smiley face—and a message forged in yellow lettering: *Have a Nice Day.*

I almost kicked the door open, my anger doubling and redoubling as I considered my ruined yard, my scared wife, the punks in the deli, the private photos distributed throughout Powers, Morgan, and Greene, and all of it occurring at the whimsy of a man who had the audacity to greet visitors with a *Have a Nice Day* doormat.

The side of my fist pounded the door four times. No answer.

Five, six, seven.

Nothing.

I jabbed at the doorbell as if trying to break it.

Still no answer.

I tried the knob, tried to twist it from the door.

Locked.

Maybe he wasn't even home. I ran to the end of the narrow hallway and peered out of a window and down and at the parking lot. No El Camino in sight—which may or may not have meant anything. Then I ran back to #262 and pounded again, my heart racing, pulse pounding. "Plott! Open the door! Now!" Again I pounded, this time with both fists. "Abner Plott! Answer me!" I hit the door until my fists ached and my head rested against it. "Plott. Plott you coward."

I imagined him sitting calmly in some tattered chair, listening without expression or reaction as I called him names and beat on his door. I imagined old shag carpet stained and ugly, empty cans of Spam licked clean by a man so focused on my destruction that he allowed himself no time for utensils.

"Plott! Abner Plott!"

My voice weakened first and then my legs, and like the plants in my pool I began a slow, eerie descent.

"Plott! Answer me, Plott!"

I was out of control, pounded out, and spent. My head slid down the front of the door near the knob, then I wrenched my body until I slumped onto my butt, the back of my head against Plott's apartment door.

Images of the photos, plus the fear of my having to explain this new chaos to Karen and the PMG partners, weighted my soul like ship anchors. I felt helpless and alone, as if there were no one on my side of the courtroom willing to jump up and shout an objection.

I waited, my back against his door, for over 2 hours. But Abner Plott never showed.

* * *

By dusk I'd returned home, the trials of the day pressed down and hidden while I interacted with youth. I stood in my driveway, a beer at my feet, and paid cash to Marty and Jackson for their installation of the new mailbox. Karen had fled the house before I arrived home, and she'd done so without writing a check to the boys. I had no idea where she'd gone, only that she once again seemed to be avoiding me.

"Mister, you look bad," Jackson said before peddling in circles in the street. "You in some kind of trouble?"

"Nah, just a little accident."

They did not appear to believe me. They just said "seeya' " and peddled off with the cash clutched in their hands. I went over to the mailbox, tested it for stability, and found it much more stable than myself.

Then it all boiled over—my entire day. Right there at my curb, at sunset, as the kids headed home all happy with their earned monies, I lost it. I needed to break something. Satisfaction—if ever so brief—would embrace me if I could only break something.

My beer bottle would suffice.

Perhaps only an unstable man would step back from his own curb, grip his beer bottle like a baseball, and hurl it into that curb and explode it against concrete.

And yet that is what I did.

At least I closed my eyes.

I felt the fragments hit my legs, and turned to see that the two kids had heard the glassy explosion from far down the street.

"Hey!" I shouted after them. "Wanna make five bucks cleaning up glass?"

They stopped and whispered something to each other.

Then Marty shouted back. "No thanks. You're acting kinda' scary."

* * *

Alone in my kitchen, I pulled open the fridge and grabbed the last bottle of beer.

My hurry to induce a new buzz was halted, however, when I saw the '2' flashing on our answering machine. I pressed the button and listened.

"What's new, you cheapskate yuppie? Me 'n the boys been watching you, been watchin' your house too. I really like that fancy car of yours. Seems a shame to have to blow it up. Maybe you'll find the bumpers and the wheels in your pool—on top of the plants."

A beep, and Karen's voice filled the living room. "Alex, hey, it's me. I'm…um, I'm at my sister's house. I've been thinking that we both need a little time apart, so I'm going to stay here for a couple days. I got two more harassment calls today at the house. I'll contact you soon, probably tomorrow. But I'll call. Be careful. Okay, bye."

Voice mail beeped to conclusion, and silence engulfed the house. In the midst of that silence I knew that Karen and I had just separated, and we had done so without even using the word "separated."

Already I wanted to drink the pain away. But already an inner voice jolted me with the seriousness of separation, and I took my untouched beer into the kitchen and turned the bottle upside down in the sink.

I needed a brother, a confidant, someone to keep me from doing something or saying something really stupid. Austin was such a poor choice for depth and brotherhood, and yet he was the friend who knew me best.

I made my way into the living room and pulled out my Blackberry and sent him a text. Then I took off my shoes, laid down on my sofa, and waited for his reply.

My head ached badly, though I ached even worse over the state of my marriage.

15

USTIN'S INVITATION TO GO TO A PUB AFTER WORK INCLUDED a walk through downtown. En route I told him all about the punks, but he assured me he would kick their butts if they showed. Austin could take care of himself; a decade earlier I'd witnessed his collegiate fight with an opposing team's pitcher after the pitcher had beaned Austin on purpose in our game against Alabama. The guy could punch.

"Where were you yesterday?" he asked, checking out the females in the crowd, his eyes hidden behind Costa Del Mar sunglasses.

"Home," I said. It was only half a lie. "After the mail incident and the accompanying embarrassment, my mind was completely fried."

He turned his head at two brunettes in mini-skirts. "We tried your house."

"Phone still unplugged. Too many hate-filled calls from foul-mouthed lowlifes."

"Sterling was looking for you. Something about the expert inter-rogatories, I think?"

I winced first. Then I grimaced.

"Crap. I was supposed to meet with him but forgot about it in all the chaos."

Austin pointed ahead at a gaggle of college girls. "When he couldn't find you, he got a bit hot. I tried to cover for you."

"Ya' know, Austin, that Mr. Big Shot Partner has ticked me off more than once recently."

"Just know that he wasn't happy."

We walked along the sidewalks for long minutes, occasionally nodding at another associate or dismissing each other's suggestions for a dinner spot. It felt good to be out among the after-work crowd with a guy who had no depth.

Easy come, easy go, Austin was fond of saying. I compared his worldview to my own and decided it was time I brought him further into my debacle.

"Austin, this Plott crap has got to stop. I have to...."

"You've got to make it stop."

"And just how would I do that?"

Austin peered over his expensive shades. And this time he focused not on some female pedestrian but on me. He leaned in close to whisper. "You're going to have to kill him."

I stopped in front of a news stand and pulled Austin to the side. He yanked his sunglasses off and looked back at me without smile, smirk, or raised eyebrow. He was not kidding.

I tugged him further off the sidewalk until we stood in the shade of a palm tree. "You're completely serious, aren't you?"

Austin nudged his shoe against a tree root and spoke to the grass at our feet. "Think about it logically, Alex. There is nothing you can do to hurt him. Since he has no assets, he makes the perfect harassment machine."

"He's really good at harassment, I can admit that much."

Austin looked about as if he might miss a stunning blond. "Sue him and you get what? A judgment? Big deal. No money for you." He lowered his voice and spoke straight into my ear. "Think a judgment would cost him his reputation, his standing in the Orlando community? Hoo hah. And what if he got sent to jail? He'd love having a better bed there, plus they'd never lock up an 80-year-old man. The big problem for you is that he has nothing to lose—except his life."

Austin's perspective felt so odd, coming as it did under a palm tree, while tanned people strolled by with tiny umbrellas protruding from colorful drinks. "That all sounds logical."

"That's because it is."

I grabbed his lapel and pulled him toward me. "Are you out of your ever-lusting mind? Plott turns up dead, and the investigators have no trouble at all figuring out that I had the best motive in all of Florida."

I walked away from Austin and headed toward a rectangular fountain, its spray intermittent and shallow. He followed me until we were walking side-by-side again, passing women pushing strollers and old men playing checkers on park benches.

"So what?" Austin chided. "Are you telling me that you, the quick-thinking Alex Lord, couldn't figure out a way to kill the guy and get away with it?"

I could not believe the conversation had reached such extremes. "Austin, you're crazier than I am. And trust me, I've been crazy lately. Last night I smashed beer bottles against my curb."

"I did that after the Gators lost to Georgia." He pointed to our right at one of his favorite bars and we walked toward its entrance. "You're a bright guy, especially when we consider that the IQ of most murderers is little more than 12 or 13. And most of them get away with it. Also, we aren't talking about a public official here. The cops aren't going to turn over every stone in the city to try and solve the murder of a poor, sick old man."

We crossed the street in a blur of pedestrians, and when we reached the bar's entrance, Austin held the door for me. I stopped long enough to share my perspective on his suggestion. "Although your idea has appeal, counselor, I really don't think I need to stoop to committing premeditated murder."

He followed me inside, maroon lights coloring our faces, Austin bobbing to the beat. He spoke from behind me. "Suit yourself. This nutty world will never miss Abner Plott. It'll just keep right on spinning, never miss a beat...and wow, check out that Latino babe in the lime green halter."

✳ ✳ ✳

By 10:30, Austin and I had meandered in and out of three different pubs and landed in a martini bar—his choice. My choice would have

129

been a shooting range. But here at the Oak Room, the patrons cooed and flashed their Cartiers and fat wallets. Austin joked that inside these walls were the last two-hundred Floridians with positive home equity. He was probably correct.

We eased past the sippers, the nodders, and the glad-handers, and found two empty seats at the bar. A young bartender, blond and tanned and looking like an extra in a South Beach video, came over and greeted us with a wide smile and very white teeth. "What can I get you fellas?"

Austin leaned in toward the guy. "I'm awfully glad you asked me that, mate. Two Belvedere martinis, astonishingly dry, slightly dirty, with three olives a piece."

Blondy-the-bartender looked impressed. "Astonishingly dry? Never heard that description before."

Austin smiled. "Just cast a glance at the Vermouth bottle as you pass."

The bartender left to fill our order, and it was then that Austin turned in his chair, faced the minglers scattered about the bar, and waved like he knew someone in the distance.

He didn't know a soul in the place.

Austin was the type who would wave across a crowded room at no one in particular, just to appear connected. Perhaps he'd seen a politician pull such stunts on the campaign trail. Regardless, it looked totally fake and yet totally Austin.

"Try it, Alex," he said. "Just wave at the far wall."

"Oh, please."

"Do it and smile. You'll feel better."

I waved at the coatrack. Neither the rack nor the Asian couple in front of it waved back. "I do not feel better. I feel like an idiot."

Austin turned back to the bar and watched the bartender prepare our drinks.

"So you got a pass from the wife for happy hour, eh?'

"Yeah. A pass."

Austin scanned the left side of the room for females. "Cool. How's Karen handling all this stuff?"

"She's about as good as can be expected." I loosened my tie and spoke over the knot. "She'll be better when all of this is over."

Austin scanned the right side of the room for females. "Then you should get it over with."

I knew at what he was hinting. Austin really thought I should consider a murder plot. Extreme revenge—heck, even a mercy killing of an old man—was just not in my nature. The last time I had plotted revenge was sophomore year at Florida, after some neighboring frat boys had lit a smoke bomb outside my room. I retaliated by flooding their frat house basement with a garden hose through a window. But *this*. This talk of taking a life! No, this was beyond my ability to comprehend, much less to plot out and execute.

"Maybe, just maybe, Abner Plott will drop dead." I said. "He wasn't really looking too good the last time I saw him."

Austin sighed as he watched a huge guy put his arm around a cute redhead at the end of the bar. "Well then, maybe you should help him."

"All right, since we're in a bar and we're talking hypothetically over Belvedere martinis astonishingly dry, how would I go about getting ridding of him?"

Austin smiled, and I realized instantly that he was not smiling at me but at the bartender, who served us our drinks with a second helping of his youthful grin and very white teeth.

"First thing you do," Austin said as he closed his eyes and savored his first sip, "is to decide who kills him. Now, if you do it yourself, you need a great alibi. Which means you'll have to be in two places at once."

In a state of semi-shock—that I could even engage in the topic at hand felt unsettling and evil—I sipped my martini and agreed that the drink was very good.

"Outstanding," Austin called to the bartender. Then he focused on me again. "Hey, I've got it. Karen and I will go off for the weekend while you're off killing Mr. Plott. People already think that you and I look alike."

I almost decked him, but this was coming from Austin, who lived his entire life in the shallow end of the pool.

He sat up straight and frowned. "Look, Alex, I'm just kidding around. I mean, Karen is okay, right? She's safe, isn't she?"

I set my drink on the bar. "She's just freaked out about all that stuff happening to our yard—and the phone calls really bother her too."

Austin set his drink beside mine, which meant he was entering into a rare period of seriousness. "What do you mean, 'freaked out'?"

I shrugged as if explanations escaped me. "She's spending a little time with her sister, that's all. She's scared and she's confused. It's really no big deal."

Austin sought refuge in the second half of his martini. "Your other option, my friend, is to get someone else to do it for you."

In an effort at kinship, I clinked my glass against his. "You interested in the job?"

"Nah. Killing Plott may sound like fun, but I can't chance getting caught and then rooming with some fat pervert for the rest of my life."

"It'd be a huge risk to involve someone else. They get caught, they talk…and *I* end up sharing the cell with the pervert."

Austin scanned the room again and added another fake wave to an unresponsive wall. "Yeah, well, I guess you need to do it. Just get a bit creative, and you'll figure it out." He sipped his drink and licked his lips. "You have a gun?"

"Nope."

"Well then, get one. Use a phony name and go buy it out of town somewhere."

I thought of Carol taking shooting lessons with her girlfriends, and I felt embarrassed that a middle-aged administration manager at PMG had more knowledge of firearms and how to use them. I made a mental note to ask her about her gun. *Perhaps I should get one regardless.* Home protection and self-preservation seemed a pressing matter these days, what with the terrorist acts enacted upon the Lord estate. "So it's that easy? Just go out of town and buy a gun?"

Austin nodded and admired the contents in his glass. "Sure. Just try the classified ads in several cities. Or even try Georgia or South Carolina. Their gun laws are some of the least strict in the nation."

For living in the shallow end of the life's pool, Austin had more random facts revolving in his head than any man I knew. "You do realize that you're becoming an accomplice for feeding me all this info."

Austin laughed, took a long sip, and laughed again. "Look, Alex, it's a simple plan. We aren't talking anything exotic here. You go to his house, you pull your gun, tie his hands, and take him to the car, which of course should be a rental. On your way to the car you walk with your arm around him, as if Plott is sick. He won't say a word and the neighbors won't think anything of it."

My fingers spun my glass in a slow revolution of sparkling light. "Okay. So he's in the car. Now what?"

"You drive for at least an hour, then you pop him behind a dumpster in another city. Wear plastic gloves and take all of his ID."

The balance of my martini went down fast and hard. "No one in Orlando would even notice he was missing, at least not for a while. And like you said before, the cops aren't going to go crazy worrying about some homeless guy's corpse."

Austin smiled as if I had just figured out a complex riddle, then he raised his glass to our young bartender. *Refill please.*

Upon the bartender's acknowledgment, Austin spoke to me out of the corner of his mouth. "Have an alibi, bro. Whatever you do, have an alibi."

✳ ✳ ✳

It is a finely tuned skill to be able to dissect from someone's questions—not to mention the *quantity* and *speed* of their questions—that the questioner has an ulterior motive. Austin Adams had asked me one too many questions, and as we left the martini bar and he walked west toward his car, I turned east and ran to my BMW.

I ran for a purpose, and I ran in order to U-turn in the street, to ease into traffic a short distance behind Austin, and hang back just far enough to follow him.

I followed him for nearly 20 minutes—until he parked in the driveway of a modest suburban house owned by Caroline Givens, a single mom who just happened to be my wife's sister.

I cut my headlights and pulled behind a minivan parked on the street. I could not see the front of the house for the woods adjacent to the Givens' residence, but I did see Austin get out of his Volvo convertible and walk toward the house.

I got out and crept down a sidewalk until I was hidden behind an oak tree. I was still three houses away but with a decent view of the porch.

Austin knocked on the door. Then he turned and looked both ways but did not see me.

The door opened and Karen came out in jeans and her soft yellow T-shirt. I knew her shirt was soft because she so often wore it to bed. I'd woken in the middle of the night many times with my face snuggled against that T-shirt.

To my relief, she didn't invite Austin inside. Instead she shut the door behind her, and they began talking on the porch.

Austin, you sorry piece of scum. Hitting on my wife while I'm distracted with the Plott fiasco.

I considered that maybe Austin was just drunk. Maybe, since he'd struck out with the females at the martini bar and all the invisible women he'd waved to across the room, he figured he could illicit some sympathy from Karen. I dug as deep as I could for any reason why my good friend might pay a visit to my wife.

I watched for several minutes, and at no time did they touch, kiss, or even hug.

Still, I tried to imagine their conversation:

Karen, I heard about the terrible things that happened at your house, and I was worried about you.

Oh, Austin, thank you. I'm fine. But what a surprise to see you.

Are you sure you're okay?

I'm as good as can be expected. Did Alex send you to check on me?

Hey, that's what buddies do for each other. But he does seem very stressed.

A pause, a knowing nod. *Maybe you can help Alex. Take him out once in a while.*

Sure. He and I haven't been out in ages. I just thought I'd check in on you.

I'll be fine. Really.

You know I'll help you any way I can.

They clasped hands like old friends and hugged for a couple seconds. Then Austin strolled to his Volvo, started the engine, and drove away. Fortunately for me, he drove off in the opposite direction.

I watched Karen shake her head as if impressed that a friend would just show up to comfort her. Then she disappeared inside her sister's house, and the light on the porch went dark.

16

FTER MY BEST NIGHT'S SLEEP IN A WEEK—ODD CONSIDERING all that troubled me—I started my day at Powers, Morgan, and Greene by calling my wife.

"Hey. It's me."

Silence and static, then a prolonged sigh.

I tried a more modest and reasoned approach. "Look, Karen, I'm really not that upset that you left for a few days. I mean, it's been rough for both of us lately, and I think a little time for each of us to pause to think through all this stuff was probably a pretty good idea."

"I need some time, Alex. Thank you for being understanding."

"I know you do need time, and I know you felt scared. But hey, why don't you move back in today or tomorrow?"

"Alex...."

"Not move in with me. I just hate that you're having to stay in that crowded little house with your sister and her kids. There really isn't room for you there. I've decided to rent a room near the office while I prep for trial."

A pause—another sigh. "I don't know."

"You won't see me. Please move back in. I've got this huge trial coming up and the hours will be insane. I'll be practically living at the office anyway. Go back to the house and enjoy your space, okay? I've got a cop checking in on our street twice a day, so I think we're safe now from the attacks. Just park in the garage every time you come home and close the door behind you."

"I'll think about it." She sounded hesitant to make commitments of any kind. "I went by the house this afternoon to get a pair of shoes, and there was glass all over the curb next to the mailbox. I think we were attacked again."

"No we weren't."

"Alex, I saw the glass. But they missed our new mailbox."

"No one attacked our mailbox. I dropped a beer bottle out there. I was just being clumsy."

"Oh."

I struggled to summon courage, since courage seemed a distant attribute of late. "Karen, I'd also like to say...."

"Alex, can't we wait and talk in person? Whatever you're about to say, I don't think I'd take it well right now. Do you mind if we wait?"

"All right."

"I'll call you about the house. I need to think about it."

"Call me anytime. Even during work."

"Okay." Another pause. "Oh, and I guess I should thank you for sending Austin to check on me last night. That was sweet of you."

"Austin? He came by to see you?"

"Yes. He said you wanted him to."

Karen moved back into our house the next afternoon. She still sounded cold and aloof when we spoke on the phone, and neither of us had mentioned Austin's little visit. By this time I'd convinced myself that Austin was merely drunk and a bit lonely, and somehow he saw himself as my concerned brother—looking out for Karen, looking out for me. The shallow man at least showed occasional glimmers of depth. Maybe.

The hotel room I'd rented was only two blocks from the office, and with the room being a top-floor end unit, I had not only peace and quiet but an unobstructed view of downtown. It also faced east, which made for great sunrise views on the tiny deck.

Onto the deck I brought my morning coffee and pondered fine solutions to the pressures that lay in triplicate before me—to endear myself again to PMG, to repair the damage to my marriage, and to use whatever means necessary to halt the harassment from Abner Plott.

Over the next two days, Karen and I fell into a routine of avoidance. She went to work and came home to our house, I went to work and came home to my hotel room. Once per day I'd call her, and once per day she'd sound as if the life had been drained from her, or, at least the joy of life.

"After the trial is over," I said with my head propped on hotel pillows, "let's look into marital counseling."

Yet another pause preceded yet another sigh. "Alex, why does a trial take priority over our marriage?"

"It doesn't. But my performance at work will lead to a faster ascent to becoming partner, then you can quit your job and we can start a family."

She exhaled her frustration. "A trial over our marriage, and your ascent to partner over the conception of our first child. Shouldn't we have another talk about priorities?"

"Yes. We should."

"Soon?"

"Yes."

We ended the call, but 2 seconds later my phone rang again.

"What now?" I asked. "More criticism?"

"No," said a deep male voice. "Just watch for dynamite under that BMW of yours, pretty boy."

That did it. If Plott and his hired goons were threatening to blow up my car—possibly even while I, or Karen, or both of us, were in the car—then I needed a potent method of self-defense. I needed to own a gun. The House of Lord, regardless of its inner bickering, needed to own a gun.

But I'd never tested a pistol in my entire life and didn't want to stroll into a sporting goods store without some degree of knowledge and research. My instinct was to find a friend who knew something about guns. I only knew one person who had a concealed carry license. Fortunately, this person worked very close to me.

It was 6:45 A.M. when I stepped off the elevator to begin my work day. Thursday mornings were Carol's day to open, and I had something important to ask her.

There stood Carol at her desk, labeling some files for me and glancing up at a weather report displayed on her monitor. A tropical storm threatened to form in the Gulf of Mexico, and I wondered if it became a named storm, would it be called Abner. No, Hurricane Abner had already ravaged parts of Florida.

"Alex," Carol said over her desk. "You're in early again."

"Can I talk to you?"

"Of course."

I pointed down the hall toward a conference room. "I'd like to talk in private, if you don't mind. My wife, Karen, has been frightened twice recently over some neighborhood incidents, so I'm thinking of getting a firearm for our home. You do carry your...."

"My rapid-fire lead-dispenser?" she said with a hint of humor in her voice. "Yes, always."

Carol slung her purse over her shoulder, grabbed me by the elbow, and pointed across the hall to a supply closet.

"In there?" I asked hesitantly.

"You said you wanted privacy."

Reluctantly, I followed. After all the negative happening inside the walls of PMG—my being served summonses the arrest, plus the ongoing office gossip that I'd spent a night in jail with Rosco-the-pimp—all I needed was for a partner to find me huddled in the supply closet with a married woman who was not my wife.

The tiny room smelled of ink cartridges as I backed against reams of paper and motioned to Carol's substantial red purse.

She stood with her back to the door and said, "So, you wanna see my pistol, eh?"

"Yeah. You seemed like a safe person to ask."

"Let's hope so." She opened her purse.

Any silence at all felt weird, so I just kept talking as she reached deep into her belongings. "Today, at lunch, I'm planning to go look at some small pistols, one that might fit either a woman's hand or a man's hand. You know, test some for comfort."

Carol drew out a small but thick black pistol, its muzzle pointed to the ceiling. She pressed a button on its side and the magazine fell out into her left hand.

She then stuck the magazine back into her purse, pulled back on the gun's action, and showed me that it was indeed empty of bullets. "It's called a Beretta PX-4," she said with pride. "It shoots 9-millimeter and holds 15 bullets."

She handed me the pistol and it felt oddly comfortable in my hand. "Nice feel."

"Point it at something," she suggested, her hand forming a finger pistol.

I moved to the center of the supply closet and turned and aimed the pistol at a tall stack of Post-it Notes, then at a flat panel monitor. Wanting to zero in on a smaller target, I turned and aimed it at a bottle of antibacterial soap.

"Please don't shoot the Dial, Alex."

I smiled and aimed again. "Great gun...very balanced."

I aimed it high, at an air vent. *Bang.* I wanted one.

"Glad you like it," she said and took her gun back. Then she inserted the magazine, checked the safety, and tucked it back into her purse. "Four-eighty-nine at Sports Authority. You can also find them for twenty bucks less on Gunbroker.com, but then you have to pay shipping, and it might be a week before you get it."

That might be too long.

"Thanks for the info," I said and pushed the closet door open a few inches. Through the opening I checked the office for early arrivals. The hall looked clear. Good.

With quiet steps we exited the supply closet. Carol spoke from behind me. "It's not just Karen who's been frightened, is it, Alex?"

"No, not exactly."

Carol's keen sense of reality lingered for all of one minute—until I returned to my office and sat and stared at the photo of Karen and me on our honeymoon. That week, and over the months that followed as we established a home in Orlando, we'd made all the blissful, long-range plans of newlyweds. In the wee hours we'd awaken and talk of our future, of giggling kids and exotic trips, of festive holidays spent with hospitable loved ones, and of well-balanced careers with our world-class marriage.

Now I contrasted those hopes and dreams with the reality of Karen sleeping alone in a quiet house, our yard destroyed, while I slept in a small hotel room, also alone, not knowing what to do other than to continue the very things that had landed me here in the first place. If the definition of insanity is doing the same thing over and over while expecting a different result, I was certifiably insane. *We* were certifiably insane.

Over the next few hours I didn't think of Karen, at least not much. Instead I lost myself in further preparations for the Bargain Mart trial—my chance to shine—a coveted opportunity to impress my superiors and gain back what I'd lost over the past month via disappointing billables.

After the trial, I would have so much more time to give my marriage the attention it deserved. I wanted to pursue Karen, date her, take her away for weekend jaunts, but there was just so little time. In addition, I'd invested so much into Bargain Mart that my preparations seemed like the one thing that was going right. I was ready to overwhelm the plaintiffs, dominate the courtroom, and celebrate victory with the partners who would reiterate their confidence in their dedicated associate.

I opened the first of three files, red pen in hand for notes and rewrites. But before I even reached the second file my phone beeped.

A press of my speaker phone, and Carol's voice filled my office. "I know you don't want to hear this, Alex, but there's a policeman up front to see you."

If I could have bounced my head off my desk and caused my entire body to carom out the window I would have done so. But I only kicked my trash can and told myself to play nice.

The cop looked unfamiliar, an older fellow than the last one. He stood next to the twin sofas in the lobby, all business, his arms folded across his chest. Several clients sat to his left, each of them in suits, briefcases at their feet. Another busy morning at Powers, Morgan, and Greene.

I greeted the officer with a wave and stopped within a few feet of him. "Hello, sir. What have we got today? Civil or criminal?" I showed him my wrists. "Or perhaps you'd rather arrest me?"

He handed me a single sheet of paper. "Mr. Lord, I'm serving a temporary restraining order on you. You are to have no contact of any kind with Abner Plott, and you may not get within 250 yards of Abner Plott. Do you understand these specifics?"

I accepted the paper and clutched it to my chest. "Very good, officer. Mr. Plott does not require my company and he's requested a restraining order on me. I understand perfectly. Anything else for me today?"

The cop appeared annoyed at my tone. "No, sir. That is all."

He walked toward the elevators, and the second door opened as if it knew he were coming.

I waved as he took his place in the elevator and waited for the door to close. "Thank you very much, officer. Always a pleasure. I'm sure I'll see you tomorrow."

The elevator door closed, and I heard footsteps.

"Alex."

I turned to see Richard Sterling standing behind me. He looked to the clients on the sofas, nodded to them, and placed a hand on my back. "Alex, could I see you for a moment, please?"

I had no idea how much he'd heard of my exchange with the officer. His clinched jaw, however, told me he had heard a lot. Perhaps all. "Sure."

Sterling did not walk down the hall, he marched. He marched like a man about to undertake a duty he'd rather not undertake. Suddenly he turned and motioned me into a conference room. I entered to see it absent of anyone except the two of us. Sterling reached behind me and shut the door.

Neither of us sat. We just stood a few feet apart, and I knew from experience that I should wait for him to speak first. "Just what in the world was *that?*"

Stay calm, Alex. "I was served with a TRO, Richard. Another gift from Mr. Plott."

Sterling shut his eyes and exhaled in a manner that told me I was off topic.

"I'm talking about your little comedy routine in our lobby."

"You mean what I said to the cop just now?"

His hands reached his hips and stayed there, though I figured he would prefer his hands around my neck. "Yes, Alex, your comments to a police officer. The same officer who just served a restraining order on you in our reception area—which just happens to be filled with our clients!"

I studied Richard Sterling's face to determine his degree of seriousness, and I determined he was quiet serious indeed. "Do you really think anyone was offended by what I said?"

"Yeah, I certainly do. I think they are offended to come into our firm, where they pay a lot of money, and see one of our lawyers being served like some ghetto stalker. And *then* acting all smart-alecky about it."

Oh, man. This was over the top. "Ya' know, this kind of over-reaction is exactly what I've come to expect from you."

His reaction toggled between incredulous and ticked off. "What!"

I backed against the door and crossed my feet in a manner that suggested a more casual chat. "Plott continues to mess with my life, and you don't care about anything except my hours or some client reading the newspaper."

"In case you have failed to notice in your years here at PMG, hours and clients are quite important. They provide your sustenance, Alex. They pay for the nice office in which you work, that BMW you wash every weekend, and that upscale house you purchased."

I let his point settle for a moment. "Did you know Plott was a total nut-job when you gave me his case?"

Sterling glared at me in a manner that was almost as cold as Karen's phone voice. "Just what are you suggesting?"

"Is that why you didn't want anything to do with the case? Is it? You knew Plott was a deranged and vindictive scumbag?"

"You're on thin ice here, Alex. I suggest you think long and hard before you start tossing accusations at me."

"I'm not accusing you of anything, Richard."

He stepped back until his butt rested against an office chair. "When I gave you the case, I really thought you could handle it, that it would be for you a simple task. You've proven me wrong."

Our stares met like a clash of swords. I felt like anything I said at this point would be refuted, so I decided to let him finish. But he took his time. He even walked around the conference table to the far side and stared out the window.

"I can't rely on you anymore, Alex. You're off the Bargain Mart trial."

No way he just said that. "But I've worked on that case for nearly 3 years!"

He turned and glared at me again. "I need people working on the case who can give it their full attention, not someone caught up in daily distractions."

"I want to see my work to its conclusion. I'm valuable to this trial."

Sterling came around the table toward me. "What you want has nothing whatsoever to do with my decision."

He brushed past me and opened the door.

"Richard, please. I just...."

"Austin will take your place."

17

*A*USTIN. *W*ILL. *T*AKE. *Y*OUR. *P*LACE.

Sterling's words repeated in my head like the chorus to a bad pop song.

Alone again in my office, the door locked, I grabbed my Ping putter from the far wall and swung it sideways. I swung it like a baseball bat but stopped short of going full-bore madman. After several minutes of maximum-force swings, perspective washed over me and convinced me that this was a needed activity—a cardio workout with a dash of anger. As Sterling's demotion echoed again, I didn't throw the putter through my window, though I was tempted.

Above my desk lamp, I initiated one more swing of increasing violence, "Eeiiiiiiiiiiyah!"

It took me 30 minutes to calm myself to the degree necessary to confront Austin. I was beyond ticked. After he'd remained pretty calm about the Plott thing for a couple days, this news of him replacing me was too much. Maybe he was just next in line to work on the case, but after not telling me that he was going to check on Karen, and then taking my place in the most important trial of my career, he needed to be confronted—and without the buffer of Belvedere martinis.

My determined walk toward his office grew even more determined when I passed two partners and three fellow associates, none of whom spoke or even made eye contact. If I wasn't yet a PMG pariah, I was well on my way.

My initial peek revealed just what I expected—Austin's wing-tips resting across the corner of his desk, the man himself reclined in his chair, his hands holding a Bargain Mart file, which hid his face.

I moved quietly up to his guest chair and gave it a firm kick in the leg. "Didn't waste any time wedging yourself into my territory, did you?"

He lowered the file. His confused and shallow face stared back. "Alex, look man, I don't know what's going on around here. Richard Sterling came in this morning and tells me I'm now working on this case, and that I should make it my top priority."

"And that's just fine with you, isn't it?"

Austin pulled his feet off his desk and sat up straight. "Why are you ragging on me, man? Sterling is a partner and he tells me what to do, what to work on. What am I supposed to do, say 'no thanks'?"

His innocent act enraged me. "Austin, I swear, sometimes you just…."

His raised hands were a weak effort to maintain peace. "I'm your friend, Alex. I'm not the bad guy here. Just take a step back and think through it."

It was no use. I turned for the door, and he called after me.

"Don't get all angry with me, Alex. You've brought this on your-self, man."

I left his office and got only halfway back to my office before my phone rang.

"Hello?"

"Still ain't found no dy-nee-mite under that BMW, pretty boy?"

I shut my phone and made for the exit.

"Alex!" I turned to see Wayne Haubert calling for me from way down the hall.

I could not handle any more partner scoldings, so I waved once to Wayne and bolted down two flights of stairs. I entered our lobby, head down, and made for the brass-colored front doors of Powers, Morgan, and Greene.

Today I was taking a 24-hour leave of absence—one day to right my life and deal with the leeches who would drain me of all I had if I did not act.

✳ ✳ ✳

Shopping for a gun for the first time felt very much like my first day at Powers, Morgan, and Greene—just act like you know what you're doing, and do your best to hide the fact that you are, for all intents and purposes, naïve and incompetent.

At Sports Authority, I discovered that there is a pistol chambered in .380, slightly smaller than a 9-millimeter, though the ammunition is more expensive. This made no sense to me, so I dismissed .380. The salesman then showed me a .45 caliber Kimber, their top-of-the-line model. This I dismissed as too heavy and far too expensive. A Browning .22, while sleek and light, seemed too much like a pea-shooter and not the sort of gun necessary to confront men threatening to blow up one's car.

After a half hour of pondering options, I decided to broaden my search. Just as I didn't take the first law firm offer that came my way, I would not take the first handgun offer.

My second stop was at Traders Gun Shop, a visit that, to my surprise, took only 20 minutes, as their stock of Beretta pistols was beyond impressive. The speed with which an unarmed citizen could become an armed citizen made me even prouder to be an American. Driving out of state to purchase a gun would have taken too long, and I just didn't have the time. I wanted a self-defense gun today; I wanted to feel its heft in my hand and know that I had the power to stop further threats from Señor Dynamite.

I purchased a Beretta chambered in 9-millimeter, plus three boxes of ammo containing 50 rounds each. The pistol I bought was not the

PX-4 model that Carol had shown me. The gun that fit my hand best was a Beretta FS. According to the older salesman who assisted me, the longer barrel yielded more accuracy.

Yes, Mr. Salesman, I agree, accuracy is good. Sell me some accuracy.

I smiled with poise and grace while he explained the features of the gun, and when he'd finished I assured him that my father and I would enjoy our target shooting at the farm over Thanksgiving. Family tradition, you understand.

I could not believe how fast I invented lies, and how the habit felt so ingrained—as effortless as breathing. *Yes, Karen, I dropped a beer bottle at the curb. Yep, Mr. Salesman, I'll be shooting targets with my dear old dad over Thanksgiving.*

I disliked my ability to lie. Before long, I'd be waving at nobodies across a crowded bar and telling gold diggers in low-cut dresses that I was a partner at PMG. I left the gun store with my weaponry and some coupons for a pay-to-shoot indoor range. On the way to my car I decided that a pay-to-shoot range felt too conspicuous, too common, and much too risky. Someone who knew Plott, or perhaps one of his punks, might see me. I needed a more private place to practice shooting. Or, at least to practice threatening.

I had no friends with acreage; all the associates lived either in condos or cookie-cutter neighborhoods. The partners, of course, lived in sprawling upper-class estates.

So I just drove—out of downtown and onto I-4 toward Jacksonville. The interstate, however, provided the kind of monotony that enabled the thought demons to surface again.

Austin. Will. Take. Your. Place.

Found any dy-nee-mite under your car, pretty boy?

Austin. Will. Take. Alex, I'm staying with my sister. Please thank Austin for coming by to check on me.

Dy-nee-mite your car. Austin will take your place.

Tell Austin thanks. There's glass on the curb.

Mister, you're acting scary.

A truck honked and I swerved back into the slow lane. Sweat dripped from my nose and chin; wild thoughts and negative scenarios were coming so fast and so random—I'd forgotten to turn on my air conditioning.

Forty miles outside of Orlando I decided the hell with it. I would make my own private shooting range. On a wooded stretch of interstate, I waited until there was a lull in the traffic, slowed to allow two trucks to pass, and pulled over onto the shoulder.

From the backseat I grabbed my new pistol and the bag of ammo. Then I got out and opened my trunk and pulled out the backpack full of targets that I'd packed in a rush.

A hot wind blew dust into the trunk while I exchanged my work shoes for sneakers. Then I shut the trunk, locked the doors, and sprinted for the woods.

Halfway there I looked up to see a hawk circling. This stretch of interstate contained more roadkill per mile than any other in Central Florida. What it amounted to—at least for the hawks and buzzards—was a 40-mile buffet. If I tried hard enough, I could envision a punk's corpse as part of that buffet.

I reached the woods, pulled twisting vines aside, and entered a forest of fractured light.

The wild calls of hidden birds registered as both greeting and alarm, and the traffic noise decreased as I moved further into the unknown. Nature, however, did not like this intruder. Bugs lit at my eyelids and burrowed into my hair. I stopped multiple times to set the bag of ammo on the ground and swat the pests.

There were no paths in these woods, not even any boundary markers; I figured the land was state-owned. My goal was to tromp at least a quarter mile off the interstate, to maximize privacy and dilute the crack of gunfire.

Dry branches cracked underfoot. Vines tried to strangle me. I pushed and pulled through it all, then I stopped and caught my breath. The distant sound of 18-wheelers barely reached this forest. Past a fallen log I came upon a small clearing, which was really just an absence of undergrowth with a plethora of wild grasses. The clearing was back-dropped by pine trees, a natural wall at which to shoot.

From my backpack I pulled the targets I'd brought along—a Kissimmee, Florida phone book, an unopened can of Diet Mountain Dew, an apple, and a black and white target of Osama bin Laden's head, which the salesman had thrown into my bag for free.

I set the phone book against the base of a pine tree and balanced the Diet Mountain Dew atop the phone book. I debated setting the apple on top of the drink can but figured I might want to eat the apple on my hike out of the forest. Then I pushed a thumbtack through the photocopy of bin Laden and pressed it into the pine tree at eye level. Good. A straight shot. It was time to load my gun and find out if I could shoot.

Pressing bullets into a magazine felt good, satisfying. One by one they clicked into conformity, the tension in the magazine growing tighter with each new entry. At 10 bullets I stopped, figuring that a nice round number like 10 was plenty for now. Besides, I couldn't wait to aim and pull the trigger.

I faced the phone book against the tree and stepped back six paces. The loaded pistol felt heavier but very balanced. I chambered a bullet, switched the safety to the off position, steadied my grip, and aimed at the Diet Mountain Dew can.

At first I couldn't pull the trigger; I kept gripping and regripping the pistol, making tiny changes in finger positions and grip pressure.

Bang, I missed.

Bang bang. I hit the phone book. Twice.

Bang. Miss.

Bang. Miss.

"Crap. I suck."

Bang. Yellow soda exploded from the can, and the can toppled from the phone book. From its horizontal position on the forest floor it spewed its contents—until I walked up to the can and shot it dead from point blank range. *Bang bang bang bang click.*

Surges of adrenalin ran through me. I felt the power, the control.

Then my cell phone vibrated in my pants pocket.

"Alex Lord."

"Pretty boy must be scared, seein' as to how he left a gun store with a little pea shooter."

Another hired voice. It wasn't the voice of Plott, but I knew he was behind it. Probably paid the guy with food stamps. I shut the phone and tossed it into my backpack. Then I loaded the second magazine, inserted it into the pistol, and moved to within four paces of the black and white photocopy of bin Laden.

Steady aim, Alex.

Bang. A hole in bin Laden's right ear.

Bang bang. One miss, one through the edge of his turban.

Bang bang bang bang bang bang bang.

I had emptied my gun a second time and it felt very good. Satisfied, I knelt beside my backpack and opened the box of ammo. Time to reload one more time and practice my threatening posture and some rapid fire.

The third and fourth bullets pressed into place inside the magazine. A fifth pushed them lower. I pulled a sixth and seventh bullet from the ammo box, but before I could insert them a branch snapped behind me.

Man or animal? I did not turn. I just stayed low, frozen in place.

A distant crunch of footsteps grew louder. Whatever it was had seen me. Possibly yet another hired goon. I wanted to load the gun and turn, but reason got the better of me.

I set the gun atop the backpack and stood and turned slowly.

The young man walking through the pine trees wore camouflage and a week's worth of facial hair. He was maybe 20, if that. The scoped rifle he carried was large and intimidating, though he held it with the muzzle pointed down and away from me.

I waved a timid hello.

He nodded and came up beside my tattered phone book and the tattered remains of my bin Laden target. He stopped beside them and checked my shot pattern.

"A dead Mountain Dew," he said to the ground. "Diet."

"Yes. Mountain Dew. Very dead."

A long silence ensued as he looked off into the woods to his right, then past me and back toward the interstate. "This your land?"

Relief. If he was asking that question, he was either being sarcastic or he too was a trespasser. "No. Your land?"

He rested the butt of his rifle on the top of his shoe. "Nope. But you scared off a good-sized deer with those pistol shots."

Fully aware that his gun was much bigger than mine, I tried to engage him further in conversation. "But it isn't even deer season yet, is it?"

"Nope."

"So...you're poaching?"

He frowned and ran his right hand up and down the length of his rifle barrel, caressing it like a faithful friend. "Surviving. My daddy lost our house after he lost his carpenter job. Said we'd have no meat this week unless I shot somethin'."

I wanted to ask him if I could take a few practice shots with his rifle. I'd never shot one and his rifle appeared capable of great long-distance accuracy. But no, I'd just scare his deer further away—and that might make him really mad.

"Ever see anyone else in these woods?" I asked.

He brought his rifle up and rested it back over his shoulder. He spit to his right and shook his head. "Nah. You the first."

"I see. And now you're angry 'cause I scared away your deer?"

Again he shook his head. "Nah. But can I ask you somethin'?"

"Sure."

"Why are you wearin' dress pants and a nice button-down shirt to shoot a pistol out in the middle of nowhere?"

C'mon, Alex, think up a lie. Quick. "Well, um, I only had a 30-minute lunch hour, plus I just bought this gun. The guys at my company are having a shooting contest next weekend."

He studied me as if I were some strange beast. "Oh...okay."

"Sorry I scared away your deer."

He looked back the way he'd come. "Yeah, well, I'm gonna go stalk him now. You done shooting?"

"Yeah." I removed the empty magazine from my Beretta and checked the safety. "All done."

"Good."

He tromped off between the pine trees, pausing every few steps to spit. I considered myself fortunate and grabbed my gear, half suspecting that when I emerged from the woods, a highway patrol officer would be inspecting my car on the side of I-4.

Nope. I came out of the woods with my backpack over my shoulder, no cops in sight, and just a single tanker-truck steaming up the interstate from the west. For whatever reason—embarrassment or shame or some combination of both—I tugged at my zipper as I neared my car.

The trucker honked.

Yessir, I couldn't wait.

In actuality, what I could not wait for, was to find Plott.

I had no idea what I was going to do. I doubted my ability to actually use a gun under duress. But could I threaten him with a gun? Probably. Threaten his hired punks? For sure.

I just needed to end the terrorism—once and for all.

18

LEFT MY CAR IN A DOWNTOWN PARKING GARAGE AND TOOK A CAB out to Plott's apartment building, my backpack in my lap, my mind trying to repress violent thoughts despite a fully loaded Beretta in my possession.

The cabbie let me out at the corner and I paid him with a 20. Keep the change.

At a walking pace that broadcast ease and nonchalance, I made my way up a cracked sidewalk and past a neglected yard, full of weeds and a pair of old hubcaps reflecting the afternoon sun. I entered the building as if I lived there and hurried up the old stairwell to the second floor.

For once, my timing was excellent.

I'd waited less than 5 minutes in the stairwell when Plott entered the narrow hallway from the opposite direction. With gloved hands I held the stairwell door open, perhaps an inch, just enough for a glimpse. I heard him rattle his keys, my signal to tuck the Beretta into the back of my belt and make my move. With my foot I nudged my backpack into the stairwell doorjamb to keep the door from closing and making noise.

Then I entered the hallway and moved quietly toward him.

Plott's back was to me as he fumbled with the keys and struggled to unlock a large deadbolt. Pulse pounding, I tiptoed toward him, my right hand gripping the pistol behind my back.

Plott unlocked the deadbolt and pushed open his door.

The door began to shut but I lunged forward and grabbed it, my gloved fingers holding strong. He felt my presence and tried to resist.

Too late, Mr. Plott.

I shoved the door with my shoulder and felt him let go. He tumbled backward onto his filthy floor and remained there, staring up at me and a drawn gun. I held the Beretta to my side, not yet ready to aim and fully threaten him. I wanted him to squirm for a moment.

Flat on his back, palms down on the floor, Plott appeared helpless—and he was. At last, I had control.

To emphasize that control, I waved the pistol about in the manner of a loose cannon. "So, *this* is your command center? From *this* high-tech post you command legions of punks to stalk and harass Alex and Karen Lord? Is that correct, sir?"

I waved the gun across his legs, up at his ceiling, at his barred window, then back across his feet. But for some reason I couldn't point it at his head or torso.

Wide-eyed and frightened, Plott stared up at me as if his life had only seconds remaining until someone draped a sheet over him.

"Don't," he whispered, true fear in his voice. "Don't shoot me."

I pointed at a rotary phone on his soiled kitchen table. It was unplugged, its cord spilling down into a wicker chair unraveling at the armrests. If this was indeed his command center, he was operating on a shoestring budget. "How many harassing calls were you planning tonight?"

He still didn't try to get up. "Don't shoot."

For a brief moment I admired my pistol and relished the adrenalin rush of reversing roles with a tormentor.

Abner Plott now looked not only helpless but ridiculous. "Please," he said, a deeper pleading in his voice. "Please don't shoot me."

I thought of the Diet Montain Dew can and the clean hole I'd shot through its center, yellow liquid spewing out in carbonated pain. Drink cans and paper targets were one thing. Before me on the floor, however, was a fellow human.

Despite what this tired old man had done, I knew I couldn't shoot him. I couldn't even scare him anymore. And though the power emanating from my Beretta still felt good as I tucked it back into my belt, I doubted my ability to use it and questioned if I should even keep it, since deep down I feared the severity of consequences in the afterlife if I took the life of anyone—even an enemy.

"Sir, I am not going to shoot you."

Relief flooded his haggard face though he did not attempt to stand.

I stood beside him, my right hand still hovering near the pistol grip in case he tried anything. If threatened again, I figured I could hit him with the butt of the gun. "I want you to tell me, Mr. Plott, exactly what it will take for you to cease all harassment and leave me and my wife alone."

His fearful stare became a series of confused blinks, as if he were simultaneously trying to hide pain and figure out what I might do next. He kept wincing up at me. I figured he'd hurt his back when he fell, and I knew in his weakened state he wasn't going to fight; what he needed most urgently was a more comfortable posture.

I reached out a hand, and he tentatively met it with his own. Then I pulled him to his feet, ushered him over to his old wicker chair, and told him to remain seated.

"Mr. Plott, I am about to lose my job—because of you. I have lowlife thugs following me on the street—because of you. And my wife just left me as well."

He picked at a strand of wicker on the armrest but said nothing.

My fist banged his table. "This all ends today, you understand! One way or other, this ends. It's your choice."

Abner Plott turned his head and gazed out his kitchen window, a gesture that seemed out of place, an insult of silence and dismissal.

I pounded his table a second time. "Are you listening, man! I'm not leaving here without this getting resolved. I'm not prone to violence, Mr. Plott, but I can be if you push me any further. I will not let you destroy my life!"

He turned his attention back to the wicker strand, his eyes blank, shoulders slumped. Still he would not speak.

I leaned in and grasped him by both shoulders, not to shake him but to command his undistracted attention. "Talk to me, Mr. Plott! Don't you understand? Don't make me—what do you want? Just what exactly do you want from me?"

Plott met my determined gaze and held it for long seconds of contemplation. "I want to sit on my porch and read my newspaper and watch my dog play in the yard!"

His answer stunned me, not at all what I'd expected from a terrorist with an AARP card.

I let go of him and stood up straight. "You *what?*"

He clasped his hands in his lap and focused on the floor near my feet. "My dog was named Chester. He was 12 years old, and every morning I would let him out to run after I got my mug of coffee. I'd sit on the porch and read, and he'd do his business and chase the birds. My house, my porch, my dog, my newspaper, that's what I want, Mr. Lord."

His answers made no sense to me although they did serve to drain away the hostility I'd felt when I arrived. "I don't understand. If all you want are those simple things, why would you...."

He spoke to the floor, his eyes watery and blinking. "Chester is gone! They wouldn't let me bring him here, and this dump was all I could afford. He wouldn't have wanted to live here anyway."

Reality settled upon me like slow rain. A lonely old man had lost his house and his dog, the simple pleasures of his golden years, and he blamed the system and chose a young lawyer as a target for vengeance. Great.

I backed against his yellowed refrigerator and folded my arms across my chest. "I can't get you your house back, Mr. Plott. And to be honest, I'm still waffling over calling the cops on you, considering what you've done to me and my wife the past couple weeks."

He broke off the strand of wicker and used it to dig dirt from under his thumbnail. "Perhaps I was a little bit harsh on you, Alex."

"A bit harsh? You pulverize my yard, take a Louisville Slugger to my mailbox, curse my wife, threaten to strap 'dy-nee-mite' under my BMW, and you call that a *bit harsh*?"

In a whisper he said, "I was kidding about the dynamite."

For a moment all I could do was put a hand over my eyes and shake my head. "And just who were those thugs you hired?"

"Laid-off roofers. I paid 'em ten bucks each for an hour of harassment."

Unbelievable. My head rocked back and rebounded off his freezer door.

"I would've paid him 11 dollars to spend an hour NOT harassing me."

Plott worked on his fingernails. "I'm sure you would've."

Minutes passed while I contemplated what to do and Plott cleaned his nails. Richard Sterling was right—I should never have let an old man distract me like this, not when all Plott could afford was to hire a couple of unemployed roofers to follow me around and spew insults.

Still, I wondered what it was like to reach his age, lose his home, and wind up in this dump. "Look, Mr. Plott, I realize it kills a man's spirit to have his house taken away. But maybe there are alternatives to enacting vengeance on young lawyers. If I weren't so ticked off at the damage you caused, I might even help you find a new place."

He brushed the dirt grains off his table and unto the floor. "Another place doesn't make it my home. My wife and I lived there for 40 years. Forty years! It was ours, and I should never have borrowed against it. We had a beautiful backyard with a birdbath, a garden…tomatoes as big as softballs."

Caught between surprise and a growing sympathy, I remained silent and let him finish.

"When she passed, Alex, it was just Chester and me left to look after each other. Plus the house. Now it's just me. Just me in this rat hole." He motioned around the room, and I did expect to see a rat scurry past, if not something larger.

"How did you end up *here,* anyway?" I asked. A glance at his sink revealed a week's worth of dirty dishes. Abner Plott was big on vindication but not much on domesticity.

He sunk further into the wicker. "I'm not telling you anything else. You can figure it out yourself. You're a smart lawyer. Why don't you just leave me alone?"

"Oh, please. Don't play the victim. I'm trying to understand what led you to end up here."

He nodded at the Beretta tucked into my belt. "First I'd like to thank you for your patience with that 9-millimeter there."

Patience. Yes, I was showing great patience. "Just how did you know it's a nine?"

"Muzzle bore is too small for a 45. I served in the army. Had a Beretta-9 on my hip for years."

Great. Both my secretary and Plott knew more about guns than I did.

Any lingering desire I might have had to return thuggery with thuggery had faded there in his living room. Among his dusty shelves and his dirty rug and the foul smells emanating from the kitchen sink, an unfamiliar flow of compassion coursed through my veins.

But first things first. "Can I have my appointment book back?"

He motioned to my left. "It's in the pantry, inside the Eggo Waffles box."

I opened the pantry to see only two cans of pinto beans, a bag of rice, a box of Corn Flakes, and an Eggo Waffle box.

I reached for the box, and my appointment book fell out at the first shake. I blew crumbs from its cover and set the box back on his shelf. "Would never have looked in there."

Plott smiled. "And I would never have strapped dynamite under your car."

When I'd surprised him at his door minutes earlier, I'd figured the least I would do was hit him—just once for the yard destruction.

The hired punks I could forget more quickly; I didn't see those guys on a regular basis, and their juvenile insults didn't linger much past the initial utterances. But each time I pulled into my driveway, and each time Karen pulled into the driveway, the ugliness of our yard greeted us without apology.

Instead of hitting Mr. Plott, I pulled up his version of a guest chair, a wobbly wooden thing that did not match his tattered wicker. I turned the chair around backward, sat in front of him and studied him for a moment. "I want to ask you again, how did you end up here?"

His slow shake of his head relayed frustration, as if I could never understand his troubled soul.

"Mr. Plott, please. Tell me."

"I made the mistake of getting sick," he said with an air of resignation. "It was 2 years and 3 months ago. Spent 2 months in the hospital. Their doctors took things out of me nearly every week. Big tubes stuck out of me. I felt like a lab experiment. Then the dang insurance company said they wouldn't pay."

Now he really had my interest. "What exactly do you mean by 'wouldn't pay'?"

He checked his dirty nails again. "Oh, they paid a little bit at first, but just a little. Denied me coverage on all the rest."

At last—motivation. "Did you bring a claim against them?"

Plott looked at me as if I were the epitome of the ambulance-chasing attorney. "Mr. Lord, that is exactly what I expected you to say. In fact, it's exactly what the lawyer I went to said. 'Sue 'em!' So we did. And after 8 months of my paying him, he tells me some sob story about how we can't win. Then the sorry scum skips town. He left a whole lot of people high and dry, not just me."

My first instinct was to defend the profession, but my questions were not motivated by money so much as they were motivated by my desire to identify who really disappointed Abner Plott to the degree that he'd hire punks to harass lawyers. "Did you ever see another attorney? Ever try a different firm?"

"With what? My rust-bucket El Camino? I have no money, and you know how attorneys—you're one of them—won't talk to you without a couple thousand bucks up front."

"Not all attorneys are...."

"No one wanted to sue the insurance company. Said it'd take too long, that we can't fight them and they have too much money. Told me I'd be dead and gone before it ever went to trial."

I ignored the stab of my own words coming back to haunt me. "So, you made the attempt to pay your hospital bills, and because of those payments you couldn't pay your mortgage and you lost your house?"

His shoulders slumped, and he spoke to the floor again. "That's pretty much it. I had a big home equity loan, and when I'd spent all that on bills and medicine, I had nothing left. The bank was real understanding."

"Mr. Plott, I don't know what can be done about your house, and I don't...."

"I don't either. Nor do I know why you'd want to do anything for me... 'specially after I tossed your Japanese maples into your pool."

"The trees and plants don't concern me much. The private photos of my wife and I, however, those are what...."

His raised hand interrupted me. "I didn't order that! That was someone else! I don't do smutty stuff like that."

I leaned in and studied him for any sign of falsehood. His slumped posture told me that he was a broken man, and in that instant a horrible reality jolted me—if Plott didn't take the photos, and Plott didn't order the photos taken, then the photos *were* taken by someone else.

Plott rubbed a place on his back. I let the photo issue go and zeroed in on the macro question. "Why me? Why heap all your terrorist crap on Alex Lord?"

"Because *you* are the problem. Or at least you represent the problem. You and your kind. Millions of you bloodless dolts running around worshipping big corporations, ruining people like me, then clinking your martini glasses and driving off in your fancy cars.

That's why. And none of you ever even consider how many lives you destroy. Then you don't even have the decency to help a man up that you knock down in an elevator."

I still maintained that he fell on purpose in that elevator, though it had happened so quickly that I could never be sure. As for being a bloodless dolt, well, I'd been called much worse.

Whatever tidbits of shame I felt over past legal victories, I hid them beneath a new round of questions. "Mr. Plott, do you have any of the papers from your old lawyer? Anything at all from the insurance company?"

He paused and sighed. Then he looked up at the ceiling and focused there, as if the peeled paint might jog his memory. "Yeah, I got some. They're some of my few remaining possessions."

I stood and pushed my chair back under his kitchen table. "Would you mind if looked at those papers?"

Abner Plott stood, walked methodically toward his tiny television, and picked up a cardboard box from the floor. He turned, handed me the box, and said, "Why not, Mr. Lord? Have all the fun you want. I could care less at this point."

I set my appointment book atop the box and carried the stash toward his apartment door. "I'll call you in a few days, if that's all right with you."

He sat on his sofa and shrugged. "No phone."

"Then I'll come by."

He offered not even a wave goodbye, so I shut the door with my foot and went to the stairwell to retrieve my backpack full of ammunition. On my way down the stairs I called a cab.

A new cab met me curbside and took me to a bus station near the parking deck where I'd left my car. At the station I rented a small locker and placed my Beretta—wrapped securely in a navy blue towel—inside.

No way was I bringing a pistol home, or to the office. The ice was so thin with Karen, and perhaps thinner still with the partners at PMG, that I was taking no chances.

I wasn't even sure I wanted to keep the pistol. If I lost my job, I'd be much better off with a rifle anyway. At worst case I could drive out to the woods again, park near the 40-mile buffet, and poach deer with Camouflage Boy.

19

CALLED KAREN ON MY WAY TO THE HOTEL BUT ONLY REACHED her voice mail. I tried her again after my shower, with no luck. My third attempt occurred after I'd spent a couple hours reading through Plott's file, trying to make sense of the notes left from his previous lawyer—the one who'd dropped his case.

"Karen," I said to her voice mail, "I feel certain that the house is safe now, and that Mr. Plott will not be sending any more goons our way. Call me when you get a minute, and I'll explain."

I'll explain. The majority of my conversations with her had become explanations of one kind or another, or else excuses masquerading as explanations, or perhaps justifications posing as excuses masquerading as explanations. Regardless, she was still avoiding me, and somewhere deep in my gut I knew I could hardly blame her.

A text buzzed in on my Blackberry. It was Austin, at the gym again, wanting me to hurry over and join him. At least he wasn't half-drunk and convincing himself that he was just the man to comfort my wife.

With Plott's file in my lap I texted him back: I have to work tonight, Austin.

Ten seconds later: But u shud see the two babes here in pink tights…one for each of us!

Chinese take-out kept me going until midnight, Plot's insurance file and its tangled contents begging for an unraveling. I fell asleep on a too-soft mattress and woke to a sore back and with a steely determination to confront Richard Sterling.

At 8:45 A.M. the hallways of Powers, Morgan, and Greene teemed with legal lemmings hell-bent on extracting money from somewhere—anywhere. I was still one of those lemmings, though my perspective had shifted. I entered Richard Sterling's office and took my subservient seat across from his massive desk.

Richard turned from his window and settled into his chair. "Alex."

"Richard, I need to apologize to you for my actions and words of last Friday. I was way out of line, and I'm sure I let the stress get to me. It will not happen again."

He peered down at me for several seconds before the first crease of a smile bent his upper lip. "I understand. These things happen."

My inner confidence surprised me. "I've been thinking about the Bargain Mart case all weekend, and I know that the trial team is stronger, much stronger, with me there. I can help you, and help the firm."

Sterling smiled as if I were PMG's true prodigal son, returning to scorch the earth in search of revenue. "What about your archenemy, the conniving and evil Mr. Plott?"

"I believe I have found a way to take care of Plott. His situation is something I would also like to talk with you about."

He frowned like only a displeased partner could frown. "And what if Plott starts harassing the trial team instead of just you? What then? I can't have some loony tune breaking into our suite and sabotaging our computers."

He had a point. But that point was no longer valid. Not after the happenings of yesterday. "I talked to Mr. Plott. I mean, I really talked to him—in person."

Amusement flooded Sterling's face. "How could you have spoken with him in person when there's a restraining order on you?"

I inched my chair closer to his desk. "Yes, there is a TRO. But look, Mr. Plott was sick, and at one point he was very sick. A couple years ago he spent a lot of time in the hospital."

"Just what are you driving at, Alex?"

"His medical bills were nearly half a million dollars."

"You've completely lost me."

"Richard, please. Let me finish. The insurance company wrong-fully denied Plott his coverage. He has a textbook bad faith claim that could bring millions in punitive damages."

If there were a phrase that pricked the ears of every partner from Sterling to Wayne Haubert, that phrase was "millions in punitive damages." It was akin to saying to a group of weekend golf hackers, "We tee off at Augusta National at 10:16 A.M." Everything stops—possibility floods the imagination. The hearer is instantly transported into a state of bliss, and all the messenger need do is to sit back and wait to be showered with praise and appreciation.

Except this was not a normal hearer; this was Richard Sterling, and his gaze drilled a hole in my head. "Please tell me why we are talking about this?"

My logic weakened, as did my confident tone. "Maybe PMG could take his case."

Sterling considered my words for all of two seconds before burst-ing into laughter.

"I'm serious, Richard," I continued, the words coming fast now. "Maybe we should. It would generate some great publicity for the firm if we helped the little guy out for a change. And besides, we always need a few more pro bono hours. Plus if we win, we could get a huge fee."

He sat back in his opulent chair, and just as quickly his chuckle faded into an exhale of frustration. "What are you doing, Alex? Are you telling me that you now want to *represent* Abner Plott, the man who's been wrecking your life?"

"Yes. That is what I'm telling you."

"Who, pray tell, is the insurance company?"

"Yorkshire Mutual."

Sterling winced. "Alex, we represent them."

This isn't happening. The Blunder of the Day award goes to Alex Lord.

He nodded slowly and deliberately, affirming the unpleasant fact that made me slink into his guest chair. "Peter James, our head of the associate evaluation committee, is our point man for Yorkshire. They've been his client for years. You really didn't know this?"

"We have 700 lawyers," I said in my defense. "I'm sorry that I don't keep up with every single client of Powers, Morgan, and Greene."

Sterling narrowed his eyes as if he didn't appreciate my comment. "Even if we didn't represent Yorkshire, there is simply no way we would take that case. We don't represent plaintiffs, Alex. We don't erect billboards that beg victims of dog bites and old men who lose their homes to drop by and see us. What would our clients say if we began suing companies who were just like them? What kind of message would that send?"

I tapped on the Plott file in my lap. "I would hope that our clients would support us when they saw what Yorkshire did to Mr. Plott."

"There is not one partner in this entire firm who would allow you to bring in that case."

"Fine." I stood, tucked the file under my arm, and decided to change course. "As for Bargain Mart, I'll have the summaries of the expert interrogatories to you this afternoon."

He let me get two steps from the door. "What are you talking about?"

I turned and feigned confidence. "Sir?"

Richard Sterling stood tall behind his desk and ran a hand through the gray hair at his temples. "You're off the Bargain Mart trial. End of discussion. I'll have some new cases for you to work on next week. Oh, and go see McDowell in bankruptcy about some work. Those guys need help down there."

McDowell in bankruptcy. Might as well have assigned me to McJanitor in toilet stoppage. Half of Florida was filing for bankruptcy, and I could just envision the routine: Billy Joe BigHouse borrowed against his home equity, the real estate market crashed, his teaser interest rate adjusted upward, Billy Joe couldn't make payments, so he ran up his credit cards and now he's broke.

Sign here, Billy Joe. Your credit rating will suffer but at least you can survive. And tell the next person in the lobby to come in when you leave.

Bankruptcy cases—especially in this lousy economy—felt like being demoted to the minor leagues.

* * *

I left work at 6:00 and drove out to check on the house. To my surprise, Karen's Nissan was parked in the driveway. Karen was kneeling in compost to the right of our front steps, gloved hands packing dirt around new plantings.

The entire front yard had been stripped of grass and fertilizer. Fresh dirt, spread evenly and ready to host new greenery, covered what was previously a scorched and ugly front yard.

I parked on the street and came up the sidewalk.

Several varieties of plant and flora lay on the ground behind her, awaiting their turns—some long-stemmed something-or-others with a single yellow flower, a pair of Holly bushes, four symmetrical clumps of exotic grasses.

I was sure she heard me park, and now as I walked up behind her, my instincts told me to employ a lighthearted manner. "How much do ya' charge for your labor, young lady?"

"I took a half day of vacation," she said over her shoulder. I hoped she would stand, perhaps even hug with me with her gloved hands. But no, she only leaned forward on her knees and dug the next hole.

I remained a couple steps behind her and turned to admire what would someday be a new lawn. "The yard looks ready for grass seed. Smells a lot better too."

"I ordered sod."

"Sod...okay. Sod is good."

She enlarged the hole in front of her and reached to her right for a clump of zebra grass. "They'll lay it all tomorrow, if it doesn't rain."

168

"Austin didn't volunteer to help you, did he? I mean, with him being Mr. Comfort and all the other day."

She shook her head. "No. Not a peep."

I moved around to her side and knelt a few feet from her, the exotic grasses waving between us. "Karen, do you miss 'us'? I'm starting to miss 'us.'"

Her hands paused in the dirt. "C'mon, not now."

"I was just thinking about what you said, about my putting work as a priority over marriage, and so…"

"Alex, I'm just trying to relax and improve my yard…I mean *our* yard."

There was enough tension between us now to wither every plant in the neighborhood. I remained kneeled beside her but changed the topic. "Ever think of asking those neighborhood kids to help? They did a fine job with the pool and the mailbox."

She packed dirt and compost around the zebra grass. "They really don't come around anymore. They act scared of you and me—like we're evil or something."

I hoped evil wasn't the only reference to us-ness she could conjure.

"Ya' know what, Karen? You say I put work before our marriage, and yet today I leave the office early, come here and try to engage you in conversation, and you in turn prefer planting stuff in the dirt to talking with your husband. Doesn't that tell you that we both need to make some changes?"

She looked up at the sky as if to consider fully my comment, which must not have moved her like I figured it might. She reached for the next clump of zebra grass and placed it in the hole adjacent to the first. "Yes," she said, "I suppose we do."

Unsure of what to do next, but knowing I needed to do *something*, I decided to ask my wife for a date. "Why don't we go get some dinner tonight, talk through everything, and come up with some solutions."

"Not tonight, Alex. I can't."

Out of options, I stood and retreated a couple steps.

She went about her work with great concentration, as if trying too hard to draw life from an activity that in reality would have been an ideal way for two people, especially man and wife, to interact and bond together.

"You sure?" I asked.

"I'm having dinner with my sister."

Perhaps today was just a bad day to engage her. Regardless, her original brand of no-eye-contact coldness was a product for which I desired no coupon. I could only hope that I was mistaken in my sense that something in her—something in *us*—was gone.

"Seeya' later," I said on the way to my car. In reply came only the sound of a spade shoveling dirt.

* * *

Fish sandwiches. McDonald's Filet-o'-Fish sandwiches called my name, my second choice for dinner behind dining with my wife. I bought two sandwiches in the drive-thru, along with two sweet teas, and drove across town to talk with my former worst enemy.

The sound of talk radio greeted me in the hallway of Plott's apartment building. Before I reached his door the talk show host blared out, "Are we going to let the government continue to intrude in our lives, steal our monies, and limit our freedoms?"

Not if we all buy a Beretta like Carol.

I knocked twice and turned the knob. Surprisingly, it opened.

Plott was seated in his wicker chair, which now contained a thick blue cushion. He waved as I entered and he seemed in a better mood, though he'd done nothing to clean his shabby apartment.

"Can you turn that down?" I asked and pointed to his transistor radio, still blaring political exaggerations from his kitchen table.

He reached over and lowered the volume. "Hello, Alex. I wasn't expecting you."

"Brought you some dinner." I set a large sweet tea on the table beside him and handed him his Filet-o'-Fish and a couple of napkins.

He unwrapped his sandwich and sniffed it. "How'd you know I like fish?"

I sat opposite him and took a swig of tea. "Wild guess. Just hope they didn't sell us filet of carp."

Plott chuckled. "I actually ate carp once." He took a bite and smiled as he chewed. "But I prefer mahi mahi."

"Yeah, and I'd prefer not having to re-landscape my entire front yard."

"I told you I was sorry."

"Eat your fish, Abner."

We ate and listened to the talk radio guy spew opinions: "We cannot continue to elect politicians who bring along lawyers to help them pick our pockets—and most of the politicians are lawyers themselves. How can we expect any degree of fairness when...."

Plott turned off his radio. "You probably don't like that guy, do you?"

I swallowed my last bite and reached for my drink. "I'd prefer classic rock or 80s music, to be honest."

Plott gripped his cup with both hands, like a kid. "Lots of angry people in this world, ya' know. But that's the only station that's comes in good. The Rays baseball game comes on in 30 minutes."

I collected our wrappers and wadded them into a ball and stuffed it all into the McDonald's bag. "I looked at your file. And you should know that you had a good case. Possibly very good."

Plott fingered the antennae on his radio. "That insurance company shouldn't have done what it did to me. They owed, and they should have paid up." His countenance looked drained now, tired of the fight. "But they didn't pay, and they never will."

For one of the few times in my career, I felt interested in a case because I truly felt compassion for a victim. The fact that a successful conclusion to Plott's case might endear me once again to the partners at PMG was not my concern. Frankly, I didn't care what the partners thought. "Mr. Plott," I said over my sweet tea, "Yorkshire would never pay without some strong pushback. I wanted to push them for you. I wanted to take your case."

"Wanted to?"

"My firm, um…it *represents* Yorkshire. I just found this out today." I studied him for reaction but he only nodded as if he expected such news. "And even if we didn't represent them, suing the insurance company would be bad for the firm's hardened image."

Plott clasped his hands in his lap. "Yes, I could see that. After all, Powers, Morgan, and Greene doesn't like to be sued."

Touche', Mr. Plott. I smiled at his wit, and he managed a brief smile of his own.

"I'm going to help you find a lawyer. Though I can't represent you, I can at least help you locate someone who can. We can set this right and get you what you are owed."

He shook his head, the smile long gone. "I'm too sick, and I'm too tired for legal fights."

Straw to lips, I spoke over my cup. "Two days ago you told me you wanted your porch and your dog."

"Yeah, well, two days and one visit to the clinic can change lots of things, Alex. Let's say we go ahead and sue the tightwads again, and we win. Just how long do you figure it'll take till I get money in my hands?"

I couldn't lie. Not to this old man in a dilapidated apartment. "It's hard to say… maybe in a few years."

"Do I look like I have a few years?"

His sense of humility and his awareness of the brevity of life seemed to suck all the language from me. For a moment I compared my life to his and wondered—if I made all the wrongs moves, a task at which I was beginning to excel—if I too might end up poverty stricken and alone, hoping someone—anyone—might bring me a Filet-o'-Fish sandwich on a Thursday afternoon.

Plott slurped sweet tea through his straw and licked his lips. "I want to say something to you, Alex. I spent my life doing everything I could, or nearly everything I could, trying to be a good man, a decent man, only to let it all get away from me in the end. I guess you can say I'm like a pitcher with a no-hitter going, who gives up a home run in the ninth inning."

His analogy contained more truth than he knew; at one time I'd felt like my marriage was World Series caliber. Now, I was in real danger of being swapped for a player-to-be-named-later.

Plott made a throwing motion. "You like baseball?"

"Yeah, I do."

"I loved it with a passion when I was a boy, back when players played because they loved the game. Somewhere over the years, love of the game shifted to love of money."

"You're saying lawyers don't love lawyering? They just love the money?"

"That's what I'm saying." Plott smiled as if he'd jabbed me with great stealth. "I appreciate your trying to help me, what with going through my file and all. But you should know that you've already helped me quite a lot."

Say what, Mr. Plott? "How's that?"

He sat up straight, rested his elbows on the table, and interlocked his fingers. "Hating you—and your type—gave me something to do, gave me energy to get up in the mornings. Heck, it probably kept me alive. Now that you've refused to shoot me or beat me up, and instead brought me dinner, well, that hate is gone like that no-hitter."

Not beating him up a day earlier took a tougher act of my will than he knew. But his case gave me something pure to believe in, and I felt good about myself for the first time in weeks. "I've been meaning to ask you something, Mr. Plott. Just how did you figure out all the legal stuff?"

"I used common means. Books, the public library, the library computer. I made most of it up as I went along. I'm sure I misspelled some words."

"Nah...you did pretty well."

He checked his watch as if he couldn't wait for the ball game to start. "Anyway, the thing is, I too have something to ask."

I prepared myself for any and everything. "All right. Shoot."

He leaned forward over the table, serious, demanding my attention. "I was wondering if you might...if you could somehow find it in your heart to forgive me?"

Whoa. Attorneys at Powers, Morgan, and Greene were neither trained nor prepared for such requests. But perhaps he was asking me human-to-human, not victim to lawyer. Regardless, I was moved by his request. "Yes, Abner, I forgive you."

He looked relieved, and his gaze fell to the table in a further gesture of humility. "Thank you." Then he looked at me and pointed to the door. "Now, go on and get out of this wretched place. Aren't you married?"

I didn't get up. Not yet. "Yeah, I'm married."

"Well then, go spend time with your wife. Life's too short to sit around here with me, trying to cure some insurance fiasco that'll never be resolved."

I stood and shook his hand then he followed me to his door. I paused there and turned to him. "I'm going to make this right. This Yorkshire thing… I'll make it right."

With a gentle hand to my back he pushed me out the door. "Go on. Get."

20

THE HUM OF VACUUM CLEANERS AND THE WHIR OF FLOOR SHINERS pressed against my office walls, the sounds of late-night office cleaners going about their duties. To my knowledge, I was the only employee in the building, and for sure, the only one accessing the database of Powers, Morgan, and Greene to view the records of a long-forgotten case involving Yorkshire Mutual.

Three clicks of the mouse and I had what I sought—the file number, plus the location of said file. All that was left to do was to take the elevator up three floors to where the file was stored, in the corner office of Peter James, the partner who claimed Yorkshire Mutual as his longtime client. I rarely interacted with Peter, and tonight I was sure he'd be home, asleep at his estate, with visions of lawsuits dancing in his head.

To play the part of a sneak disturbed my sense of right and wrong. But on this night I saw myself as an associate mouse just looking to sample a specific piece of cheese hidden deep within one of Peter's five-drawer filing cabinets. This cheese, I would turn into justice. I could sniff this cheese; its scent led me out of my office and on to the elevator.

Before the elevator door closed, however, a middle-aged Asian woman in a white apron shuffled past, pushing a vacuum down the center runner. I prepared to smile and wave, but she never looked up.

The fifth floor of PMG was somewhat familiar—associates often ventured here at the request of a partner, to locate a file or research firm history. At 1:20 A.M., such tasks were perhaps not so common. An associate sneaking into a partner's office at 1:20 A.M? That never happened.

I turned his brass doorknob and entered. His curtains were open, and beyond his desk the bright lights of Orlando twinkled in the night.

I pulled a small flashlight from my pocket and went to the first of four filing cabinets. Open, shine, no luck. Open, shine, files not even in alphabetical order.

Crap. And this guy's a partner?

I opened and shut drawers as quietly as possible—until I reached the bottom drawer of the fourth cabinet. Bingo. Yorkshire Mutual. A modest file, perhaps an inch thick.

My pulse raced. I closed the drawer slowly—deliberately. All that was left for me to do was exit the office unseen, followed by a nervous stroll to the elevator.

The hallway clear, I made my dash and centered myself in the elevator. The door slid shut, and the three little beeps sounded to me like the first notes of redemption.

My first instinct upon arriving back on my floor was to make copies of everything.

And I did.

In mere seconds, two sets of copies ran through the printer behind Carol's desk, the only interruption coming from a young man pushing a floor cleaner. I saw him coming and knew he suspected nothing.

"Mind if I move this trash can?" he asked.

"Here, let me get it." I moved the can to the rug under Carol's chair, and while I was there I borrowed two blank manila folders from her supply drawer and labeled them. *Alex Lord Personal 1* and *Alex Lord Personal 2.*

Now I felt good. Now I had evidence. Now I just needed to make it down the hall to my office.

"Alex. Hey!"

I turned to see Wayne Haubert, PMG partner of 20 years, striding toward me in deck shoes, khaki shorts, and an ocean-green fishing shirt.

I'm dead.

Sunglasses hung from Wayne's neck, along with a pair of nail-clippers on a lanyard. In his left hand he toted a tackle box.

My nervous smile sufficed as greeting.

Wayne looked happy to be alive and surprised to see me there. He checked his watch and said, "1:25 A.M.? Man oh man, when I was an associate I never worked past 1:15."

I tucked the three folders under my arm. "Yeah, Wayne, it's all part of my job. You logging late hours too?"

He smiled and stopped on the far side of Carol's desk. "No way. A long-awaited fishing trip begins in less than 2 hours. Forgot I'd left one of my tackle boxes in my office."

He jiggled the tackle box and it sounded full of lures.

Why a PMG partner would keep a box full of fishing lures in his office was beyond me, but perhaps such pursuits were a secret perk. Regardless, he seemed in a very good mood, so I figured my chances of being interrogated were slim.

"Where you headed on your trip?" I asked, my voice one degree short of steady.

Wayne looked past me at the cleaning people for a moment and seemed satisfied that all was well. "Bonefishing in Abaco, Bahamas. Charter flight leaves at 3 A.M. We'll be on the water fishing by 7." He glanced down at his wardrobe. "This is why I'm dressed so...formally."

I faked a chuckle. "Yessir, you look the part. Hope you catch a thousand."

I figured he'd leave then, but no, tonight Wayne had turned chatty. "Andrew and Bryce, from our Entertainment division, are going along, as well as Jack Lesley, whom you spoke with at your review. Jack and I believe in you, Alex. You just hit a rough patch last month."

Time to be Mr. Agreeable. "Yes, I believe so too. Tonight, I'm just adding a few billable hours to the total."

He pointed at me and winked. "Good job."

"Thank you, sir," I said, and wondered where to go with this wee hour conversation. "Do you four fish a lot together?"

Wayne Haubert grinned and switched his tackle box to his right hand. "Twice a year we plan something. The Caribbean this time. Last couple of years it's been salmon fishing in Alaska, pike fishing in Canada, and peacock bass in South America. Our goal is to leave no waters un-fished." He came over and patted me on the back twice, as if to reward me for my late-night diligence. "You keep working hard, Alex, and you'll certainly make partner, and then on our next trip we just might have room for a fifth man."

"Thank you, Wayne."

He whistled his way down the hall, his tackle box swinging in his hand, a silver bonefish embroidered on the back of his shirt.

Sure, I'd fish with those guys some day. If I tried hard, I could convince myself of such inclusion. Deep down, however, I knew that at the rate I was going, I'd do no better than bait their hooks.

* * *

By 3:30 A.M., I'd read every page of the file twice and had even flung it against the wall in disgust. The insurance rider that Yorkshire used to deny Abner Plott his due coverage actually did no such thing. Had the issue ever been presented to a judge and a jury, Yorkshire surely would have had to pay him. Mr. Plott had been hoodwinked, deceived, and defrauded, the victim of big money and intimidating corporate lawyers who were paid large sums to protect Yorkshire from paying out even larger sums. Collectively, the whole thing disgusted me.

I fell asleep in my office chair and woke at 5:58 A.M., the sun not yet stirring over eastern Orlando. My goal was to jog two blocks to the hotel for a shower and a shave, change clothes, and prepare my case for another 2 hours. Then I would head across town and confront counsel at Yorkshire Mutual on the small matter of their stinginess and fraud.

But as I shut the door to my office and found the hallways empty, I could not help myself. I had to peek into Austin's office, just to see how deep he was into Bargain Mart preparations. It still stabbed my gut to know that *he* had been given my role.

I crept into Austin's office—just three doors down from my own—and turned on the lights and saw a single Bargain Mart file atop his desk, right in front of a framed photo of Tatiana. Except that the back of the picture frame was loose, and it appeared that more than one photo rested behind the glass. I pulled out the first photo and found four more behind it—a blond, a redhead, a Hooters gal, and yet another blond, this one in roller skates and a pink halter—rotating bimbos. No wonder the guy was still single.

21

THE OPULENCE OF YORKSHIRE MUTUAL'S HEADQUARTERS PUT Powers, Morgan, and Greene to shame. Through heavy brass doors and past statues of unfamiliar heroes, I entered their lobby. Everything around me, under me, and before me appeared polished, marbled, and reeking of profit. These insurance uppity-ups had both the revenue to afford it and the gall to display it.

A receptionist with Miss America hair and a ballerina's physique pointed with red nails to the lobby, and I obeyed her command. My appointment with Yorkshire's General Counsel, Jonathan Marshall, had only been approved because of their long relationship with PMG. Even so, Jonathan Marshall had warned me that he could only spare a few minutes, from 10:00 to 10:20 A.M.

I tapped my foot on a Persian rug and noted the time as it rolled forward to 10:01, 10:02. Then Miss Red Nails summoned me to her desk and instructed me to go up the spiral staircase, turn left, and go to the corner office at the end of the hall.

Jonathan Marshall—his suit pinstriped, his head full of perfectly coiffed gray hair—greeted me as I entered. He didn't wait behind his desk but met me halfway, his smile sincere and his handshake firm.

"I'm Jonathan Marshall," he said. "I don't believe we've met."

I shook back with something less than gusto. "And I'm Alex Lord, with PMG."

He motioned me to his guest chair and I continued talking, if only to try to put him at ease. "No sir, I don't believe we've met. I practice labor law, for the most part, and occasionally dabble in bankruptcy."

He nodded and sat with the ease and graciousness of one meeting with a friend of a friend. "Well, I prefer not to dabble in anything related to bankruptcy, Alex. We at Yorkshire are allergic to bankruptcy." He motioned to the fine art and small sculptures along his walls, as if to emphasize his point.

"No sir, no money shortages today."

Jonathan Marshall shifted with ease into business mode. "What can I do for you today, Alex?"

To the point. Good. "A couple years ago, my firm handled a case for you involving an older gentleman named Abner Plott."

He fixed his attention somewhere above my head and mouthed the words "Abner" and "Plott." A kind of measured blankness filled his countenance, as if the name were too common, too simple, to maintain registry in his memory. "Nope. Doesn't ring a bell."

My sweaty hands opened the file in my lap. I debated whether or not to show it now, or wait a few minutes. No time like the present. "I didn't think his name would be familiar to you."

Across his desk I handed him the file. He accepted it with an air of suspicion, his head cocked to the side as if he preferred to sneak a peek at the contents rather than give a direct perusal.

Seconds became minutes, and I watched his eyes for signs of recognition and annoyance.

Recognition won out. "Ah...yes," he said. "Now I remember. What about Mr. Plott? His case has been closed for a long time now."

I was glad to have spare copies, one in my old briefcase and another in the trunk of my car, right beneath the phone book I'd shot dead in the woods. "Yorkshire denied coverage to Mr. Plott, and did so without a legitimate basis for that denial."

Marshall shut the file as if he'd now saved all of its relevant information into his brain. "There were exceptions in the riders that precluded coverage. You should know that."

"No sir. There were no legitimate exceptions."

He appeared stunned by my statement, a General Counsel unfamiliar with such boldness from an associate attorney. I remained resolute, however, in spite of my low status. Abner Plott's case gave me a cause to pursue, something pure to believe in within a corrupt and selfish world, never mind that the possibility of millions in fees might save my career with PMG and vault me back past Austin in the eyes of Richard Sterling.

The old competitive nature had arisen in me, and though I felt a growing compassion for Abner, I also recognized that his case was a football that I intended to march down the field for my own glory. The opposing team, however, was led by the frowning and disappointed man sitting across from me in his opulent office.

"Alex, what is this really about?"

My instincts told me to lock on his gaze and emphasize my opinion. "This is about doing what is right. You owed Mr. Plott coverage, and I think you should pay him."

His expression toggled between shock and incredulity. "What? Has the man sued us again?"

"No."

Relief flooded his face. "Then why, pray tell, would we consider paying him?"

I was a steel girder, unmoving and unapologetic. "Because it's right and because I *want* you to."

Marshall did not simply appear displeased; he had the look of a man who wanted to swat the bug that had lighted in his guest chair. "Mr. Lord, what are you saying?"

"I'm saying that your rider exception was a joke, a farce, and you knew it the whole time. Plott was poor, old, and of very limited means, and you knew if the case ever got really heavy, you could finagle things and settle with him for far less than you owed. But it never got that far, did it, Jonathan?" I reached across his desk and reclaimed the file he'd closed minutes before. "Remember a letter you wrote, in which you included the sentence, 'It is undeniable that his policy offers coverage?'"

He shook his head. "No, I don't remember that. In fact, I have no recollection at all of it. And I didn't see any such letter in the file."

"That's because I have the original."

Fear shown in his face. "What exactly do you want?"

"I want you to pay Plott's claim or I will take this file and that letter and make it all public. I will show the world that you consciously destroyed a man in order to save a few dollars for Yorkshire Mutual."

Marshall grabbed a pen and tried to stick it through his desk calendar. "You do that, Mr. Lord, and you'll breach the attorney-client privilege and you'll be disbarred!"

I stood and looked down at him. "And the day after that, the national news will run the story of what you did to this sick old man, and within a week over a 100,000 people will cancel their policies."

He motioned me to sit again. I didn't budge.

"C'mon, Alex. Let's just calm ourselves a bit here. You don't really want to throw your career away by threatening us, now do you?"

"No, I don't. You simply pay Plott what you owe him, and we all can keep our jobs."

He looked as if his head might explode. Then, somehow, a kind of forced calm overcame him. "Look, if what you say is true about the rider, then perhaps we should take another look and revisit our coverage decision."

Spoken in perfect non-committal legalese.

He extended his hands, his palms upturned in a gesture that begged me to hand him back the file. "I'll review the file this afternoon."

I tucked it back under my arm. "I'm sure that somewhere within the marbled headquarters of Yorkshire, you have your own file."

I opened my briefcase, set the file inside, and slammed it shut.

"You're making a huge mistake, son."

Son? What arrogance and condescension. "I've reviewed the file several times, Jonathan, and you do owe Plott the money. You should listen to me. After all, I'm one of Yorkshire's lawyers."

His vein-popping stare continued without any offer of a handshake.

I turned and left him to his thoughts. I'd said all I came to say.

* * *

My drive back to Powers, Morgan, and Greene passed in a blur of opposing thoughts. *What did I just do? What if this actually works? Could I surpass my previous worst day ever by being disbarred by noon? If so, should I stop at Walmart and buy some camouflage?*

Carol saw me enter the hallway, her concerned face telling me all I need to know. One glance past her desk and down the hall revealed my office door closed. When I left to visit Yorkshire, my office door was open. Someone, or more likely, several someones, now waited for me on the inside.

Carol mouthed, "I'm sorry," as I passed her. In reply I made a finger pistol, put it to my skull, and pulled the trigger.

My guess was that my reception party consisted of at least two PMG partners—probably Richard Sterling and Wayne Haubert. No, Wayne was off fishing the blue waters of Abaco, so it had to be someone else. At my door, I switched my briefcase to my right hand, paused to prepare myself, and reached for the knob. I pushed on the door, which seemed to open on its own.

"Alex," Richard Sterling said. He looked grave, a bearer of bad news. He motioned me inside. "Come in."

Across the room, between my desk and the window stood Austin Adams. The drawers to my desk were open, as were the drawers to my two-drawer filing cabinet.

"Find anything interesting, Austin?" I asked.

A brief smirk. Nothing more from my former best friend.

Sterling closed the door behind me, and I moved to the center of the room, wary of being caught between two manipulators. "You've been under a lot of pressure lately, Alex. I hadn't realized just how much pressure."

Briefcase still in hand, I stood between the two, Austin to my left, separated from me by my own desk. Richard, to my right, positioned himself next to the wall and very near my diplomas, as if he might at any moment grant himself authority to snatch them from their perch and declare them invalid.

"Actually, Richard, I'm doing much better."

Austin folded his arms. "No, you're not."

His verbal arrogance was exceeded only by his pompous expression, like he'd elevated himself to partner-in-waiting and was practicing how to belittle an associate.

Sterling moved in front of me and stood there inspecting me, observing me in my habitat.

I felt like a salmon filet behind a grocer's glass. At any moment I expected Sterling to sniff me for freshness. Instead his chin rose high, and he too appeared to be trying his best to look down upon me. "We all get so caught up in our work, we miss the signs."

I could not deal with vagueness. "What exactly are you talking about?"

Sterling looked at Austin, and Austin shrugged as if he'd conceded the interview to his superior. "For you to risk your career and the reputation of the firm, you must be desperate."

"Really desperate," Austin added, the lover of bimbos now talking like a parrot.

I nodded at Sterling. "Yorkshire didn't waste a minute calling you, did they?"

"Alex, it's not too late for you. Not too late at all. This can be fixed with our client, and fixed with the firm. We're good at fixing things around here, and we can also help you deal with Mr. Plott."

This was too much. "Really now? And just how are we going to do that?" I turned to Austin. "Shall we kill him?" I wheeled around to face Sterling. "Because I know we're not going to *represent* him! He's too small—too trivial."

Sterling took a step toward me, a trace of fear in his eyes. "We can help. We can help and we can fix everything for you. But first I need the original file."

Both Sterling and Austin were no longer looking at me; they were focused on my briefcase. I tightened my grip on its handle. "You want the original file? For what reason?"

Sterling sighed. "That file belongs to Powers, Morgan, and Greene. Please, you need to start acting in a manner that will help yourself."

"Your manufactured compassion is really touching, Richard. Almost as touching as Austin taking it upon himself to comfort my wife. The reason the two of you are in my office has nothing to do with helping me."

Austin came around the desk and stood next to Sterling. "Alex, stop playing the martyr! We are here to try to keep you from destroying your legal career."

I met his gaze and envisioned his head as a hollow place, devoid of anything but empty platitudes and the memorized phone numbers of nightclub floozies. "You fit right in, Austin. Stick around and you'll go far."

"Alex!" Sterling scolded.

"Richard, this meeting is over."

I turned for the door, and Austin lunged for my briefcase. I expected such, however, and in one motion I switched the briefcase to my left hand and watched him miss. I reared back and hit Austin Adams with a clenched right fist, and I hit him harder than I ever hit any punching bag. I hit him square on the cheek, and he fell sprawling back into the front of my desk.

Sterling reached to take my briefcase, but he was slow of motion and whiffed his attempt. "Alex. Give it to me!"

I backed toward the door, and he lunged again.

I sidestepped him and swung the briefcase sidearm. A corner of the case caught him in the belly. His air left his lungs and he dropped to his knees and gasped. "Ohhhh. You…you idiot!"

I stood over this so-called partner, whose main partnership bonded him not to co-workers but to corporate purse strings. "Sterling, you make me sick."

I opened the door to leave but I could not. A policeman blocked my path. He stood in the doorway as if his sole duty in life was to keep me quarantined in my office.

Sterling came up behind me, and I watched him like the animal he'd become. Austin remained propped against my desk, rubbing the side of his face and wincing.

"Officer," Sterling said, one hand still supporting his stomach, "this man has in his possession stolen property from this law firm. It's in his briefcase."

I faced the officer. "If you want to look in this briefcase, sir, then you first get a search warrant."

The officer backed away, and I moved past him and made for the elevators.

"Sir!" the cop called from behind me. "Wait just one minute. Come back here."

I stopped and considered running, but my sense was that more law enforcement might be waiting at the exits. In addition, Carol was no longer at her desk, and I wondered if they'd warned her to get to a safe place. Dangerous Alex Lord was on the loose, terrorizing all of Orlando with his mighty briefcase.

"Sir!" the cop repeated. "Come back here."

I turned and approached the small crowd—Sterling, the cop, Austin with his hand on his cheek, plus a couple of other partners who'd wandered onto the third floor and happened upon the scene.

The cop checked on Austin, noted that Sterling looked pale, and said to them, "You guys okay? What just happened in there?"

Sterling shook his head. "Nothing happened."

Austin glared at me as if he wanted to bore twin holes through my skull and pour gas on my corpse. "Officer," Austin said, his eyes never leaving me, "this is nothing that I can't take care of myself."

The situation felt odd as I stood in my employer's hallway and wanted to run, but instead faced a confused cop who stood in front of the partner whom I'd just leveled with my briefcase, and a former best friend who now hated my guts. "Officer, why are you keeping me here? Please tell me what I've done wrong."

The officer looked at Sterling, then at Austin, then at my briefcase. "Sir, just hold on a minute. Will you let me look in your briefcase?"

"No. I will not."

Sterling pointed at me and told the cop to arrest me.

The officer raised a finger of caution. "I need reasonable suspicion to believe that a crime has been committed here."

"And you have none," I shot back.

He turned to Sterling. "Well? Is there anything to give me reasonable suspicion?"

Austin stepped around Sterling and in front of the cop. "I saw him put firm property in his briefcase."

"You lying sack of...."

Austin pointed at me and raised his voice. "A file—of the firm's—I saw him put it in there."

"Good enough for me," the officer said. He brushed past Austin and approached me. He appeared annoyed at the proceedings, like he wanted to be anywhere but in some quarreling law firm. "Sir, open the briefcase. And do it slowly."

Now I had them. I had them all, and I determined to enjoy the moment.

After a pause for dramatic effect, I raised the briefcase slowly to eye level and stepped closer to Austin, wanting to give him a perfect look. Then I reached up and flipped the latch and opened the briefcase high over head. I even shook it so that all the air might fall out because that was all my briefcase contained—air.

"Remember our poker games, Austin? Back in Gainesville? You never could run a bluff."

Sterling gasped, the cop nodded, and Austin—veins bulging in his neck—glared at me with a hatred that bordered on insanity.

"You're free to go," the cop said.

"This isn't over, Alex." Austin warned.

Still facing him and the partners, I stepped backward and retreated toward the stairwell. No elevators this time. "I'm done with you, Austin. I'm done with all of this."

I pushed open the metal door to the stairs with my butt and took one last look at my antagonists. Richard Sterling wore the expression of a man so immersed in payola that he held no concept of truth, or why anyone would want to pursue truth. Sterling seemed—and I thought the same of Austin—a chocolate bunny of a man, attractive on the outside but oh so hollow on the inside.

I ran down the stairwell, fully aware of the problem of applying heat to a chocolate bunny—under high temps it doesn't disappear, it merely reforms into an uglier version of the original.

22

To consistently lean on alcohol as a source of comfort was neither my goal nor my inclination. I just needed a temporary retreat, a place to ponder, and at least 1 hour to gather my thoughts and prepare for what was to come.

Otis refilled my glass with sweet tea and wiped a couple drops from his bar. "So let me get this straight," he said, and he poured himself half a glass. "You now wanna help the guy who threw your plants into your pool, you've done blown it with your bosses, and now you gonna blow it for everybody involved? Gonna take down the entire ship?"

"Just the captain and first mate." I sipped the sweet beverage and looked around at the empty innards of Otisology. It was 3:25 in the afternoon, and the only other customer had just paid and departed.

My new favorite bartender stooped and lifted a case of Corona and set it atop the bar. "And he was your best friend and he try to frame you? Right there in front of everybody?"

"He did, Otis. But he was too stupid to pull it off."

Otis opened the case of beer and plunged the bottles one by one into round ice. "My sophomore level advice is…stick to sweet tea. This ain't no time for inebriation."

"No," I said, and gulped down the balance. "No, it's not."

A delivery guy summoned Otis to the back door, and he left me there alone with my thoughts and my empty glass. What Austin and Sterling might try to pull by the end of the day was a question that both confounded and frightened me. I had felt so tough, invincible even, in the hallway with the cop and the partners. I'd called Austin's bluff and watched him fizzle. But now I shook from fear. These guys were capable of most anything—and I regretted leaving my Beretta locked away in a bus station locker.

My personal fears morphed quickly into concern for Karen. I speed-dialed her and felt relief when she answered on the first ring.

"Karen, hey. It's me."

A 2-second pause. "Did you hit Austin at work earlier?"

That manipulating piece of scum. "And just how would you know about that? Did he call you?"

"Maybe."

"I can't believe that guy."

"Well, *did* you hit him?'

"Yes, but he came at me first."

"Oh that's just great, Alex. We have debts, we have a house losing value like every other house in Florida, a landscaping bill for our war zone of a front yard, and you go off and ruin your career over some spat with Mr. Plott."

"It wasn't a spat, Karen, and it wasn't with Abner Plott. Powers, Morgan, and Greene acted with Yorkshire Mutual to defraud that man, and he's owed large sums because of that fraud."

"Austin said you're acting crazy and out of control, that you stole firm property and you're dangerous to be around."

"Karen, listen to me. Austin set me up. You have to believe…."

"He advised me to avoid you until this all settles out."

"Karen, do not listen to him."

"I have to go, Alex."

"No. Don't hang up."

A pause. "Where are you?"

"What?"

"Tell me where you are. Right now. I want to know what you're up to."

"I'm in a bar."

"See. Austin said he thought you'd be drinking."

"I'm not drinking. I've had two sweet teas and some peanuts."

"You're in a bar, Alex."

"I needed some time to think."

"You're scaring me."

"Karen, please."

Click.

I sucked a melting ice cube from my glass and crunched it into bits. I might as well have been crunching my job and my marriage, so shattered and damaged were they both. I'd met manipulators before, but no one came close to Austin Adams.

"That didn't sound too good," Otis said from behind an armful of boxes.

"Much worse than no good."

He set the boxes on the counter behind the bar, his gray hair tinted red by the Budweiser neon sign above him. "Lemme' fetch a couple more cases from out back, and then we'll talk."

I stood and shook my head. "Can't do it, friend. Gotta go."

* * *

By nightfall, I returned to my rented hotel room a few blocks down from the office. I tried three times to call Karen but she would not pick up. My growing fear was that she believed Austin's words over my own. I considered driving out to the house to talk with her, though I wondered if she were even home. In an effort at stealth, I used the hotel phone and dialed our home number.

No answer.

The knock on my hotel room door came as a surprise, and from the lightness of the knock I expected a female. I opened the door, however, to find that the knocker was none other than Richard Sterling, still in his pinstriped suit but no longer holding his belly.

I looked past him to scan for cops but saw none anywhere. Although I was filled with doubts over his motivation, I invited Richard inside. Cautiously, he stood in the doorway and looked around the room, as if I too might have set an ambush. "Alex, we need to talk."

"Why are you here, Richard? Why are you *really* here?"

He turned and perused the hallway to both sides. Then he sighed and stepped back until he had propped himself against the wall, directly across from my door. "Sometimes things get complicated in a hurry. We panic; we say things; we do things that later we regret."

I gripped the doorframe with both hands. "What do *you* regret, Richard?"

"You and I have worked closely together for more than 4 years now, and believe me when I say that I know what a fine lawyer you are. The firm has invested a lot in you, and we would really hate to lose you."

He was feeding me a load of crap and I refused to sample a single spoonful of it. Powers, Morgan, and Greene wanted that original Yorkshire file, and they wanted it bad. Richard Sterling was today the PMG bird dog, sent to sniff out under which bush that file might be hidden. It was hidden well.

"Go on," I said. "Tell me more of why you'd hate to lose me."

He shifted his weight onto his left side and propped the sole of his right foot against the wall. "I've learned quite a bit from all this. We at PMG need to change the way we operate. We need to understand our associates better, and we're committed to doing just that. You'll see."

"Nah. I'll just read about it."

Sterling appeared surprised by my words, like he had conjured in his head exactly how his little drop-in visit would play out, and I had just missed my line and thrown the entire production off course. But that was the calculating world in which he thrived: If they zig, we zag. His problem today was that he had shown himself as a zigger, and I, unexpectedly had zigged even further. Nothing like expecting a zag but getting a zig, eh Richard?

"Alex, we do want you back."

"No you don't."

"Yes, we want you back. No good can come from destroying careers and companies. You'll be placed back on the Bargain Mart trial. I'll insist on it."

His offer surprised me in one sense—that he would use the firm's best possibility for a megamillion fee to try and lure me back. But I knew that once I agreed to anything, I'd be demoted once again, doing bankruptcy cases for every two-bit condo flipper south of the Georgia state line. Bargain Mart was simply a bargaining chip, and that chip was an optical illusion that would disappear as soon as I reached for it. No thanks.

I shook my head in disbelief.

Sterling seemed anxious. "Alex, you were right, you know. The trial team is far better...far, far better, with you there."

"What about Plott?"

"He gets paid. Yep, he'll get his check very soon. I confirmed that with Jonathan Marshall on my way over here."

"Just like that, huh?" The liar—the shallow, conniving, money-grabbing liar.

He pushed away from the hotel wall and assumed the stance of a used car salesman preparing to explain the fine print—feet spread wider than normal, arms crossed at his chest to hide his black heart. "Not quite. There are just a few conditions. First, you come back to work and you return the original Yorkshire files."

"Then what?"

"You'll then sign an agreement with Yorkshire stating that if you disclose any of their confidential information, you will pay them substantial damages."

There it was—conditional legalese from the calculating lawyer. I remained poised in the doorway and showed no fear. "I tell the truth; I destroy myself."

"Mr. Plott will get the money, Alex. Isn't that what you want? Or do you also want to scorch the earth?"

"Right now, Richard, I'm not sure what I want."

He smiled as if he'd weakened me into submission. "Come on back, Alex. Do Plott a favor. Do *yourself* a favor."

Out of words and tired of his act, I just met his twisted gaze and dared him to say more.

Richard Sterling, of course, could always say more. "We all need to do ourselves favors at times. Even partners like me." He winked, walked off down the hall, and offered one last comment over his shoulder. "At least give it some thought."

He ducked into the hotel elevator, and as the three beeps signaled his departure, I slumped to the carpeted floor, my energy spent, my legs sprawled in the hallway like the leftovers from last night's room service.

I was going to take the deal to help Plott, but my career at Powers, Morgan, and Greene was finished. Sterling would do anything in his power to keep Yorkshire Mutual as a client, including offering me a deal to entice me to return. I was just another associate he could throw under the bus when the time was right. I was already a distant memory at PMG. Austin and the other associates had probably already divided up the spoils from my office. As soon as I signed anything, Sterling and the partners had me. They'd eventually cut my salary, remove me from important cases, pass me over for promotions, force me out, and never give me a decent referral.

The interesting thing was that I no longer cared. At least Plott would get his money.

I reached up for the doorknob, pulled myself up from the floor, and decided I should go tell Abner the news—he could expect a check very soon.

At least someone in my orbit would have a good day.

* * *

Before driving out to visit Plott I swung by the house to see if Karen might be home. The sun was setting over the palm trees when I turned on to our street, and for a moment I reflected on better times, when whoever got home first would set the table and ease the other's burden, when we'd take our after-dinner wine out to the pool and sit and download our days—followed by a swim, perhaps a mutual massage. I knew that kind of companionship was rare; those memories fled my conscience when I saw that Karen was not home. The only surprise were the rectangular clumps of Zoysia sod laid out in uniform lines across our front yard, needing rain, sun and a few months of time to stitch themselves to each other and bond for life.

But there was no life here for me this evening, so I turned into my driveway, backed out, and headed across town to tell Plott the news.

* * *

Being the bearer of good news—even when your own world is crumbling—comes with certain therapeutic benefits. My sense was one of relief—Plott would get his due—and also one of optimism. Although I knew I'd soon lose my job, I had my integrity. I could find another job—even begin a new career if I wanted. After all, I was only 30 years old. Plenty of people had switched gears later than that and ended up just fine. Happier, most of them.

I passed the Baptist church again en route to Plott's apartment and parked on the street outside the ratty complex. For a couple minutes I remained in my car and practiced in my head how to tell him the news. *Abner, you've won. Yorkshire is paying what they owe you. I know you can't buy back your wife, but at least you won't have to live in this dump anymore.*

By the time I stepped out of my car, night had blackened the city, and only a few windows in the complex were illumined with light. Who knew, maybe most of the units sat empty. Or perhaps the place was so full of transients and ne'er-do-wells that only one in three tenants paid their power bill.

I hustled up the sidewalk and went inside. The metal stairs to the second floor creaked underfoot, and I imagined again the surprise on Plott's face when I informed him of Yorkshire's concession.

I knocked twice on the door and listened for footsteps.

Figuring that he was napping, I knocked again, this time louder. "Mr. Plott? You home?"

I tried the doorknob, and it turned fully. The living room was total darkness, and when I flipped on the light I nearly vomited.

"No!"

Abner Plott lay in the middle of his rug, blood under his head, blood matted into the hair above his left ear. A pair of roaches scurried from the body as I neared him.

God. No. Not this man! Not here, not tonight.

My stomach wretched violently as I noted the pistol in his hand—a Beretta FS. My Beretta, I was certain.

I fought the urge to vomit, and kneeled beside his body. I felt gutted and numb beyond reason, unable to move.

My eyes filled with tears, and through watery lenses I took in the awful surroundings of his last day—the dirty carpet, the peeling paint on the walls, the dim light, all of it serving as a backdrop to the overwhelming sense that I'd been set up.

My hand eased down to the pistol and I pried it gently from Plott's fingers. I checked the serial number above the trigger guard and knew then that the killer had used my gun. The killer had to know that I'd stored the pistol in the locker at the bus station. He'd followed me, or had someone follow me, broken into the locker, and came here and shot Abner.

Already I knew who.

Still on my knees beside the body, I took stock of Plott's possessions and saw the cardboard box that held his records from Yorkshire Mutual next to the TV. I moved the safety on the Beretta to the on position before reaching over and setting the pistol on the box. I listened for sirens but heard none. Surely someone had heard a gunshot. And surely I needed to flee very soon.

I was not a man who prayed often, or hardly at all, for that matter. But there beside his body, I felt the need to say something, anything. "Mr. Plott, it should not have ended like this—you deserved better, a lot better—oh, God…God bless you, sir."

I stood, box in hand, and exited the apartment. Then I closed the door and used my shirttail to wipe the doorknob.

I drove in a daze, forgetting where I'd come from and unaware of my destination. I just drove—and not very fast. Memories of Karen and

I flashed uncontrollably in my head, only to be shoved out of the way by images of Austin comforting her, then by images of Austin shooting Plott in the head. Finally, an image held fast—that of the photos taken from the pool area of Karen and me during an intimate moment.

Now I saw it all with clarity. When Plott had asked me if I had a wife, I should have put it all together. If he had been the one who took the photos, he would have already known that I had a wife.

Abner Plott had told the truth when he'd said he had nothing to do with those photos. A much lesser man—a man highly competitive and impossibly cruel—had taken those pictures.

Direction came instantly. No longer driving randomly around Orlando, I headed straight for Austin's house. I not only saw his motive, I saw his plan and how he went about it. He'd taken the locker key from my desk, found the gun in the locker, and concocted his plan.

It took only 10 minutes to reach his townhouse, but it stood dark and vacant, his Volvo convertible nowhere in sight. I U-turned in the street and headed for downtown. It was him or me, and now I knew just what to do to build a case against Austin Adams.

* * *

The parking lot beside Powers, Morgan, and Greene sat empty of all but two vehicles—my own, and the disabled van belonging to the local printer company. It had been there for days, ever since it broke down during a delivery. PMG's offices were mine to search, and one office in particular called to me in the night air.

Less surprising than having no guard posted to keep me away was the fact that my key card still worked. Maybe the partners were so busy trying to figure out a way to nab me and get the Yorkshire file that they'd forgotten small details like my possession of a key card.

I entered quietly and ran up the stairwell toward the third floor. En route, I summoned clarity and held tight to my theory—Austin had shot Abner Plott in the head with my clean gun, which the cops would immediately figure for a murder, even though the killing was set up to look like a suicide. There'd be no gunpowder on Plott's hand, plus the wound angle looked strange. No way all of it would match up with a suicide. Austin figured the cops, in time, would trace the gun back to me—and they'd know I had a compelling motive, given what Plott had done to my yard.

I reached the third floor and something—whether it was pure whimsy or perhaps my desire to tell someone honorable the absolute truth—possessed me to stop at Carol's desk and leave her a note. I pulled a Post-it from its brethren, scrawled a quick message, and stuck it in her top drawer.

> Carol, I did not do it.
> Please believe me.
> A.L.

I shut the drawer and ran down the hallway.

Austin's office door was open. Good. Even better, his Costa Del Mar sunglasses rested upon his desk.

I searched his drawers, his closet, beneath his desk, but did not find what I wanted. Then I looked behind his credenza, and there it was—shiny and leather and virtually unused. The new briefcase that Karen had gifted me on my birthday—the same one that disappeared from my car at the convenience store a few days later—was squeezed into the narrow opening between Austin's credenza and his wall.

Oh, Austin.

I reclaimed what was mine and returned to his desk. There I drew a Kleenex from a box beside his phone and lifted his sunglasses by the nosepiece. I needed to leave all fingerprints intact. With his shades in my left hand and my new briefcase in my right, I hastily left Austin's office on the third floor and fled Powers, Morgan, and Greene.

This hand of poker had but two players remaining, and I was all in.

23

TROUBLE CIRCLED ME LIKE BARRACUDAS AROUND BLOOD. WHEN your opponent is crazy enough to steal your pistol, commit murder to put you away and remove you from the competition, it becomes hard to fathom the depths of his depravity. Austin Adams had dropped a bomb into my life, and I was determined to dodge the shrapnel and return fire.

Why I drove back out to my house is a question that still haunts me. But I did drive there. Maybe it was habit. Maybe, in the midst of raw emotion and panic, I forgot that I had taken up temporary residence at the hotel near the office, and so I drove toward the house figuring I would spend the night there—like always. I wasn't thinking clearly. I probably wasn't thinking at all.

My headlights shown first on the new mailbox, rigid and sturdy, standing sentry over new sod. But then I drove closer and saw in the driveway Austin's Volvo, parked snug behind Karen's Nissan.

I truly wanted to shoot him. In another time and place I might have pulled the Beretta from my trunk and busted through the front door and shot him in the head and dipped my finger in his blood and scrawled "Revenge of Plott" across his chest. But that was not the way to redemption.

I parked on the curb and left my car idling. Trance-like and still numb, I made my way up the sidewalk, the smell of fresh sod engulfing me as I prepared for the worst.

My instincts told me to avoid the front door, so I crept between two of the newly planted clumps of zebra grass and peeked inside through the bay window.

Between the curtains I saw them, their backs to me. Austin and Karen sat shoulder-to-shoulder on the sofa, a glass of red wine in their right hands. They were watching TV—the Travel Channel—of all things. I watched the two of them watch a blond lady stroll Bondi Beach in Australia. Then I watched Karen lean into Austin and whisper something into his ear.

He turned to her and nibbled at her earlobe.

It felt so surreal, nightmarish.

Austin clinked his glass against Karen's and they drank in tandem. Then I saw it—the bottle of Ferrari Merlot, a wine I'd purchased months ago with the intention of opening it on the day I became partner. I remembered spotting the bottle on a rack in a Total Wine store and asking a male clerk about it. We'd joked about never being able to afford a Ferrari, but at least a guy could enjoy the wine. So I'd bought a bottle and proudly told Karen that someday we'd celebrate together.

Tonight, however, I stood on fresh mulch and spied through my own window while Austin drank my Ferrari Merlot and snuggled on the sofa with my wife.

I raged inside, but it was all directed at Austin. At that moment I didn't know what to feel about Karen—betrayal, obviously—although my desire to kill Austin quashed any feelings of retribution against her. I'd deal with one sinner at a time. Right now, I was on a fast track to the electric chair—unless I thought through this and reversed the panic unto my opponent.

He put his arm around Karen, and I nearly put my fist through the window. But I held my anger in check. Part of me had to hand it to Austin—very few people would even attempt to pull off anything close to his wickedness.

He sipped my wine again, and I knew from his posture and the arrogant raise of his chin that he was congratulating himself on having a pretty good day.

This day, however, was not over.

* * *

At 10:40 P.M., I re-entered Plott's apartment, pulled a Kleenex from my shirt pocket, and placed Austin's Costa Del Mar sunglasses on Plott's kitchen table. Even in the low light of the kitchen, I could see Austin's fingerprints on the lenses. This felt amazingly good. Scary good.

Then I stared again at Plott's dead body and felt incredibly sad. A brokenness came over me, a feeling that I could no longer order the events of my world, that happiness would forever elude me.

In the waning minutes before I turned the tables on Austin, I went to Plott's body and reached into his pants pocket with the Kleenex and drew out his keys. My plan was for these keys to soon turn up in Austin's possession—either in his townhouse, his Volvo, or perhaps in his coat pocket. But they would be found by law enforcement. Yes, they'd definitely be found.

I touched Plott's hair and told him again that I was sorry. Then I bolted out the door and down the stairwell and walked calmly into the shabby courtyard fronting the complex.

On my Blackberry I located Austin's number and dialed. I envisioned him still on the sofa with Karen, sipping another glass of my wine.

"Hello?" he said in a voice trying to hide nervousness.

"Hi, Austin. It's Alex, and I need to see you."

The pause was brief and awkward. "Um, this isn't a real good time for me, buddy. I'll see you at the office tomorrow."

"No, you will see me tonight. At Abner Plott's apartment."

A second pause, and I heard the TV go mute. "What are you talking about, buddy?"

"I'm talking about your shades, the ones you love so much. You left them here on Plott's table. Not a very smart move for a lawyer of your intellect."

"Hey, look...."

"No. You be here within 20 minutes or I'll have the cops over with a fingerprint expert. You want to try and explain your sunglasses at the scene of a murder? And by the way, there's a Hispanic lady from across the street who saw you come in this afternoon and leave in a hurry. She ID'd your photo."

That was enough, and I hung up.

Austin didn't need to know that the Hispanic lady was a figment of my imagination. He just needed to fear the consequences.

It took Austin only 12 minutes to arrive. By then, I had moved my car one street over. I'd also turned out the lights in the second floor hallway, plus the lights in Plott's room.

From the side of the building I watched Austin exit his Volvo and walk tentatively toward the apartment complex. When he took the stairwell to the right, I hurried inside and took the one to the left. I watched from the end of the darkened hallway as he pushed open the door to Plott's apartment. He turned on the light and said, "Alex?"

I knew Austin Adams; I knew that he'd go straight for his sunglasses in the kitchen and then scram. He had the shades in hand when I slammed the front door and locked the deadbolt from the outside. The inside of the deadbolt I'd removed with a screwdriver long before he arrived.

I heard him run across the living room and pound on the door.

"Alex! You idiot!"

His footsteps pounded back across the living room and faded to silence.

But Austin could not escape; the bathroom window was protected with iron bars—same for the bedroom window. All the windows of these ratty apartments had bars. Steel bars were the burglar alarms.

I had caged a psychopath, and the psychopath went wild.

A dish shattered against a wall. If Austin hadn't been so pitifully naïve, and Plott hadn't been so absolutely dead, I might have laughed.

A second dish shattered, and then I listened with my ear against the door.

Austin called someone. "Karen," he said, his voice frantic, "it's Austin. He did it!. Alex murdered Mr. Plott! I'm scared for your husband...No, don't call the police until I know more. Just know that Mr. Plott is dead...How do I *know?* Because I'm in the apartment...Look, I can explain, but you've got to get me out of here. Alex locked me inside after he killed Plott...I'm at 200 West 70th in apartment 262...Then look it up on MapQuest!...And bring a couple screwdrivers and a hammer...bring a cordless drill if you can find one...Just hurry and get me out of here!"

She wouldn't be going anywhere if I could get to her first. I ran out to my car and hoped a BMW could make the trip in 10 minutes or less. I sped across the city—the traffic light at this late hour. I figured it would take her a few minutes to look up the directions, a few more to find the tools. Maybe I could delay her an extra minute or two.

I dialed her cell.

"Hello? Alex?"

I hung up.

I dialed her cell again.

"Alex?"

I hung up again.

I did this four more times, and by the time I turned onto our street and switched my lights on bright, she had yet to leave the house.

She came running out the front door—a piece of computer paper in one hand, a toolbox in the other—as I pulled into the driveway. She hurried to the door of her Nissan and turned and stared into my headlights. I blocked her in and left my engine running.

In the illumination of the headlights, she appeared as frightened as I'd ever seen her. I got out with my hands out, a gesture of peace. "Karen...."

She set the toolbox on the ground and backed against her door, eyes wide, panic in her face. "Alex, what are you doing here?"

I stopped some 10 feet away. No need to scare her further. "The question, dear, is what was *Austin* doing here? Why was Austin Adams sitting next to my wife on my sofa, sipping my wine?"

"Alex, stay away from me. I mean it."

"You walk away from me, tell me you need some time, and then you hook up with Austin? AUSTIN? Why not just take a knife and plunge it through my chest?"

She sighed to the night sky. "It's…it's not what you think."

I moved a step closer. "Not what I think? Sure, the lying, back-stabbing Austin Adams isn't fooling around with you. You expect me to believe that?"

"Alex, I know about Mr. Plott. I think you should just go. Just leave and go to Mexico or wherever it is you plan to flee."

She was clueless, and I moved to within a foot of her. "What do you mean, you *know* about Plott? You don't know anything."

She pressed her palms back against the driver's door, fear flooding her soft features. Her mouth moved but no sound came forth.

"Austin killed Plott, Karen! He killed him earlier this evening…with *my* gun."

She put her hands over her ears and shook her head violently. "No! I'm not going to listen to this. I know you did it!"

I grabbed her left arm. "Karen Lord, you don't know anything! Your boyfriend is a psychopath!"

She shook her head again. "No! He didn't do it!"

"Yes, he did!"

"No!"

"How could you know that?"

"Because he's been with me all afternoon and all night!"

Daggers of pain shot through me. Our eyes met and I could feel her abandonment. We stared at each other like strangers but said nothing. Finally, I let go of her arm but not her eyes. The years together, the excitement of college romance, the plans, the future, kids, all of it reversed course in seconds, as if a dastardly time warp had sucked back the joy of an entire decade and left me with no hope.

It was gone. All of it. All of *us*. Trust—the trait we had shared on the highest level, had completely vanished.

"Karen, why?"

"Just leave me alone, Alex. Go."

She began to cry as I climbed back into my car. In a tiny act of compassion, I switched my headlights to dim so as to spare the neighbors the sight of my cheating wife.

I backed out and sped back toward the caged psychopath, who I presumed was still locked inside the apartment with the body of the man he'd murdered.

I owed the psychopath something, and it had nothing to do with any bet.

* * *

Have an alibi, he'd said. Whatever you do, make sure you have an alibi. I had no idea if he'd brainwashed Karen or somehow hypnotized her or what, but he apparently had his alibi. At the time of the murder, however, I was in my hotel room—alone.

I drove wildly, my thoughts racing. With no alibi, I had only my rage to unleash on Austin, to give him his comeuppance before any authority got hold of me. I no longer cared what happened to me. I felt empowered, fueled in my anger by a combustible mix of images—my cheating wife sleeping with my cheating best friend, all of it boosted by the high octane of revenge.

His Volvo was still parked curbside when I arrived back at Plott's apartment. Even from the first floor I heard the pounding and clanging upstairs. If neighbors were alarmed, they didn't show it. No one came out of their apartment units. No one, apparently, had called 911. This was the kind of neighborhood where talking to the cops meant that you'd be marked as the next victim. *I ain't seen nothin', officer.*

The pounding continued as I scaled the stairs and entered the second floor. Wham! The door of #262 splintered in the middle.

Wham! A sliver of wood shot out of the door's middle. Wham! Another strike, another splinter.

Then Austin's hammer broke through, although he wasn't using a real hammer. He wielded an iron skillet—apparently all he had found in the house to try and break down the door. He grunted and hit the door again. Then he yelled, "Aaaayhh!" and fractured the center further.

I jammed my key into the deadbolt, and as his next hit splintered the door anew, I kicked the door and sent Austin sprawling back onto the carpet. The skillet landed at my feet, and I left it there.

Austin stood and took a wild swing at my head. I ducked and hit him square on the nose. He fell backward and landed in front of Plott's body.

"What was it, Austin?" I said as I stood over him. "The punch in the office? The golf wagers? The rush to beat me to make partner?"

I kicked him hard in the ribs and he howled in pain.

"Was it your lust for Karen? What made you do this?"

He curled into a ball. I almost kicked him again, but Plott's tragedy overwhelmed me. *An innocent man, shot…in order to frame me.*

It all crashed down on me like sandbags of guilt, and I stood over the body and wept, tears falling onto bloody carpet.

Austin needed to feel the weight of what I felt. I grabbed him from behind at both shoulders and dragged him backward beside Plott. "This is what you do, Austin? This is what you do to get rid of me? I was helping this man! It was going to work out for him!"

Still dazed, Austin offered little resistance as I turned his head and pushed it into the sticky blood that had drained into the carpet from Plott's head wound. "Take a look at him, Austin! You would kill a man just to get to me?"

Austin's foot came up and snapped into my knee. I hollered and fell to all fours beside him.

I turned to hit him but his fist caught my temple.

Neither of us reached our feet; we just swung wildly from our knees—until my hands grabbed his throat and his hands grabbed mine.

In seconds, I couldn't breathe. He was too strong. I tried to stand but slipped in blood.

"Austin," I gasped, "you framed me, you…."

"Freeze!" It was a cop, his gun drawn.

The traitor's hands at my throat relaxed their grip, and I fell across Plott's body and landed on his right side. Austin, on his knees to Plott's left, faced the door and raised his hands into the air.

"Do not move!" the cop shouted. "Either of you!" His gun moved from Austin to me and back again. "Both of you turn slowly, backs to me, and put your hands behind your head."

Austin blurted, "But officer, Alex here...."

"Shut up!"

A second officer entered, and a cold click of handcuffs locked my wrists. A third and fourth click locked Austin's. Through Plott's barred window, blue lights flashed, and from the street, sirens wailed.

Pulled to my feet and shoved toward the door, I heard Austin curse behind me. The second officer told him again to shut up, and he did.

I knew better than to try and immediately explain my presence at the scene of a murder—I wasn't an emotional buffoon like Austin. So I went peacefully and entered the hallway as instructed, the first officer's hand pressed into my back.

We neared the stairwell and he spoke into his two-way: "Suspects in custody. We're bringing them out."

24

AIL SUCKS. My entrance into confinement greeted me with the slurred cusses of street drunks, the boastful graffiti of gang members, and the stench of tiny cells in need of fumigation.

Not that there were any drunks or gang members confined with me—from what I could tell, suspected murderers got their own cell.

Falsely accused and having no one to step forward in my defense, I felt cut loose from the moorings of life, adrift from reality, so far removed from my comfort zone that the charges didn't scare me so much as they hovered around me in the abstract.

My first hour as a suspect passed quickly; during the second hour I was twice escorted from my cell—once to collect samples of dried blood from my hands and arms, and then a second time to sit for interrogation.

I had no idea where they'd put Austin. But I was certain that savvy detectives were already taking his story in umpteen ways and comparing it to my own.

I had told them the truth. I told them everything—my desire to help Abner Plott after discovering he was defrauded, my buying a gun for protection, Austin stealing my gun, and Austin shooting Plott and making it look I did it, using my wife for an alibi. One of the two detectives had appeared to believe me. The other—the kind of bald, ultra-thorough guy who might as well have been the son of Kojak—looked very, very doubtful.

They had at least allowed me to call and arrange an attorney. Sadly, I didn't know who to call. The only partner at PMG whom I trusted to point me in the right direction was Wayne Haubert, so I left him a voice mail to call me when he got a chance. I knew the peer pressure inside the firm might keep him from offering assistance, but he was much better potential help than Richard Sterling.

At sometime around 1 A.M., I woke on the cot in my reeking, graffiti-marred cell and called out to the dark in anger, "Austin, where are you?!"

No reply. They had taken him elsewhere.

I didn't know what I would have said to him anyway—perhaps cursed him just to see if it made me feel better.

An hour or so later, unable to sleep, I tried again. "Austin!"

"Shut up," came the raspy voice of some old bum in the next cell. "Just shut up and sleep off your drunk like the rest of us. You'll be outta' here in the morning."

Yeah. Sure I would.

Morning dawned slowly and through the bars of a tiny rectangular window I watched the pink prelude to sunrise. The window was just a slit in brick, a tease from the heavens. Then a clang of doors, and one by one the bums and the drunks, the street brawlers and the pimps, were let out of their cells. Each new clang of a cell door reverberated in my head and reminded me that I was going nowhere. I had not asked any authority yet, but I assumed I was being held without bond.

When the cop had first burst into Plott's apartment, my initial thought was, *Yes, this looks really bad but they'll figure it out quick and only arrest me for assault.* The idea that I really could look so guilty of murder, that they'd hold me, at best, as an accomplice to murder and at worst hold me as the person solely responsible for that murder, didn't register until sometime in the wee hours of the night.

Just as reality settled over me, a sliver of sunlight glinted through my slit of a window. Then a guard moseyed down the hall and opened two more cells. Five more one-nighters shuffled past me, most of them stoic and inexpressive, as if this morning's protocols were routine and they were now free to return to the streets and resume their bad habits.

The last one—he wore a black stocking cap, stringy gray hair sticking out at odd angles—paused outside my bars to look me over. "You'll be outta' here soon, buddy," he said as the guard urged him forward, "Might wanna lay off the hard stuff."

"I'll do that, bro."

Bro. I had never called anyone "bro" in my life. But here in the slammer I wanted to fit in. Already I'd stripped off my button-down shirt and wore just my T-shirt, untucked over black trousers with a few dried blood stains.

The hallway fell silent again, and a hopeful thought overcame me—that Austin by now had confessed to all he'd done, and within the next few hours the authorities would figure it all out and let me go.

They did not let me go.

The next few hours, in fact, passed without incident or interruption. No one came by. No one else was escorted to a cell. Apparently, between 8:00 A.M. and lunchtime, all of Orlando remained perfectly behaved.

I passed the next hour by thinking of all the crime that gets committed at night. The muggings and the burglaries, the drug deals and the drive-bys, the arson and the murders—most of it done under cover of darkness. I had been arrested at night, my worst behavior of my life had occurred at night, and as I sat staring at a small crack in the concrete floor, I remembered what Karen had said a year earlier, after two brutal murders on successive nights had frightened our side of the city. "Evil loves the darkness, Alex."

I had never associated my name with evil, much less dark evil. For that matter, I could not recall associating my name with good, either. I had never seen myself as Alex Lord, the good guy; or Alex Lord, the bad guy; or Alex Lord, the Christian; or Alex Lord, the atheist. No, I was just Alex Lord, the lukewarm successful guy with a pretty wife and all the trappings of a highly motivated, 30-year-old attorney.

The life change that can occur, however, between age 30 years, 2 weeks, and 3 days, and 30 years, 2 weeks, and *4* days, can stagger a man. The rate of that life change felt even more astonishing than the reality of the change—and several standard deviations more astonishing than a Belvedere martini.

* * *

Happy hour in the city jail comes early, and they combine it with lunch. At 1:00 P.M., I was given a bottled water, a small hamburger sans condiments, and a cookie of undetermined vintage.

"Got any ketchup?" I asked the guard as he continued down the hall.

"No."

I counted his steps—18—until the door to the hallway clanged shut again.

I ate the burger and thought of Karen. I didn't know if she knew yet, or if the local news had already broadcast photos of Alex Lord and Austin Adams along with a caption referring to us as alleged killers. Then I wondered—if Karen did know—if she'd drive over here and try to bail me out or would she first try to bail out Austin. Now there's a fine choice for a woman to face—whether to first bail out her workaholic husband or his best friend with whom she'd spent the evening creating for him an alibi while he snuck off and murdered the old man who'd thrown her plants and shrubs into her pool.

What is "None of the above for 600, Alex?"

The clanging of the hallway door interrupted my efforts to make sense of my plight.

The footsteps grew louder, and I counted them down—14, 15, 16, 17, and there he was again—Son of Kojak, observing me like I was already tried and found guilty.

He unlocked my cell and escorted me to a small room. The room boasted fluorescent lighting, two metal chairs, and a small table bolted to the floor. Bright lights shone off his bald head. He motioned for me to sit, and I obeyed. He sat opposite me and folded his arms, a notepad and pen on the table before him.

"Alex, the story you gave me yesterday is rather hard to believe."

"Yes, I can see how you'd view it that way."

"Yesterday we also spoke with Mr. Adams, and he was ready to testify against you."

"*Was* ready?"

"His story changed a bit today."

A glimmer of hope. "Changed for the better or for the worse?"

My interrogator stared back at me, and after a while it became so awkward that I lowered my gaze and read his name tag: Detective Sherman. *Oh, man, one of his ancestors torched Atlanta.* Finally he uncrossed his arms and said, "For the worse."

"I'm not admitting to something I did not do."

"Just what *did* you do, Alex?"

I knew that he was watching me for signs of lying, traces of nerves, but I remained steadfast, too scared to lie. "I hit Austin Adams in the side of the head with my fist, and I hit him quite hard."

Son of Kojak stood as if to intimidate me. "And why did you hit him?"

"Because he murdered an old man with my gun in order to frame me."

"Is that all?"

"No."

"What else?"

"Austin had been hitting on my wife."

"*Hitting* on?"

"I saw them snuggled on my sofa, drinking my wine."

"What kind of wine?"

"Ferrari Red. I was saving it for a special occasion."

He sat again and jotted on his notepad. "Ferrari makes wine? Or are you just making that up?"

"They really make wine. It fits, ya' know. Ferrari cars are usually red, so it would seem natural that they would also make red…."

"I don't need an explanation out of *Wine Connoisseur* magazine, Alex."

"No, sir."

He wrote something else on his pad. "What were Austin and your wife doing on the sofa? Making out? Making love?"

"They were watching the Travel Channel."

"What time of night was it when you saw them?"

"About 10:30."

"And that's when you left to go kill Mr. Plott?"

"No. Plott was already dead by then. Austin had killed him and returned to my house to use my wife as an alibi."

He set his hand atop his notepad and interlocked his fingers. "Admit it, Alex. You and Austin killed Plott together."

"I had no part in the killing of Abner Plott."

"You and Austin killed him to eliminate a pest from Powers, Morgan, and Greene. You're both associates on the fast-track to partnership, and you murdered Plott to remove an obstacle to your making partner."

"You just made that up. Been drinking red wine yourself this morning, detective?"

His face flushed. "Shut up, Alex! I'll ask the questions here."

"Ask away. I'm telling you the truth."

He leaned back in his metal chair and breathed deeply, as if to calm himself. Then he reached out, grabbed his notepad, and flipped to the second page. "Alex, how long have you owned a Beretta FS?"

"About a week."

"You kept the gun at home?"

"No, I had it locked in a bus station locker."

"Why the bus station? Hoping to make a quick escape on a Greyhound? Flee to Miami? The Keys?"

I shook my head in disgust. "There you go again, making stuff up. I kept my gun in the bus station locker because I didn't want it at the office, especially with psychopaths like Austin only steps down the hall."

He nodded as if that particular explanation made sense. "You practice much with your gun?"

"Just once."

"Where?"

"Out in the woods."

"Why the woods?"

"For privacy."

"Anyone see you there?"

"Just a deer hunter."

His eyes widened and he dropped his pen on his notepad. "It isn't even deer season yet."

"I told the guy that."

Detective Sherman pinched the bridge of his nose and shook his head. "Deer poachers. I hate those guys."

"You a hunter, Detective?"

"Shut up! I'm asking the questions today."

"Yessir."

He stood again and backed up a couple steps from the table, as if the longer distance might grant him clarity. "Alex...."

"Yes?"

I'd interrupted him, and he glared at me again. "Your story is so full of holes that I might as well have shot it with buckshot. When are you going to tell me the truth?"

I stood, but he pointed me back to the chair. Again I obeyed. "Look, detective, I've told you the absolute truth. Austin Adams really did steal my gun, really did shoot Plott, really did try to frame me, and really was hitting on my wife during a difficult time in our marriage. If I'm guilty of anything, it's for battery on Austin Adams—because I *did* hit him—and also negligence toward my wife, because I've been working too much and not giving her the attention she needs." A pause to reflect on tangential sins— "and if you want even the smallest details of truth, know that I also ran three red lights in my dash across town to confront her."

His expression softened a degree, though not much. He remained silent for a minute or so and wrote something else on his notepad. "I'm going to escort you back to your cell now, Alex."

I stood and he came around and put a hand to my back and urged me toward the door.

"Can I borrow one sheet of paper from your pad?" I asked.

"For what?"

"I'd like to pen a letter to my wife."

* * *

During my second questioning they'd removed my paper plate from my cell, along with the uneaten half of my stale cookie. They'd left the bottled water, however, and it served as a reminder of my new limitations and forced me to accept the scope of a suspect's restraints.

Until you've been confined, you can't appreciate the narrowness and imposition of it all—the inability to call a friend; the inability to jump into your car and drive to the grocery store; the absence of entertainment. You even lack the freedom to go to the fridge for a snack. Instead of producing things and reaping rewards, you're instantly part of the dependent class, waiting for some monotone government employee to bring you a basic necessity.

It all felt so third-worldly, surreal even, and the leaving and returning to a cell only reinforced the tight parameters of my new world.

I sat back on my cot, my head against a cinder block, and reminded myself that I could not control what Austin might be telling the detectives. He'd have to pile lie atop lie in order for his story to make any sense at all. Under the scrutiny of Orlando's finest, he'd wither into contradiction and become the very evidence needed to convict him.

I rested in that knowledge and unfolded the piece of notebook paper I'd tucked into my back pocket. Then I grabbed the dull pencil issued to me by the detective. What I wrote was not well thought out; it was simply raw emotion merging with an ample dose of confession:

> *Karen,*
> *I'm not thinking clearly right now, so I apologize if my words seem rambling. Here in this awful place, I see now my misplaced priorities. Watching you sip wine with Austin hurt me more than you know, but it was also the reminder I needed of what I stood to lose. Will you visit me? Come and talk to me, say you forgive me,*

and I'll tell you a thousand times that I forgive you for believing Austin. We'll go to counseling if necessary. I'll start a new career if I must.

Open your mind to the truth, Karen, and I will tell you all about Austin and the blackness of his soul. I may eventually serve some time, but Austin will rot in a prison—if they don't put him on death row.

Will you come visit? I do not belong here. Come to see me and we'll talk about the path to forgiveness. We can at least do that, can't we? Isn't restoration what they preach at that church you attended? I know, I know, I should have gone with you. I should have done a lot of things.

Come visit me. Please.

I still love you.

Alex

25

I T TOOK A WEEK FOR THE COPS, DETECTIVES, AND PROSECUTORS to figure out what had happened—or at least what they thought had happened. What they did not believe was my denial that I conspired with Austin to have Plott killed. How could they have believed otherwise? The evidence and the motivation stuck to me like pinesap. But the authorities did figure out—despite Karen's alibi—that Austin had pulled the trigger. The gunpowder residue found on his hands spared me from a murder charge.

Thanks to a friend of a friend of Wayne Haubert, I had a savvy lawyer, a guy better than I could ever afford. I suspected he'd taken my case partly because he believed me, and partly because he'd once lost a key courtroom battle to Powers, Morgan, and Greene. To shine some light into the PMG cavern of cover-up and manipulation—even if it was just a brief mention in the newspaper, seemed to give our side an extra dose of adrenalin. Still, my lawyer was concerned about going to trial, a feeling I shared. I mean, what juror across the fruited plain would believe the truth—that Austin Adams acted alone?

Perhaps such a juror existed somewhere, but no way would I risk my life on him or her showing up for jury duty on the day of my trial.

We met with the prosecutors three different times. They wanted me to plead, and with expectant faces they urged me to offer up evidence against Austin. Truth is, I would have invented evidence, manufactured evidence, even summoned higher powers of evidence creation if that is what it would have taken to pin that slimeball to his sins.

I also knew that Austin would end up spending a lot more time in prison than I ever would, and in fact he might even be sentenced to death, what with the premeditation involved.

I expected the investigators to find evidence on Austin's hands. What I did not expect, what I could not expect, was the unlikely witness who wandered into the police station the following Monday and told the authorities that she would testify against him.

Tatiana Gomez was not such a bimbo after all. Suspecting Austin of cheating on her, she'd followed him to my house on the afternoon of the murder, then she'd followed him to Plott's apartment. She had no idea what had taken place inside the apartment; she just suspected Austin had yet another girlfriend waiting for him there. Her three cell phone photos of Austin's Volvo, however, put him at the scene at the time of death. Those photos, plus the evidence found on Austin's hands, renewed in me a sense of justice that would keep me from facing life in prison.

For hours each day I sat in my cell and wondered what I would miss, what it would cost me, if I was sentenced to 3 years, 6 years—10. With each mental calculation, the costs of longer and longer sentences, the strivings to make partner, and the insane hours of my PMG career faded into something well short of critically important. What flooded in on me was a sense of brevity, of precious years passing quickly, and that what I really wanted was simply a job I enjoyed and a faithful woman with whom to build a life. I now had neither, and an unfamiliar feeling of hollowness came over me, as if I, too, had become a chocolate bunny of a man.

* * *

Before escorting me for a third time to the small room with the metal table bolted to the floor, Detective Sherman reiterated how fortunate this new evidence was for me. He spoke matter-of-factly, as always, though I detected something more coming from him beyond another round of questioning.

"What's that in your shirt pocket?" he asked, his inquiring gaze darting back to his notepad, which held all sorts of jottings and notes, many of them underlined, some in all caps.

"It's the letter I wrote to my wife. I keep hoping she'll come by to visit and I won't need to mail it, but I don't think she's gonna show."

Detective Sherman reached out his hand. "Want me to mail it for you?"

His offer surprised me. "Sure. Address is on the back. I'll have to owe you for a stamp and an envelope."

He smirked and tucked it into his own shirt pocket. Then, as if he had second thoughts, he pulled out my letter, unfolded it, and began reading.

"Hey, that's personal."

"Hush. This too could be evidence." He read quickly and then appeared to go back and read it a second time, his head slowly shaking as he reached the end. "This is the same kind of crap every repentant husband writes to his wife from jail." He folded it again and stuck it back into his pocket. "Of course, yours is a bit more poetic."

"Thank you...I think."

"No problem."

"So, you'll really mail it?"

He nodded. But then he paused again, and I could tell he had something much more substantial to say to me. "I have some news for you, Alex."

He said this with the blank-faced countenance of one long experienced in delivering bad news.

"Someone else is lying about me? Richard Sterling, right?"

He shook his head. "Nope." Then his clean-shaven face became an alternating picture of duty and consternation. His breathing grew heavy.

"Go ahead," I urged him. "Tell me the news."

"Be glad you're sitting down."

"Austin confessed to everything?"

Again he shook his head. Then this tough detective sighed as if he'd rather be elsewhere, perhaps running a drink stand on a beach in Pensacola—anywhere but here. Finally, he leaned in and rested his elbows on the table, his thumbs under his chin, his eyes locked on mine. "An hour ago we found Austin Adams dead in his cell. He hung himself."

The shock of this factoid faded as I regretted not being able to see Austin sentenced in a court of law. The cheater had cheated me one last time.

"Alex, you okay?"

"No."

No, Detective, I was not okay. A murderer had just excused himself from life on this planet and left me to answer for him.

But of course it would end this way. Of course Austin Adams would find a way to excuse himself from responsibility and leave me dealing with the aftermath. It is the inevitable consequence of selfishness and stupidity—your burdens do not go away, they don't evaporate like a mist in July, they just transfer onto the back of someone else.

Today, the weight of a friendship gone bad strained my back like nothing I'd ever felt.

Thanks, Austin, for exporting to me a 10-ton crate of disappointment. You finally crushed me, golf buddy. You finally won.

And all it cost you was your life.

26

AT THE URGING OF PROSECUTORS, AND FOLLOWING A conciliatory nod from my lawyer, I pled guilty to conspiracy to commit murder. To face trial meant a very good chance of life in prison—for a murder I did not commit. David beat Goliath once, and though I remained impressed by his triumph, I knew that I was no David. All slings were now owned by the state, and any flying stones would not be slung by me but *at* me. No thank you.

I got 10 years in a state penitentiary—possibility of parole in 7 years if I behaved myself.

Surely, I could behave myself. Surely, I wouldn't meet any clone of Austin Adams lurking in the next cell and planning my demise.

Surely.

* * *

Pre-sentencing, Karen never showed up to visit. For that matter, she had yet to visit me after the sentencing. All I'd received from her—and it took her nearly 3 weeks to write—was a 1-page letter in reply to the one I'd sent her:

> *Alex,*
> *I'm sorry it has taken me so long to write. I kind of freaked out after your arrest and Austin's death, and I fled Orlando. Guns and blood and men with tempers will do that to a woman. I hope you*

are being treated decently. I also need to be very honest with you: I still want children, and I want the father of my children to be in the house with me, not in prison.

Even if we could repair the damage we both caused (and yes, I'll admit that I am partially to blame), by the time you get out I will be nearing 40, and that's too much to ask of me, especially now.

I still don't know what to think about Mr. Plott—still don't know if you and Austin acted together or if one of you lied to me or both of you lied to me, which is the direction I'm leaning. Austin killing himself, however, does lead me to think he was the instigator, and that he somehow convinced you to go along with his plan. Regardless, I can't take any more chaos—not in a marriage, not in the legal world, and certainly not in my house and yard, which should be a place of refuge, not a war zone. I need peace, Alex, and rest. You have no idea how tired and worn out I have felt for the past year. I imagine that you too feel tired and worn out, and I do feel for you. I wish things could have turned out differently.

Two weeks ago I moved into a townhouse rental in Savannah, a few miles from my parents. I found work here. Plus, I've been visiting a local church, where I've begun to make new girlfriends and rediscover faith.

This next part is hard to write, but I know it is the right thing for me, and for us. Next month my attorney will begin divorce proceedings. Please know that I do not want anything from you, Alex. As you know, we don't have much left. The house is now worth less than our mortgage, so perhaps you should rent it out if you can. I did take the bed, my dresser, and the cedar chest given to me by my grandparents.

I wish you the best. We tried. I know we both tried. Thank you for some good years, Alex Lord.

Prayers for you,
Karen

I just felt numb again. Just cold and numb and unable to process a coherent thought. Then numbness turned to denial, then to anger, sorrow, bitterness, and regret, until the frequency of shifting emotions made me numb all over again. At some point I tucked the letter under my state-issued pillow, as if sleeping on it might change its message.

For hours I lay back with my hands under my head, staring at a gray ceiling that offered neither wisdom nor compassion. Soon the numbness left me for good, and I began to shake. Reality spread over me with all the surety of nightfall, and I curled into a ball and wept.

27

FTER 8 MONTHS AS AN INMATE, I'D WITNESSED OVER A DOZEN fights in the cafeteria and one stabbing in the courtyard. But those skirmishes were the exceptions. The penitentiary largely served as a fortified bank into which prisoners deposited huge chunks of their life spans.

I lived on B Floor, where across the hall from me resided three ex-bankers serving 5 years each for securities fraud, and two brothers convicted of stealing from investors in a Ponte Vedra condo investment scam. What we had in common was our little concrete and steel neighborhood; what we didn't have in common was guilt. They'd each been convicted after lengthy trials. I was here because I'd pled guilty in order to spare myself an even worse sentencing. No one cared, though. If you were here, you deserved it.

Guilty or innocent, I loathed my inability to set my own schedule. Most days it felt like the giant hand of the state held a remote control with three buttons: 1. Time to Eat, Alex; 2. Recess Time, Alex; 3. Back to Your Cell, Alex.

But as the days turned to weeks, and the weeks to months, the monotony became a kind of blessing in disguise. Though time had become a slow-motion arc of dullness and repetition, I used much of the time to read, even about incarceration. One of the goals of incarceration—a goal many inmates tend to overlook—is to allow the prisoner enormous amounts of time to reflect on prior decisions, the impact of those decisions on his life, and what he should do to change his behavior so as not to earn a return trip.

I had no desire for a return trip. Not with only 6 years and 4 months left till parole.

Flat on my back on my narrow bed, I'd reflected a little on Austin, a little more on how I'd dealt with Plott, but mostly I reflected on Karen and what had happened to our marriage.

I tried not to think too negatively about either of us, but that was perhaps the hardest aspect of imprisonment—I'd end up turning over every issue so many times in my head, seeing everything from every angle—I inevitably came face-to-face with my shortcomings. And that in itself was a new experience. Sure, a prisoner can find camaraderie with other convicts—and I did—but inside me grew a knowledge that I was deeply flawed, so flawed that my actions had demonstrated a potential threat to society and forced the state to protect that same society from people like me.

Yet another thought to occupy my head while I waited for lunchtime—that I was seen as unfit to interact with normal society. Coupled with the fact that my wife thought me unfit to interact as the male half of a husband-and-wife team, I often caught myself fighting an overwhelming sense of failure. I kept returning to Karen's words during the worst of my workaholic weeks and the worst of the attacks on our home. After her emotional plea, I'd told her that I was trying to provide and protect.

Her reply still orbited inside my head: *I also need you to pursue me, Alex.*

The more I thought about the "p" words, the more I convinced myself of failure—on all three counts. While initially I'd given myself credit for trying to be a great provider, in reality I'd placed the importance of provision—and the attraction to the lawyer lifestyle—ahead of pursuit, and in Karen's eyes this was all so very backward. She recognized it intuitively 10 months earlier; I only recognized it in hindsight—from behind bars, when it was too late.

A glance at the clock revealed less than a half hour till lunch, and in the waning minutes I reflected again on my shortcomings as a spouse.

What I concluded next nearly jarred me from my bed—that my application of the protection aspect of manhood was not just a shortcoming but an epic failure.

To want to protect all who dwelled under my roof was fine. Even to purchase a gun to bolster that protection was fine. But to take that gun and go in search of my tormentor to threaten him to stand down and cease his attacks, while at the same time excluding law enforcement from their rightful role, had caused me to turn a Plott molehill into a Plott mountain.

High upon that mountain, of course, stood the dark silhouette of Austin Adams. From on high, he had looked down at me in my struggles, more than willing to push boulders over the side to thwart my ascent. Then he'd laugh and watch each jagged rock careen down at me. That is the problem with turning a molehill into a mountain—gravity can so quickly work against you. The resulting landslide had devastated not only my career but also, more importantly, my marriage. It was the irony of ironies—my overzealous effort at protection had resulted in the crushing of the very thing I desired to protect.

A plastic cup rapped against steel bars. "Almost mealtime, A-man!"

The voice was that of Frankie T, my tattooed and gregarious friend in the next cell, alerting me to the approach of lunch hour. He was the first inmate I'd met at the penitentiary, and he'd nicknamed me A-man on my second day, as we tossed a football in the prison yard.

"No coconut shrimp today, Frankie," I said in reply.

I noted 6 minutes until lunch, 36 minutes until the start of Saturday visitations. Although I did have a visitor scheduled for today, I had not given it much thought, simply because I kept slinking into regret over my most severe failure of manhood—that of pursuer.

The idea of a husband continuing to pursue his wife was not something I'd had modeled for me in my youth. Sins of the fathers?

Probably. With the benefit of hindsight, I concluded that my wife had been correct about my misplaced priorities. Though I'd been a leader at work, at home I'd been the passive chip off the old passive block. After months of reflection, I no longer saw Karen as a cheater but the victim of an inattentive husband. Sure, on her bad days she had a cold streak in her, and I supposed I had the same tendency. But that's what we had signed up for on the day of our marriage—to love each other through the bad and help each other back toward great.

I still wanted great, and over the next 6 years and 4 months, I was determined to re-enter the world a more balanced man, one who not only *wanted* great but one fully capable of bringing great to a relationship. Whether or not Karen Lord came back to me, I was not going to make the same mistakes. Alex Lord 2.0 would know better.

Karen offered no further communications. All I had received from her was a preliminary document from her attorney explaining divorce proceedings. But that document had arrived 4 months ago, and I'd heard nothing since. Maybe she was reconsidering. I could always hope.

Two loud buzzes across B Floor signaled the call to lunch, and in seconds our row of doors opened in a symmetry of automated release. I stepped into line behind Frankie T and did my part to form an orange line of jump-suited conformity.

"Hungry, A-man? Frankie whispered over his shoulder.

"Very."

Seconds later, after the guards were satisfied with our alignment, the hand of the state pointed its remote at me and pushed button #1.

Time to Eat, Alex.

On Saturdays they served us roast beef sandwiches on sesame seed buns. Saturdays were a big day at the state pen—lunch, followed by visitation, followed by an hour of recess.

We were given 30 minutes to eat, and we usually ate fast so as to leave time for inmate stories and prison gossip. They'd heard my animated version of Plott destroying my yard at least twice, but no one could match Frankie's journey to incarceration. Apparently,

Frankie had been a bulldozer operator and had once gotten so mad at some golf course developers—a husband-wife team he described as prissy and upper-crust—that he'd raised the blade of his bulldozer and dropped it on their new Lexus, smashing it over and over again until the car was mangled beyond recognition.

"How many times did you smash it, Frankie?" I asked over my last bite of sandwich.

"At least 20 or 30 times," Frankie said and admired the mermaid tattoo on his forearm. Then he broke into a grin and spread his arms wide, one hand around my shoulder, the other around an ex-CFO in the pen for embezzlement. "All I know is I crunched it enough times to end up living here with you fine fellows. I got 4 years for assault with a deadly bulldozer."

Two guards, stationed at the door and bulked up to the size of NFL linemen, shook their heads as if they'd heard it all before. Before I knew it they had motioned us up from the table, and the biggest one said, "Lunch is over, ladies."

On his command we stood, formed a line, and carried our trays to the conveyor. We were then taken back to our cells, where we waited to be escorted, one at a time, to visitation.

While waiting I caught myself over-thinking everything again, my mind toggling between regret and hope. In an effort at distraction I picked up a day-old newspaper to see how the world outside was faring.

On my narrow, state-issued bed, I read for a second time an article about the ongoing real estate depression in the Sunshine State, along with an estimate of how many citizens had been forced into bankruptcy. At Powers, Morgan, and Greene I had recoiled at the idea of working bankruptcy cases; today I'd have given anything to be able to sleep in my own home, go to work for half the pay, and do nothing but bankruptcy cases from dusk till dawn.

Perspective—sometimes it only comes with a prison sentence.

The flip side of my regret was that I felt freer inside of prison than I had outside of it. Not physically free but free from the peer pressure and the associated politics of working for a top law firm, free from the frantic pace and the life-sucking burden of 12-hour days. If I wanted to, I could now spend 12 hours per day planning how to begin anew once I walked out of this monotonous, razor-wired shrine to punishment.

* * *

The burly guard came and escorted me off of B Floor. With his massive hand clutching my elbow, we walked side by side down a flight of stairs toward the visitation room.

Although the escorting I received and the uniform I wore annoyed me, I clung to hope and found it in small doses—sometimes through the simple act of checking off another week on my mental calendar, but always via these biweekly visits from a faithful friend.

I didn't know Otis Bettencourt very well when he first came to visit me, but we seemed to understand each other, even though we came from polar opposite socio-economic backgrounds.

On the way to visitation, as hard-core criminals shouted insults from A Floor, I wondered what I'd get to discuss with Otis. At first our conversations had centered on the local economy; we'd speculated often on just how bad things would become in our beloved Florida. I even wondered how many future Abner Plotts would lose their houses over the next year and perhaps blame the system. So many Floridians owed so much, on homes worth so little, that they were walking away—like Karen—or else living rent-free until the mortgage holder finally foreclosed. The situation was horrible for the banks and great for the homeowner. Word around the prison—and a number of the inmates were homeowners—was that so many homes remained ahead on the docket that the next homes to be foreclosed upon would not be dealt with for at least 18 months, and possibly for over 2 years. It was a giant blood clot in the vein of capitalism, and it made for an odd opportunity for Otis and me.

Otis had lost his bar business in the recession. Not only had he closed his establishment but he'd also lost his basement apartment, where he'd lived for the past 6 years. So he and I came up with an agreement: He'd live in my house, maintain the place, and contribute 400 dollars to my 1300-dollar per month mortgage payment. I directed my bank to pay the other 900 out of my IRA, an account that would be largely depleted by the time I left here.

In my favorite orange jumpsuit, I entered the visitation room and saw Otis signing in on the free side of a row of inch-thick windows, the clear barriers that relegated all visitors to talk but not touch. Otis was always punctual, and ever since his first visit I'd thought of him as a confidant.

The guard directed me to the third of eight seats, the thick glass before me smudged with fingerprints. I sat and brought the phone receiver to my ear, anxious to talk, aware that the penitentiary limited visitation to 30 minutes.

"You're still here?" Otis said into the visitor phone. "I never can remember if you got 6 *months* left or 6 years."

"Very funny, Otis. What's up?"

He wore a purple button-down shirt with thin black stripes, and he looked as if he'd been given a haircut. "You're looking good, Alex," he said. "Pumping a few weights?"

"A few. Running some laps too. What's the latest in the bar business?"

He frowned and looked about the room for a moment. "Three more bars closed last week. One belonged to a friend. I may never go back to serving drinks."

"No?"

"Might go work for the mouse. Drive a tram from the parking lot. Help park cars, whatever. I got me a connection."

I smiled and gave him a thumbs up, glad to hear he was moving forward. "How's my house?"

He nodded in the affirmative. "Good. Last week I made a trade with your pool service man. Traded him four of my old bar stools for his service. Said he'll keep the pool clean through September."

"Even trade?"

"Even trade."

I nodded and fought a growing sense of jealousy. "Nice." I really missed my pool. "So, you're using the pool a lot?"

"Mornin' swims, mostly. Oh, and I got a cord run out there for your HDTV. Me and a couple of nephews gonna watch Florida's opener next Saturday."

I had forgotten that college football began in a week. "So you're moving my Sony…out by my pool."

"And your grill. Bought a few steaks with my food stamps. Them kids from down your street are coming over to join us."

"The entrepreneurs on bikes?"

He nodded. "Every weekend they try to get work from me, but I tell 'em I can't afford much." Otis reached into his pocket and pulled out a folded piece of notebook paper. "Them kids wrote you a note."

He held it up and a guard came over. The guard inspected the note and said, "All right." Then the guard brought me the folded paper, and I read a short message scrawled in green ink:

> *Dear Mister Alex,*
>
> *Jackson and I know you're in jail and all, and you probably don't have much money 'cause you're not working, but your grass is getting really long, and Mrs. Fox has been complaining about it. We can cut it for you. We have a push mower. And a weed trimmer too. You can pay us when you get out, I guess. You're getting out soon, right?*
> *Sincerely,*
> *Marty Huntley, Jackson Dore*
> *M & J Lawn Service, Bike Service, and Pool Cleaners, Inc.*

Instantly I regretted throwing that beer bottle into the curb and scaring them. But I supposed that the resiliency of youth had sent them rebounding back for summer jobs.

"Otis?"

He checked his watch. "Yeah?"

"I kept five twenties in an old metal vase. The vase is hidden in the…."

"Found it already."

"You took my twenties?"

"No, still there. Last week I was about to put some flowers in the vase, add some atmosphere to the house, but I found your money instead."

"Take two of those twenties," I instructed, "and give it to the kids. Twenty bucks each to cut my grass *and* trim the edges."

He pursed his lips. "They might want gas money too."

"Then haggle with 'em. Tell 'em they can swim in my pool for a week."

Otis smiled and pressed a crease from his shirt. Then he looked at me with the sincerity of a friend who cares. "You miss her, don't you?"

His instinctual accuracy was intimidating. "Karen hasn't come by for anything the past couple weeks? A piece of furniture? Her garden tiller?"

He shook his head. "No, sorry."

"Not even the china?"

"Nope."

I paused and thought of the new mailbox and what might arrive there. "Any letters or postcards?"

"I'm sorry, Alex."

With no updates forthcoming about Karen, I transitioned awkwardly to Otis's ability to continue paying his part of my mortgage.

He assured me that in November he'd be turning 62 and would qualify for early Social Security. "That is, if the government don't raise the minimum age. Things change quickly nowadays, Alex. Feels like all of life has sped up."

"You should try living in here for a month."

He was staring at me again, his eyes boring holes through chit-chat and searching for truth. "You really are missing her, aren't ya?"

It felt so awkward, being transparent while burly guards stood just feet away, acting as if they weren't listening. "Yeah, I do. I miss what she and I had."

Otis twitched his mouth as if he had much more to say. "Remember that first night you came to my bar, when I told you not to stay if you were going to drink in order to get yourself in a mood for revenge?"

"I remember."

"Well, there's another side to that. And it's what I wanted to tell you that afternoon when you were drinking sweet tea and looking all anxious. But you left before we could finish our talk."

"I had things to do, people to see."

He flinched as if he wished upon me a do-over. "Well, what I was wanting to tell you is that I thought you should slow down and consider if you were trying to cover all the bad in your life by doing one good deed for Mister Plott."

My defenses surfaced and ruled my reply. "Trying to help Abner Plott was one of the few pure things I've ever done."

Otis studied me for a moment. "I just thought you might be trying too hard to redeem yourself."

"You're saying a man can't be redeemed?"

"No, I'm saying a man can't redeem *himself.*"

The guard came over, stood beside me, and pointed at the clock.

"Otis, I know you once led a church, and you're…."

He shook his head again. "Nope, you got that wrong. I was assistant pastor for 3 months, but I couldn't get nobody to tithe so I opened up the bar with my brother."

"Still, if you're gonna start preaching…."

He waved me off with both hands. "Naw, naw, not if I only got 2 minutes. But lemme tell you something else."

I knew there'd be something else. "Yeah?"

"Last time I visited, you told me all about how you regretted not pursuing your wife."

"I still regret that."

"Well, you can still pursue her."

"From prison?"

He straightened the collar on his shirt and nodded in the affirmative. "Maybe not on foot, but you can write her every week. Heck, write her three times a week if you got enough to say."

I had plenty to say. What I lacked was confidence. "But what if she never writes back? I haven't heard from her in months."

"Well, now that's what makes a man, don't it? He pursues her *regardless* of what she does. At least that's what I tried to do with my wife, back 'fore she passed from the cancer."

I considered his words and glanced at the clock. "I may need to borrow some stamps."

The guard tapped my shoulder. Thirty seconds left.

I leaned forward near the inch-thick glass, the phone receiver tight to my mouth. I felt like I owed Otis something for his efforts to have an impact on my life. "Otis, you might as well enjoy the opening game to the fullest. In the back of my closet there's an original Tebow jersey I bought 2 years ago in Gainesville. You could...."

"Fits perfect, Alex. I wore it to the mall yesterday."

The guard grasped my elbow, and I stood and waved goodbye to my friend. My salt of the earth, school of hard knocks, ultranosy friend—Otis.

✳ ✳ ✳

Each day at recess I yearned to walk in the sunshine with the group of inmates who'd befriended me, including the ex-bankers and the condo fraudsters. Daily we hung out along a long strip of grass we called our football field and sometimes on the volleyball court. The drug dealers and the more hardcore criminals mostly kept to themselves, usually near the weights and the basketball goals. It was their territory, their claimed space, and for the most part neither group interacted with the other.

At the entrance to the grounds I passed inspection and made my way into the prison yard, where the group was gathering as always on the same patch of grass bordered by the 10-foot fence topped with razor wire. Beyond the fence, a wide ditch ran parallel to the prison grounds before curving off toward the woods beyond.

For weeks the rumor among us was that a gator lived in that ditch. The rumor became fact shortly after I stepped on someone's half-eaten roast beef sandwich. I figured one of our obese guards had thrown the sandwich to the ground after eating several others, so I picked up the squashed section and squeezed it into a ball. Then I reared back and flung the chunk of sandwich far over the fence.

In seconds a small gator emerged from the ditch as if expecting its meal. A dozen of my fellow prisoners watched with glee as the little monster waddled up the bank, exposed a mouth full of teeth, and gobbled the morsel.

I turned to check if any guards had seen my toss. They had either not seen it, or were debating what to do about it—if anything. But no whistle blew and no guard shouted; we all remained standing along the fence, our gazes locked on a reptile enjoying its freedom.

Seconds later, Frankie T pressed a football into my back and asked if I'd help him practice quarterbacking our prison team.

"Sure," I said, and left the others to their gator watch.

Frankie gripped the football and stretched his right arm in a warm-up motion. "When you gets out of here, A-man," he said as he re-gripped the ball, "you watch out for them gators. They'll eat anything in their path."

That they will, Frankie. That they will.

He motioned for me to go long.

I sprinted across the prison yard, my head turned to spot the football's launch. Beyond the ball a seagull soared, and Frankie's pass spiraled tightly through a blue Florida sky.

About the Author

Ray Blackston is the author of the comedic novels *Flabbergasted* and *Last Mango in Texas*. He lives in the upstate of South Carolina. *The Trial of Alex Lord* is his seventh novel.

Acknowledgments

Special thanks to Art Ayris of Kingstone Media, and to screenwriter Chris Carlyle, for trusting me with this project. Chris and his wife Shannon provided an enormous amount of input and advice, all of which was excellent. Additional test-reading excellence came from Jonathan Darling, of Clemson University. A tip of the cap to Bill White and Matt Williams for teaching me the importance of the "p" words. Thanks also to Amanda Peck, who provided hospitality and a tour of EPCOT during my research trip to Orlando.

As always, my family and friends offered up the encouragement and support that is so vital in the crafting of a book. Love to all of you.

Ray welcomes reader feedback through his website, *www.ray blackston.com.*